P9-DDF-976

continued . . .

Murder Past Due

"Combines a kindhearted librarian hero, family secrets in a sleepy Southern town, and a gentle giant of a cat that will steal your heart. A great beginning to a promising new cozy series." —Lorna Barrett, *New York Times* bestselling author

"Courtly librarian Charlie Harris and his Maine coon cat, Diesel, are an endearing detective duo. Warm, charming, and Southern as the tastiest grits."
   —Carolyn Hart, author of the Bailey Ruth Mysteries

"Brings cozy lovers an intriguing mystery, a wonderful cat, and a librarian hero who will warm your heart. Filled with Southern charm, the first in the Cat in the Stacks Mysteries will keep readers guessing until the end. Miranda James should soon be on everyone's list of favorite authors."
   —Leann Sweeney, author of the Cats in Trouble Mysteries

"*Murder Past Due* has an excellent plot, great execution, and a surprising ending. This book is a must read!"
   —*The Romance Readers Connection*

"Miranda James begins the Cat in the Stacks Mysteries with a bang . . . [An] absolute breath of fresh air."
   —*Fresh Fiction*

"Read *Murder Past Due* for the mystery and an enjoyable amateur sleuth . . . You'll find yourself wishing for the next book to catch up with Diesel." —*Lesa's Book Critiques*

Please visit Diesel the cat at
facebook.com/DieselHarriscat.

Berkley Prime Crime titles by Miranda James

MURDER PAST DUE
CLASSIFIED AS MURDER
FILE M FOR MURDER
OUT OF CIRCULATION
THE SILENCE OF THE LIBRARY

A Cat in the Stacks Mystery

OUT OF CIRCULATION

Miranda James

BERKLEY PRIME CRIME, NEW YORK

THE BERKLEY PUBLISHING GROUP
Published by the Penguin Group
Penguin Group (USA) Inc.
375 Hudson Street, New York, New York 10014, USA
Penguin Group (Canada), 90 Eglinton Avenue East, Suite 700, Toronto, Ontario M4P 2Y3, Canada
(a division of Pearson Penguin Canada Inc.) • Penguin Books Ltd., 80 Strand, London WC2R 0RL,
England • Penguin Ireland, 25 St. Stephen's Green, Dublin 2, Ireland (a division of Penguin
Books Ltd.) • Penguin Group (Australia), 707 Collins Street, Melbourne, Victoria 3008, Australia
(a division of Pearson Australia Group Pty. Ltd.) • Penguin Books India Pvt. Ltd., 11 Community
Centre, Panchsheel Park, New Delhi—110 017, India • Penguin Group (NZ), 67 Apollo Drive,
Rosedale, Auckland 0632, New Zealand (a division of Pearson New Zealand Ltd.) • Penguin Books
(South Africa), Rosebank Office Park, 181 Jan Smuts Avenue, Parktown North 2193,
South Africa • Penguin China, B7 Jiaming Center, 27 East Third Ring Road North,
Chaoyang District, Beijing 100020, China

Penguin Books Ltd., Registered Offices: 80 Strand, London WC2R 0RL, England

This is a work of fiction. Names, characters, places, and incidents either are the product of the author's
imagination or are used fictitiously, and any resemblance to actual persons, living or dead, business
establishments, events, or locales is entirely coincidental. The publisher does not have any control over
and does not assume any responsibility for author or third-party websites or their content.

OUT OF CIRCULATION

A Berkley Prime Crime Book / published by arrangement with the author

PUBLISHING HISTORY
Berkley Prime Crime mass-market edition / February 2013

Copyright © 2013 by Dean James.
Cover illustration by Dan Craig.
Cover design by Lesley Worrell.
Interior text design by Tiffany Estreicher.

ISBN: 978-0-425-25727-2

BERKLEY® prime crime
Berkley Prime Crime Books are published by The Berkley Publishing Group,
a division of Penguin Group (USA) Inc.,
375 Hudson Street, New York, New York 10014.
BERKLEY® PRIME CRIME and the PRIME CRIME logo are trademarks of
Penguin Group (USA) Inc.

PRINTED IN THE UNITED STATES OF AMERICA

10 9 8 7 6 5

ALWAYS LEARNING   **PEARSON**

*In loving memory of my two feline companions,
who provided so much more than mere company
for seventeen years:*

Marlowe (1994–2011)

Booboo (1994–2012)

ACKNOWLEDGMENTS

Thanks, as always, to the usual suspects. First, my wonderful, supportive editor, Michelle Vega, and my amazing agent, Nancy Yost. This ride was bumpier than usual, but thanks for cushioning it as much as possible.

My fellow critique group members gave helpful advice as always. Thanks to Amy, Bob, Heather, Kay, Laura, Leann, and Millie for their judicious critiques. Thanks also to the Soparkar-Hairston family for their continued support and the use of their lovely home for meetings.

A special thanks to coworkers Philip Montgomery and M. J. Figard for their expert advice on archives and rare books. Another coworker contributed the title for this book, and she insisted she didn't want her name in the acknowledgments. She didn't say I couldn't put it in the book somewhere, though!

Patricia Orr, Julie Herman, and Terry Farmer continue to cheer me on, and I appreciate them more than they can ever know.

ONE

▪▪▪▪▪▪▪▪▪▪▪▪▪▪▪▪▪▪▪

"Charlie Harris, what are you doing *hiding* in the kitchen? Stiffen up that spine, young man, and get yourself in there where you're needed."

Miss An'gel Ducote didn't wait for a response. The grande dame of Athena society turned and strode back toward my living room. She had been telling the citizens of Athena what to do for more than seventy of her eighty-odd years. Far be it from me to cast aside my Southern upbringing and defy her—even if the last place I wanted to be this Wednesday night was my own living room. Confrontation unsettled me, and I had taken refuge in the kitchen, ostensibly to brew fresh tea. I wasn't going to avoid the unpleasantness that easily, however.

The tea forgotten, I scurried after Miss An'gel as fast as my fifty-two-year-old legs could move. My feet tangled together just inside the living room, and I grabbed at the door frame to steady myself.

Miss An'gel had resumed her place on the sofa with her younger sister, Miss Dickce. Her fire-engine red, vintage Chanel woolen dress provided a startling contrast to her sister's sober black. I didn't ordinarily pay much attention to women's clothing, but my actor daughter, Laura, waxed ecstatic whenever we encountered one of the Ducote sisters. Evidently they'd inherited a considerable wardrobe of designer clothing from their mother and grandmother. Laura practically swooned over the creations of Worth, Chanel, Balenciaga, and Dior she'd seen them wear, and I'd picked up enough detail to identify the designers' work. I drew the line at shoes.

Diesel, my Maine Coon cat, nestled between the sisters. His head and upper torso lay across Miss Dickce's lap, and his purr rumbled from across the room. He lifted his head briefly to acknowledge my return, but as long as the Ducote sisters remained in my house, he would stick close to them. The ladies adored my cat from the first moment they saw him, and Diesel appeared to be every bit as smitten with them.

Vera Cassity's strident tones claimed my wandering attention as I eased toward my chair. She cast a frown in my direction as she held forth. "As I was saying before Mr. Harris left the room, it's ridiculous to consider holding the gala anywhere else but Ranelagh. We have the only private dining room that can seat seventy." She leaned forward in the wingback chair and glared at the other members of the board of the Friends of Athena Public Library.

Besides Vera Cassity, the Ducote sisters, and me, the board was composed of Teresa Farmer, the library's new director; my boarder, Stewart Delacorte; and Sissy Beauchamp. The three of them appeared no more inclined than I to wander onto the battlefield.

"Vera, honey, we all know how big the dining room at Ranelagh is." Miss An'gel treated her adversary to a brief smile. "But we are not proposing to have a state dinner. We're having a *gala*, and I believe that means a *festive* occasion. Darling, there's nothing *festive* about a sit-down dinner for that many people."

"Pardon me for trying to inject some *class* into the event." Vera puffed up like a porcupine about to discharge her quills. "I seem to recall last year's gala at River Hill got downright rowdy, and there were several complaints from your neighbors. Although apparently *that's* nothing unusual." She sniffed and twiddled with the oversized collar of her dowdy pea green dress. The color did not flatter her sallow skin.

The annual duel of the antebellum mansions, I thought. From what I'd heard before I joined the Friends board two months ago, Vera and Miss An'gel argued over the site of the gala every year. Miss An'gel usually won. The Ducotes, after all, had lived at River Hill ever since it was built way back in 1838. Vera Cassity and her husband, Morton ("call me Morty"), bought Ranelagh from its impoverished owners only fifteen years ago. Vera has apparently been trying to wrest control of Athena society away from the Ducote sisters ever since.

"Can Dickce and I help it if people actually have fun at River Hill?" Miss An'gel's sweet tone fooled no one, I was sure. "The point of a gala is to loosen people up so they'll whip out their checkbooks and write numbers with a bunch of zeros in them. The looser they are, the bigger the donation, darling. Haven't you figured that out yet?"

"Getting people drunk, even in the name of charity, is downright disgusting." Vera bared her teeth in her version of a smile. "But I suppose River Hill has seen its share of heavy drinking."

Sissy Beauchamp smothered a laugh, while both Miss An'gel and Miss Dickce regarded Vera with catlike disdain. "The Ducote men have always enjoyed their liquor, I must admit." Miss Dickce coughed delicately. "Before I forget, Vera, honey, how *is* your poor brother doing these days? Is he comfortable down at Whitfield?"

Whitfield was the state mental hospital near Jackson, and everyone in Athena knew that Vera's brother, Amory Hobson, had lived there for the past thirty years. According to local gossip, Amory was crazy as a betsy bug and given to stripping off all his clothes and running around hugging anyone he saw.

Vera's face turned an angry red, and she gripped the arms of her chair so hard I feared she'd rip the sixty-year-old fabric.

Before she could form a reply, Teresa Farmer—brave soul that she was—attempted to scale back the hostilities. "Miss An'gel, Miss Dickce, Mrs. Cassity, it's really wonderful that you all want to host this year's gala. If it hadn't been for your support over the years, the Friends wouldn't be the highly effective, respected group it is. Everyone in Athena has benefited from your efforts, and I hope we can continue to work together for even more success this year." As head of the Athena Public Library now, Teresa had to play peacemaker. I knew she hated confrontations like this as much as I did, and I didn't envy her the challenges of her new job.

Sissy Beauchamp spoke next. Her sultry voice always made me think of Lauren Bacall, but with a Southern accent, of course. "I think we should be guided by the theme of this year's gala, don't y'all? We're going to be dressing up as our favorite literary characters and giving out prizes for the cleverest costumes and holding a contest for who can name most characters correctly. Who's going to have time to sit down to a formal dinner at a masquerade ball?"

Sissy—real name Judianne—treated Vera to a malicious smile. The two women loathed each other. Sissy—again according to local gossip—had recently started an affair with Morty Cassity. She was nearly half Vera's age and a real stunner, with gorgeous red hair, a creamy complexion, and a figure reminiscent of Hollywood glamour girl Ava Gardner.

Stewart Delacorte, a new board member like me, nodded emphatically. "A formal dinner would cost a lot more, too, and we need to keep the expenses down as much as possible. Finger food is a lot cheaper and works just fine with a costume party." He smiled at the Ducote sisters. No doubt at all where his sympathies lay.

Miss An'gel and Miss Dickce exchanged glances, then looked at me. "Well, Charlie," Miss An'gel said, "what's your opinion? Formal dinner or finger food?"

That wasn't the real question, and we all knew it. Was I going to support the Ducote sisters and River Hill publicly or go over to the enemy and vote with Vera Cassity and Ranelagh?

Considering that I didn't like Mrs. Cassity any more than the other members of the board did, I had little difficulty in answering, "Finger food." I hated, however, the atmosphere of hostility and dissension brought on by an absurd power struggle.

Diesel had picked up on it as well. He no longer lay sprawled across the sofa and the Ducote sisters' laps. He sat between them, and I would have sworn he was frowning. He leaped from the sofa, across the coffee table and came to sit beside my chair. I stroked his head to reassure him, and I could feel some of his tension ease.

Vera Cassity glared at Diesel, then her gaze swept upward to my face. The sheer fury in her eyes shocked me, and I looked away, unable to face her. No wonder Diesel wouldn't go near her earlier when she'd arrived. He'd taken one look and backed away, though he usually made a point of greeting guests as they came in the front door.

Miss An'gel broke the silence. "That's settled, then. We'll continue with our preparations for the gala at River Hill. Vera, honey, I was thinking that a sit-down dinner at Ranelagh would be just the thing for the fund-raiser next spring. You know, the one for the county mental health association?"

I wanted to run for cover because I expected major fireworks after that little barb. All eyes focused on Vera as we awaited her response.

Her face reddened, but when she spoke, her tone was chilly. "That's a fine idea, An'gel, my dear. I'll be happy to have that event at Ranelagh. Then I guess it'll be your turn to head the fund-raiser for unwed mothers. Or perhaps Sissy would like to handle that one?" Her eyes glittered with malice.

I risked a glance at Sissy Beauchamp and noted that her face was about the same color as her flaming hair. Miss An'gel and Miss Dickce appeared perfectly calm, however.

Diesel muttered, and I understood how he felt. The tension in the room was thick enough to make gravy. I risked another glance at Sissy and was relieved to see her looking calmer.

"I suppose you're thinking about my cousin Mary Lee Beauchamp." Sissy shot Vera an icy glance. "Poor girl just can't seem to get them to the altar until after they get her pregnant. But I do envy her those sweet little babies, don't you, Vera, honey?"

That was way below the belt. Vera and Morty had no children, and Vera was known to dote on other people's offspring. Pretty terrifying prospect, if you thought about it much.

"Little they may be," Miss An'gel said, her voice deceptively mild, "but they behave like the spawn of Satan, and you know it. It's no wonder Mary Lee can't keep a husband around for more than a year at a time."

Vera gave a snort of laughter, quickly quelled when Miss An'gel looked at her.

Sissy's mouth opened, but no sound came out. Her jaw snapped shut, and she frowned while Miss An'gel and Miss Dickce exchanged glances. They rose in unison from the sofa.

"We really must be going." Miss An'gel smoothed her silk skirt and nodded. "There's so much to do."

"Oh, my, yes." Miss Dickce's head bobbed up and down. "So much to do."

"Let me see you out." I escorted them, with Diesel's help, to the front door. I extracted their wraps from the hall closet and helped each sister into hers, Miss An'gel first.

Then each sister had to pat Diesel on the head a few times and coo at him, telling him what a handsome gentleman he was. Diesel purred and chirped, in obvious agreement.

I suppressed a smile as I waited to open the door. From the direction of the living room I heard conversation in progress, some of it sounding heated. Were Vera and Sissy at each other's throats? I hoped not. I didn't need a headache like that.

Miss An'gel shook my hand gently. "Thank you for being our host this evening, Charlie. And pay no attention to Vera, or whatever she might say once we're gone." She shared a glance with her sister, and they both smiled. "Vera won't be a thorn in our sides much longer. Dickce and I have seen to that." Miss An'gel pulled an envelope from her purse and handed it to me.

"We thought we might save the postage." Miss Dickce beamed at me. "We were sure you wouldn't mind hand delivery."

Miss An'gel nodded. "The others went to the post office this afternoon." With that she and her sister stepped out into the cool December night, and I closed the door behind them.

Diesel warbled, and I glanced down. He gazed up at me, then reared up on his hind legs to bat at the envelope.

"All right, I'll open it." The paper was thick, heavy, and no doubt expensive. By the shape I figured it could be an invitation. I managed to get it open without ripping the envelope too much and withdrew the card inside.

It was indeed an invitation—to the Friends of the Library winter gala at River Hill next Tuesday.

TWO

Fifteen minutes after Diesel and I bade good-bye to the last board member, we got in the car and headed for the town square and my dear friend Helen Louise Brady's French patisserie. After the rancor and tension of the board meeting, Diesel and I both needed to relax. Plus, I hadn't seen Helen Louise in three days, and I missed her even though we talked on the phone daily.

Diesel chirped at me when I told him our destination. He loved Helen Louise, and the adoration was mutual. She always made a fuss over my cat, and if anyone in her establishment dared object to his presence, she informed the offender not to let the door hit him on his way out.

I pulled the car into a slot right in front of the bakery. Diesel hopped out over me as soon as I opened the door, eager to see his friend and whatever tidbits she would offer.

Even before we stepped inside, I felt my mouth watering from the appetizing smells that emanated from the bakery.

Brioches, croissants, gâteaux, éclairs—the combination of these and more made my early dinner a rapidly fading memory. Perhaps I'd have a small piece of Helen Louise's sumptuous *gâteau au chocolat*, a particular weakness of mine.

Helen Louise greeted me from behind the counter, and the thought of chocolate cake receded. There stood the real attraction. Rake thin and nearly six feet tall, Helen Louise wore her dark, luxuriant hair in a short bob. The curls framed blue eyes that sparkled with fierce intelligence and wicked humor, a mouth that often quirked in amusement, and a shapely nose that wrinkled adorably when she laughed.

She came around the counter as Diesel and I approached, and we shared a hug and a brief kiss.

"Missed you." Helen Louise's words shimmered softly in the air between us, and I pulled her close again for a longer kiss.

Diesel warbled and inserted himself between us, and we broke apart, laughing.

Helen Louise grinned at me as she bent to stroke my incorrigible feline's head and neck. "We could never forget you, *mon brave. Tu es un chat très formidable.*"

After ten years in Paris learning her art, she often lapsed into French. Diesel warbled at her as if he understood her.

"He's not *formidable*, just shameless." I, too, stroked Diesel's head, and my hand brushed against Helen Louise's. We smiled at each other.

Diesel butted his head against my thigh, then did the same to Helen Louise. "Someone expects a treat, I think." I shook my head.

Helen Louise laughed. "Go have a seat, and I'll bring you both something *très délicieux.*"

Only a few customers at eight thirty in the evening, I

noted as Diesel and I moved to our usual table near the cash register at the end of the counter. Diesel waited until I sat and then positioned himself against my left leg, his head turned toward the spot from where Helen Louise would shortly emerge.

I watched Diesel's face, and his nose twitched as Helen Louise approached the table with two dessert plates. Chocolate cake for me and some bits of chicken for my poor starving feline.

"You do spoil us." I grinned at her as she set the cake in front of me.

Diesel reared up and put his front paws on her arm as she took the chair opposite mine. "You're both worth spoiling." Those blue eyes sparkled, and I thought for the umpteenth time how beautiful they were.

"Here you go, Diesel." Helen Louise tore the chicken into smaller pieces and held her hand out to the cat. Diesel wasted no time in scarfing the food out of her hand, and she laughed. "Charlie needs to feed you more, sweet boy. You're obviously wasting away into nothing."

My mouth full of sinfully delicious cake, I groaned as Helen Louise doled out the rest of the chicken. We exchanged glances as she wiped her fingers on a napkin. Diesel popped up on his hind legs again, head over the table, searching for more chicken.

"That's all, Diesel." I spoke in a firm tone, and my cat stared at me. For a moment I had the strangest feeling that he was going to stick out his tongue at me, but instead he blinked a couple of times and sat back on his haunches.

"How did the board meeting go?" Helen Louise leaned back and regarded me with an amused expression. "All-out catfight?"

I set my fork down. "Don't you know it. I've never seen

Miss An'gel and Miss Dickce strip someone to the bone, but they sure did it with Vera."

"Vera brings it on herself." Helen Louise sighed. "I do feel sorry for her sometimes, but honestly, if she'd just relax and not get so caught up in trying to be the doyenne of Athena society, people might cut her some slack."

"Not to mention that she tends to order people around like her personal peons." I recalled her behavior every time she'd visited the public library when I did volunteer duty. She sent staff scurrying like Cleopatra giving orders to her slaves.

"There's not an ounce of grace in her." Helen Louise shook her head. "She came up from nothing, and she thinks she can bulldoze people into forgetting it. Sad thing is, most people couldn't care less."

"She should be proud of what she and Morty have accomplished." I licked the fork, hoping for one last taste of that amazing chocolate. "But you know what people here are like. She's never going to be one of the Ducotes of River Hill, no matter how hard she tries." The populist in me thought it ridiculous, but attitudes about class and position changed slowly in Athena.

Helen Louise snorted. "Let me guess what happened. She wanted to host the gala at Ranelagh, but Miss An'gel and Miss Dickce declined to agree."

I laughed. "You sure you didn't hide in the corner of my living room tonight?"

"Honey, they've been fighting that same battle for the past decade or more. And the outcome never varies. I bet you anything Miss An'gel already sent out the invitations."

"She handed me mine before she and her sister left tonight."

"The Ducote sisters could teach the military how to maneuver," Helen Louise observed.

Diesel warbled as if he agreed, and Helen Louise and I both laughed. "I don't want to be anywhere around when Vera finds out." I could just imagine the explosion.

"Vera ought to be expecting it." Helen Louise shook her head. "But she always thinks she's going to outsmart them, and of course, she never does." She paused. "Sissy Beauchamp show up?"

"She did." I grimaced. "She and Vera went at each other like two cats. I swear, if every board meeting is going to be like that, I may have to rethink being a member."

Helen Louise regarded me with a concerned expression. "Now, Charlie, honey, I know it makes you nervous when people carry on like that around you, but you can't let it upset you. They need you on that board, and I know Teresa appreciates your support."

I nodded, feeling slightly ashamed. "You're right. I should stop whining. As long as they don't try to pull me into too many of their arguments, I guess I can manage."

Helen Louise leaned forward to squeeze my hand. Diesel rubbed hard against my legs and meowed a couple of times. Helen Louise and I shared another laugh as I reached for the cat's head and scratched it. Diesel's rumbling purr sounded loud even against the light background noise from the customers.

As I glanced over Helen Louise's shoulder, my attention caught by the opening door, I blinked to focus. Sissy Beauchamp strode in, her younger brother, Henry Ainsworth Beauchamp IV—better known as Hank—right behind her. He spoke to her in an undertone, his words unintelligible, but the tension between them fairly vibrated.

Sissy's mulish expression changed quickly when she spotted me. She smiled and waved, then elbowed Hank in the stomach. He stopped talking and followed the direction of Sissy's nod. He scowled at Helen Louise and me briefly before he managed to smooth his features into the bland mien he usually presented to the world.

Helen Louise cast a quick glance at me, one eyebrow raised, as she left our table and took her place behind the counter. "Evening, Sissy, Hank, how are y'all doing? What can I get for you?"

"We're doing just fine, Helen Louise." Sissy gave no sign now of anything amiss between her and Hank as she slipped into gracious belle mode. Hank nodded, but I couldn't see that he relaxed at all.

"I'd like a couple of those wonderful éclairs and a café au lait." Sissy turned to Hank. "What about you, darlin'?"

"Same for me, I reckon." Hank's deep voice always surprised me because it seemed bigger than he was. Only about five-nine, he had a slight figure and looked like a good breeze could send him reeling.

"Coming right up." Helen Louise entered their order in the computerized register and gave them the total.

Hank paid with a credit card, but when Helen Louise spoke after checking the register, her voice held a hint of compassion.

She pitched her voice low, and I barely heard her. "Sorry, honey, but it didn't go through."

Hank stared at her for a moment, then uttered an obscenity. He turned and stomped out. Sissy called after him, but he never looked back.

THREE

|||||||||||||||||||||||||||||||||

"Hank, come back here," Sissy called out to her brother, but he didn't falter. Throwing an apologetic glance at Helen Louise and then at me, Sissy scurried after Hank. The door clanged shut behind her.

Helen Louise shrugged and punched a couple of buttons on her cash register. She strolled back to the table and resumed her seat.

"What was all that about?" I asked. Diesel chirped several times as if to indicate he wanted an answer as well. I rubbed his head, and he quieted.

An excited babble of voices startled both of us before Helen Louise could answer my question. She turned as I looked past her toward the door. A group of eight young women poured inside, all talking at once. The din struck my ears and made me wince. Diesel hunched against my legs, frightened by the clamor.

Helen Louise offered a wry smile as she stood. "Sorority

sisters in desperate search of sugar and chocolate. Sorry, my dear, I have to get back to work." She leaned down and gave me a quick kiss.

"Okay, we'll talk later." I wanted to hold her for a moment, but I didn't get to my feet in time. She darted behind the counter and attempted to dim the roar to a more acceptable level.

"Come on, boy." I rubbed the cat's head. "Let's go home."

Diesel couldn't get out the door and into the car fast enough. As I drove I considered the reasons for Hank Beauchamp's less than gentlemanly behavior, but I reached no conclusions by the time I pulled the car into the garage.

Once inside Diesel headed straight for the utility room and his litter box. I let the peace of the house settle around me as I gazed at the empty kitchen. More than likely Diesel and I had the house to ourselves, except for Stewart Delacorte in his aerie on the third floor. I'd spotted the lights in his rooms as I drove in.

Justin Wardlaw, my other boarder, was probably still on campus, studying with friends in the library. Final exams loomed as the semester drew to a close, and Justin always made sure he was prepared.

Sean had told me earlier that he had plans for dinner tonight with Alexandra Pendergrast. I had to smile, thinking back to the first time Sean and Alexandra met, over the Delacorte business. The sparks flew that day, Sean sure that he didn't like Alexandra in the least. Now he thought and spoke of little else, much as I'd expected. Alexandra was beautiful, intelligent, and more than a match for my temperamental, brilliant son. I expected to hear news of an engagement any day now.

Laura spent most of her free time with her beau, Frank Salisbury, a colleague from the theater department at Athena

College. As the semester drew to a close, so did Laura's temporary job. The professor for whom she had substituted this semester came back from maternity leave in January, and Laura planned to return to Los Angeles and her acting career. At least, that was the original plan. Frank no doubt had something to say about that. He would either have to follow my daughter to Hollywood or persuade her to remain here. If I had a say in the matter, I hoped Frank could talk Laura into staying in Athena. Having her at home with Sean and me these past few months made me happy, and I would miss her even more keenly if she went back to California.

Diesel would miss her dreadfully as well. I remained his favorite human, but Laura ran a close second. She always made a fuss over him, and he loved the attention.

I sighed as Diesel ambled into the kitchen, warbling away. I poured myself a glass of cold water from the fridge, and Diesel continued chatting to me as I leaned against the counter and drank.

Christmas was little more than two weeks away, and I was thrilled that the people I cared most about in this world would all be here for it. Thanksgiving had been truly special for that same reason, and I offered up more than one fervent prayer that I could keep them all around me. I even felt the presence of my departed loved ones—my wife, Jackie, and my aunt Dottie—close by. That was as it should be.

As Diesel and I settled down in bed a short while later, I returned to the puzzle of Hank Beauchamp's behavior. He obviously had money problems if his credit card got declined for such a trifling amount. The Beauchamp family had the reputation, however, of being filthy rich. So what had happened to Hank? And did Sissy suffer from the same problem?

I reminded myself that I had no business speculating over the Beauchamp family finances and tried to relax. At my side, Diesel stretched out, already asleep. I drifted off soon after.

After a decent night's sleep I stepped out into the chilly morning to retrieve my newspaper. Two deep breaths of the bracing air cleared my head. Diesel had disappeared during the night, and I had no doubt he was snuggled up to Laura. She stayed in bed later than I did, and he liked his rest.

When I reached the kitchen, the sight of my housekeeper, Azalea Berry, startled me. I still wasn't quite used to seeing her every weekday morning, but with the additions to my household in the past few months, she had recently informed me I needed her every day. I saw no point in arguing with her, especially when she was right.

"Good morning, Azalea, how are you?" I sat at the table and opened the paper.

"Tolerable, Mr. Charlie, tolerable." She offered a brisk nod as she approached the refrigerator. "I'll have breakfast ready before long."

"Thank you." I had a sip of the coffee Azalea had waiting for me.

"There was company here last night. Cream just about gone." Azalea turned to frown at me. "And here I was gonna make one of them quiches you like so much."

"Sorry about that." I offered her an apologetic smile. "It was a bit last-minute. I made tea for my guests, and I suppose we used most of the cream."

"Ain't no never mind." Azalea shook her head. "I got to go to the grocery store anyway."

Still feeling obscurely guilty, I said, "I hadn't planned on it, but I hosted a meeting of the Friends of the Library board. We were supposed to meet at Cathy Williams's house last night, but she got called in to the hospital at the last minute. Some kind of an emergency with her nursing staff, I think."

Azalea turned to glare at me. "Then you had Miss An'gel and Miss Dickce here, didn't you?" She didn't wait for a response. "And I didn't get around to dusting the living room yesterday. I was saving it for today." She shook her head. "What on earth they gonna think of my house-keeping now?"

The living room, as I recalled it, was as spotless as it always was. "I'm sure they didn't think anything bad, Azalea. In fact, Miss An'gel complimented me on how beautifully you keep the house."

That appeared to mollify Azalea. She turned back to the refrigerator and extracted the ingredients she wanted.

"In fact, Vera Cassity said the very same thing." I picked up the front section of the paper and started to open it.

Azalea whirled around and glared at me again, an egg in her right hand. "How come you let that trash in this house?"

The venom in Azalea's voice startled me. I had never heard her speak in such a tone. "What do you mean?"

Azalea crushed the egg in her hand, and I watched in fascination as the contents oozed through her fingers and dripped on the floor. She appeared oblivious to the mess.

"That woman ain't never done a good thing for nobody, 'cepting herself. She don't deserve to be around decent folks."

Azalea furiously angry would make anyone want to beat a strategic retreat. I tried not to squirm in my chair or get up and scuttle out of the room.

What on earth had Vera Cassity done to earn this kind of hatred?

Before I could voice the question, Azalea seemed to recover herself and gazed in dismay at the remains of the egg on the floor. She muttered to herself as she stepped over to the sink to rinse her hand. I watched in silence as she then took paper towels and wiped the floor.

I decided I'd ask anyway, though I might get my head handed back to me on a platter. "Why do you dislike Vera Cassity so much?"

Azalea glared at me for a moment. "Ain't nothing you need to worry about." She turned toward the stove, her back and shoulders stiff.

I went back to my paper and my coffee. Though I still burned with curiosity, I knew better than to push the issue.

The scent of bacon frying soon perfumed the air. Azalea remained silent as she tended the stove, and I gazed at the paper without comprehending much of what I read. Did anyone in Athena actually like Vera Cassity? I had seldom encountered anyone who seemed to engender universal antipathy as she did.

Justin entered the kitchen. Diesel ambled along beside him. "Good morning, Mr. Charlie, Miss Azalea."

"Good morning, Justin." I held out a hand to Diesel, who butted his head against it. "And good morning to you, boy."

The cat chirped at me, and I could have sworn he also grinned. I scratched his head, and he purred with pleasure.

Justin helped himself to orange juice from the refrigerator while Azalea poured him a cup of coffee. He thanked her, and she nodded before she turned back to the stove.

He glanced at me with a faint frown, and I shrugged. Azalea had failed to extend him her usual greeting, and I couldn't explain why to him, not with Azalea right there. Justin shook his head as he sat down across from me.

"Exams going well?" I folded the paper and laid it aside.

"Fine, as far as I can tell." Justin took a swig of orange juice. "English lit's going to be a monster." He shook his head. "The professor warned us to expect to spend the whole three hours on it. My brain'll probably be completely wrung out by the time it's over."

"Even so, I'm sure you'll do fine. You have an A in the class, don't you?" I already knew he did. He was not only bright, but also a hard worker. He didn't accept anything other than A's in all his courses.

"Yes, sir." He blushed. "But I want to keep it, so I can't let the exam do me in."

"When is it?"

"This afternoon, at one." He scratched his bearded chin.

"I'll send good vibes your way." I chuckled. "Though I doubt you really need them."

Justin grinned, and as I regarded him, I marveled at the changes in him over the past year. When he first moved in, the fall semester of the previous year, he had been shy, gawky, and unsure of himself. After a traumatic first semester he'd blossomed into a more outgoing, physically active, and confident young man. I was as proud of him as if he were one of my own.

Azalea set plates of scrambled eggs, toast, and bacon in front of Justin and me. She glared at me when she was done. "Don't you be letting that woman back in this house. Miss Dottie like to rise up and haunt you. And I won't set foot in here again."

With that she whirled and stomped off into the utility room.

FOUR

Justin and I stared at each other. Diesel meowed several times, and I knew the tense atmosphere bothered him. He butted my thigh, and I scratched his head.

"Man, what's up with her?" Justin kept his voice low. "I've never heard her use that tone before." He shook his head. "Who's she talking about anyway?"

I answered the last question first. "Vera Cassity."

Justin's expression turned sour. "Oh, her." He had a sip of coffee.

"How do you know her?" Did everyone in Athena know and dislike the woman?

"Scholarship." Justin shrugged. "She endowed one of the four-year scholarships I received. I'm grateful to her, because it really is a good one."

"But?" I prompted when he fell silent.

"She wants a thank-you letter at the beginning and end of every semester. Plus, you have to tell her about the courses you've taken and how they have contributed to your growth as a mature, moral person." He sighed. "I guess it's really not that big a deal, but it takes up a lot of time. Because those letters sure aren't short."

"Does she actually read them?" I thought two detailed thank-you letters per semester excessive. The woman evidently needed massive sops to her ego.

"She sure does." Justin laughed. "Because you always get a letter back, and she comments on things. So you don't dare skimp on the details when you write to her."

"That's going way overboard on her part." I grimaced. "I admire her for endowing scholarships, but requiring written proof of gratitude so frequently is just weird. Not to mention the bit about *growth as a mature, moral person.*"

"Well, yeah, it is weird." Justin shrugged again. "But without that money I'd have to go to school part-time and work full-time probably."

The more I found out about Vera the more fascinating—albeit distasteful—she became.

"But why does Miss Azalea hate her so much?" Justin forked some egg into his mouth.

I shrugged. "I haven't the foggiest." Had Azalea worked for Vera at some point? I couldn't see Azalea tolerating Vera's high-handed manner, but her reaction to Vera argued a more serious offense.

"She must have done something pretty awful." Justin ate more. "I mean, Miss Azalea's not exactly a warm and fuzzy person"—his eyes glinted with amusement—"but she doesn't usually go around bad-mouthing anybody."

I agreed. Azalea's reaction implied deep animosity.

"Definitely a mystery." I had a bite of bacon, and suddenly a paw tapped my thigh. I glanced down at Diesel. His gaze riveted on the bacon in my hand, he chirped. "You're incorrigible." I broke off a piece and fed it to him.

Justin laughed. "He does love bacon."

"That he does." I fed the cat another piece. "That's all." I held up my hand to show Diesel that it was empty.

He glared at me for a moment before he turned and walked over to Justin's chair. His tail bristled with indignation.

"A couple of bites," I told Justin. "No more."

"Yes, sir." He grinned as Diesel warbled for him. He broke off almost half a slice and fed it to the cat.

"Justin." I shook my head. "That was more than a couple of bites."

My boarder ducked his head briefly, but when he returned my gaze, he grinned. I suppressed a chuckle. I couldn't be angry with him.

Justin popped the remainder of the bacon into his mouth and held his empty hands where Diesel could see them. Diesel knew what that signal meant, even if it annoyed him.

Tail once again in the air, Diesel marched out of the kitchen into the utility room. Justin and I shared a quiet laugh.

"What's so funny?" Stewart Delacorte, my other boarder, entered the room like a diva coming onstage. Once he had our attention, he preened, striking in his black suit, white shirt, and crimson tie. "Well, what do you think? Am I not simply *gorgeous* this morning?"

"Why should today be different from any other day?" Justin flashed a grin at me. When Stewart first moved in, his assumed flamboyance had disconcerted the younger man. Now, however, Justin took Stewart in his stride, and the two had become friends.

Stewart blew a kiss. "You are too, too sweet." He

advanced to the table and rested his hands on the back of a chair. "I have a meeting with the president today, therefore the professional drag." He grimaced. "I *must* have caffeine in my system if I'm going to listen to Mr. Prez blather on and on for an hour or two." He wandered over to the counter and poured himself coffee. "Now, what were you two laughing about?"

"Diesel." Justin and I replied in unison.

"How dare you laugh at that magnificent feline," Stewart chided us in a mock-fierce tone. "Where is he, by the way?" He glanced around the room as he sipped his coffee.

Diesel chose that moment to stroll back into the kitchen. He spotted Stewart and made a beeline for him.

Stewart tried to hold the cat off, because he well knew Diesel intended to rub himself against his legs. "Darling kitty, I *adore* you, but I don't want to have to de-hair myself." He glanced over at me. "Why is it that they simply *must* get their hair on anything black?"

Diesel sat on his haunches and gazed up at Stewart. He warbled twice.

"I think he may be telling you his hair is special." Justin laughed.

"It is." Stewart flashed a grin. "But not on my best suit, and not when I have a command performance." He kept a wary eye on the cat as he approached the table and took the chair to my right.

Justin glanced at his watch. He pushed back his chair. "Sorry, gotta get going. See y'all later." He waved to Diesel as he trotted out of the room. Moments later I heard him run lightly up the stairs.

"Where's Dante?" I turned to Stewart. Usually the dog made every step that Stewart made.

Dante was the toy poodle Stewart took over from my

son, Sean, a few months before. Sean had rescued the poor little guy from an owner—Sean's former girlfriend—who'd lost interest in him when she discovered he had no pedigree. Once Stewart and Dante set eyes on each other, though, it was love at first sight.

"Laura has him with her this morning. She promised to keep him occupied so I could sneak out of the house. He's had his morning walkies." He checked his watch. "I've got a few minutes before I need to head for campus." He had a sip of coffee as he regarded me with a thoughtful expression. "Recovered from last night's episode of *Everybody Hates Vera*?"

I couldn't help laughing. Stewart was outrageous, but fun. "I don't think I've ever met anyone with a talent for getting on people's nerves the way poor Vera does."

"She's had sixty-odd years to perfect her talent. Plus, she's worked really hard at it." Stewart grimaced. "Be thankful she's not *your* godmother."

I probably gaped at him after that little verbal bomb. "Are you serious? Vera is your godmother?"

Stewart shrugged. "Sadly, yes. She and my late mother were best friends in high school. They both grew up on the wrong side of the tracks." His left eyebrow arched. "They both ended up marrying money. Of course, my father inherited his, while Morty had to earn it by the sweat of his fevered brow."

"Marrying into it is so much simpler, naturally." I grinned, and Diesel warbled right on cue.

Stewart laughed. "Naturally. I have to say this for my mother, she stuck by Vera in the years before Morty had a pot to pee in—pardon the elegant expression, but it fits the subject so well." His left eyebrow quirked upward again. "When I came along, charming bundle of joy that I was, my mother insisted on naming her best friend as my godmother."

"Then you know Vera well?" This connection between Stewart and Vera really surprised me.

"Well enough, I suppose." Stewart didn't sound thrilled about it. "Vera was never that fond of me, nor I of her, but when she finally figured out I was gay, she had as little to do with me as possible." He shot me a sardonic glance. "And of course I was completely devastated."

"I'm sure it marked you for life." I kept my tone serious.

Stewart snorted. "Just another example of the way Vera endears herself to people." He paused for coffee, then set his cup on the table. "I do feel sorry for her sometimes. She tries to get people to like her; she just doesn't understand the basic principle—that you have to be nice to people yourself. Plus, she has a chip the size of Mount Rushmore on her shoulder about growing up dirt-poor. She's so sure people resent her because of Morty's money, she comes across like a lion getting ready to feast on an arena full of terrified Christians."

"Surely she's not that bad." I had no reason to be fond of Vera, based on our previous interactions, but I wouldn't compare her to a voracious wild beast.

"Well, probably not." Stewart chuckled. "She seriously needs to take a chill pill, especially around Miss An'gel and Miss Dickce. The way they were bickering last night really got to you, didn't it?" Stewart often pretended to be a complete flibbertigibbet, but he was far shrewder and more observant than he liked to let on.

"I don't like conflict, especially conflict that open." The cat meowed, and I smiled. "Neither does Diesel."

"Par for the course with Vera and the Ducote sisters." Stewart rolled his eyes. "I guess everybody else is just used to it. If Vera didn't push the sisters so hard, they wouldn't resent her so. They're really not the self-absorbed aristocrats they sometimes appear to be."

I could concur with that. In my limited experience with them I had seen their true kindness and concern for the welfare of others.

Stewart echoed my thoughts as he continued, "They work very hard, and if they were thirty years younger they'd probably be running their own companies. A lot of people have reason to be grateful to them for the good works they do." He paused for a moment. "Instead of just pitching in and getting the work done, Vera wants to be in charge. I think she wants the glory, like she has to prove herself to someone, but she doesn't want to soil her hands with actual work."

"Perhaps she needs to prove something to herself," I suggested.

Stewart nodded. "You're probably right. Miss An'gel and Miss Dickce care about helping people, and that's the point of it all. They regard it as their duty. It's how they were brought up to think."

"Vera loathes them." I paused. "At least, that's my impression."

"Maybe she does," Stewart said. "She sure as heck resents them because they thwart her all the time."

"Like with the gala. They sent out the invitations yesterday, before the meeting."

"Doesn't surprise me." Stewart laughed. "No flies on those two old girls." He glanced at his watch. "Time I was heading off to campus. Can't keep the president waiting." He pushed back his chair, stood, and then took his coffee cup to the sink behind me.

I turned in my chair to face him. "One quick thing,

before you go." I was about to be incredibly nosy, but curiosity had the better of me.

Stewart nodded. "Sure, what is it?"

"I mentioned earlier to Azalea that Vera was here last night, and I thought she was going to have a conniption fit over the woman. Do you have any idea why she would hate Vera so much?" Azalea had once worked for Stewart's family, although it was many years ago now, and I thought he might know something.

Instead of answering, however, Stewart blinked at me several times in rapid succession and tilted his head a tiny bit.

Taking his cue, I turned back to the table to see Azalea standing a few feet away.

"You best be mindin' your own business, Mr. Charlie." Her fierce expression hit me like a laser, and it took all I had not to crawl under the table to escape from those eyes. Diesel did disappear under there. "What's between me and that woman ain't nobody's business in this house. Ain't *never* gonna be." She stomped past me and moments later I heard the thud of her feet on the stairs.

FIVE

||||||||||||||||||||||

I felt about three inches tall, and to judge by Stewart's expression, he was experiencing a similar amount of chagrin.

Stewart pushed away from the counter. "Guess I'd better head to my meeting, discretion being the better part of valor and all that." He headed for the front door after treating me to a pale imitation of his usual cocky grin.

"Guess you and I had better hop it up the stairs, boy, and dress for work." I got up from the table, and Diesel trotted toward the hall. With a rueful glance at my unfinished breakfast I followed the cat upstairs. With any luck I could get out the front door without encountering Azalea again. I was frankly surprised she hadn't given me notice, but I supposed it would take more than my nosiness to make her relinquish her job.

While I got ready for work, I thought more about Azalea's reaction to my nosiness. Vera must have done something terrible to merit such loathing. I would have to be careful about mentioning Vera's name in front of my housekeeper. I didn't want to exacerbate the situation. I'd embarrassed myself enough already. Maybe if I tiptoed lightly around her, Azalea would eventually forgive me. Otherwise her baleful presence might be too much to live with.

I continued to mull over the issue while Diesel and I walked to work, but I was simply treading the same ground over and over. While I divested myself of my coat and scarf, Diesel leaped into the window behind my desk and settled down to gaze outside and eventually to nap. He meowed twice as I sat and switched on the computer. I obliged with a few rubs on his head and ears, and he rewarded me with a loud purr.

After dealing with various e-mails, several of which required detailed responses, I focused my attention on cataloging. The Delacorte Collection was my current project, and I got a tiny thrill every time I touched one of the often-rare volumes, like the first editions of titles as diverse as *Pride and Prejudice* and *Whose Body?* I regretted the manner in which the college had obtained the books—a legacy from the late James Delacorte who had been murdered—but the opportunity to work closely with such gems was such stuff as catalogers' dreams are made on.

I smiled. Laura would appreciate my slight misquotation of Shakespeare, no doubt.

Diesel dozed in the window behind me, and other than the occasional yawn or lazy warble, I heard only the music I played while I worked. Today I listened to Telemann horn concertos. The precision of Baroque music, I generally found, provided a certain orderliness to my thought processes.

My concentration was so deep, in fact, that I worked for

almost two hours without a break. Only a series of sharp raps on the office door pulled me out of a state of deep concentration.

I stood and stretched my back and arms as I glanced at the door. I figured the person who knocked was my friend Melba Gilley, who worked downstairs in the library director's office. She visited Diesel and me at least once a day.

The person who strode into the office was Vera Cassity. To my knowledge this was her first visit to the college archives, and I wondered why on earth she was here now.

"Good morning, Mr. Harris." She stopped two feet in front of my desk and frowned. Her shoulders twitched a couple of times.

It took me a moment to realize that she expected me to take her coat—a mink I regarded with considerable distaste—and to offer her a chair. I hurried to accommodate her as I returned her greeting.

The mink safely placed on another chair and Vera seated properly, I returned to my position behind my desk.

"Tell me, Mr. Harris, do you enjoy your job here at the college?" Vera cocked her head to the right and regarded me with what she probably intended as a friendly smile.

"Yes, I do, very much." Behind me I heard Diesel mutter for a moment before he subsided. Vera's presence bothered him, and I had to admit I felt faintly uneasy.

"That's good." Vera's head returned to an upright position, and her gaze bored into mine.

The silence lengthened as I waited for the woman to explain the purpose of her visit. I was determined not to speak again until she continued.

At last she spoke. "I'm sure you know my husband and I give a lot of money to the college."

I nodded. "I've heard about the scholarships for deserving students. Very generous of you." When would the blasted woman get to the point?

Vera nodded, her expression smug. "I heard that one of the lucky boys actually lives with you. Justin Wardlaw."

"Yes, he boards with me. He's a fine young man and truly worthy of your scholarship."

Vera's eyes narrowed. "Your aunt used to have boarders, didn't she?"

"Yes, for many years. I decided to continue her tradition." Surely she wasn't here to inquire about Justin, was she?

"Your aunt was a lovely lady. A pillar of the community, you might say." Vera again offered a smile.

"Thank you. Aunt Dottie was a wonderful person." Vera was trying to butter me up for something. That must be it. But what? I itched to demand that she get to the point and stop dillydallying.

"The archives have lots of treasures, I'm sure."

Vera's abrupt change of subject threw me. Now what?

"Indeed. Some excellent collections of rare books, like the Delacorte Collection, for example." I was curious to see her reaction to the Delacorte name.

Vera shifted in her chair and shrugged. "I've known the Delacortes all my life." Her tone suggested disdain for the family.

I decided to ignore that. "The archives also house manuscripts by Athena graduates and the papers of many distinguished alumni and benefactors."

"I figured as much." Vera nodded. "Some of Athena's finest families, probably."

Again that gaze bored into me. Had we finally reached the point of her visit? I was willing to bet it had something to do with the Ducote sisters. Vera probably still smarted over her latest defeat at their hands. I figured she was the type to nurse a grudge until it was ready for Social Security.

"Certainly families important to the history of the college and of the town, too."

"Like the Ducotes." Vera fairly spat out the name.

"Yes." There was no point in denying it. If she went to the trouble, Vera could find out that much by examining the library's website and the main page for the archives. The Ducote family papers were among those listed there.

"I'm interested in the history of Athena." Vera regarded me coolly. "I've been thinking about writing some pamphlets for the Athena Historical Society. I'm president of the Society, did you know?"

"Yes, I believe I heard that." From what I'd gleaned from Helen Louise, the Athena Historical Society did very little besides having the occasional luncheon for its members where they knocked back piña coladas and shredded the reputations of any members not present. The Ducote sisters had never joined.

"I thought it would be interesting to do a pamphlet on the first families of Athena."

"That could entail a lot of research." Somehow I didn't see Vera as having the commitment for a project like that. Besides, I knew her real goal. She wanted to dig around in the Ducote family papers to try and unearth a scandal.

"I'm sure it would," Vera said. "But I think I'd enjoy it. I thought I'd start with probably the oldest family in Athena, the Ducotes."

I almost laughed. She tried to suppress her eagerness, but the gleam of malice in her eyes betrayed her.

"They are certainly one of the oldest and most distinguished families." I decided to draw it out a bit before delivering the blow.

"An'gel and Dickce are so proud of their ancestors." Vera couldn't quite keep the bitterness from her tone. "I'm sure they have their reasons."

"I believe Beauregard Ducote was one of the founders of the town."

Vera ignored that as she continued, "To do the job properly I need to look at their papers, of course."

The moment had arrived. I kept my expression neutral as I responded. "Yes, that would be ideal for your project, but I'm afraid it won't be possible."

"What do you mean?" Vera frowned. "Surely I can look at whatever I want to in the archives."

"In this case, you can't. The Ducote family papers are not open to the public."

"That's ridiculous." Vera's face reddened considerably. "Anyway, I'm not *the public*. I fork out a lot of cash to this school. You can just get busy and let me see those papers."

"No, I can't. Not without the written permission of a member of the family or their legal representatives." Diesel had a better chance of having tea with Queen Elizabeth than Vera had of getting permission to view the Ducote Collection.

Vera jumped up from her chair and loomed over my desk. Her nostrils flared, like those of a bull ready to charge. "Who the hell do you think you are?"

I stared calmly back at her, though I had to struggle not to flinch. Her head was mere inches from mine. "I'm the person in charge of the archives, and it's my responsibility to uphold the ethics of the position."

"I can have you fired." Any moment now I expected her to start foaming at the mouth, she was so angry.

I made no effort to disguise my extreme dislike as I

replied, "Go right ahead. My boss's office is right downstairs. I'm sure he'd be happy to speak with you."

Diesel growled as he leaped over my shoulder to land on my desk. Papers went flying, and I had to grab a couple of rare volumes to keep them from hitting the floor. Vera jolted back and stumbled into her chair. She sat abruptly as my cat hissed at her.

"Call off that thing." Vera trembled and scooted her chair back at least a foot. "I'll sue the hell out of you if it so much as touches me."

I bit back a retort. Diesel wouldn't want his mouth on any part of her. I placed my hand on the cat's head and stroked. He calmed after a moment.

"I don't believe there's anything else I can do for you, Mrs. Cassity." I got up from behind the desk and retrieved her fur.

She snatched it away and grabbed her purse. She stomped off but paused in the doorway and turned back. "I think it's time I reconsidered some of the scholarships I give out. *And* maybe have a talk with the animal control people about that monster." She gestured rudely at Diesel before she disappeared.

SIX

|||||||||||||||||||||

All the rest of that day and the next I stewed over Vera's threats against Justin and Diesel; I replayed the scene in my head several times a day. But I saw no evidence that she followed through with either threat.

Should I have been more conciliatory?

No, the end result wouldn't have changed. I could not let her have access to the Ducote papers, no matter what she swore to do.

Perhaps Vera blustered more than she bit. Many bullies talked big but didn't follow through with their threats. I tried to comfort myself with that thought, but I remained preoccupied with my concerns. I confided in no one, though, because I didn't want to alarm my family unduly.

Vera didn't reappear at the archives or come to the public library on Friday when I did my volunteer stint, Diesel at my side. I braced myself for a confrontation from the moment I walked in the door that day, because Vera often turned up on Fridays. For all her faults she was a voracious reader and usually ripped through five or six books a week, mostly romances and thrillers. As the end of my volunteer shift approached, however, there had been no sign of her.

Miss Dickce Ducote came in a few minutes before three and approached me at the reference desk. The moment she said hello, Diesel, snoozing at my feet, perked up and stretched before loping around the desk to rub himself against her legs. I waited while Miss Dickce cooed over my cat and rubbed his head. Diesel rewarded her with purrs and chirps, and other people nearby looked on indulgently. Diesel was popular with library patrons, and I knew quite a few of them waited until Fridays to visit the library, just so they could see him.

"He is such a lovely boy. Aren't you, Diesel?" Miss Dickce kept her hand on the cat's head as she focused on me. "Charlie, I know this is a terrible imposition, and awfully last-minute, but An'gel and I were hoping you might join us at River Hill this afternoon for tea. Diesel, too, of course."

"It's no imposition at all." Miss Dickce spoke so charmingly that I couldn't refuse, even had I wanted to. I had nothing special planned for the afternoon, and I knew Diesel would love being fussed over by the sisters. "Diesel and I are delighted to accept your invitation."

Miss Dickce smiled. "You are always the gentleman." She glanced down at the cat. "You, too, you gorgeous thing." She faced me again. "How about four o'clock? Will that be convenient for you?"

I assured her that it would, and after a final pat on the head for Diesel, Miss Dickce left the library.

Diesel and I headed home soon after. I wanted to freshen up a bit before we drove out to River Hill. I toyed with the idea of changing into a suit, because somehow an invitation to tea from the Ducote sisters seemed to merit the formality. I wavered, wondering whether I was being foolish, but quickly decided that I wasn't. The sisters always dressed impeccably, and since this was my first invitation to tea with them, I figured I should live up to the standards they set.

Attired in a dark suit, white shirt, and deep purple tie, I pointed the car toward the outskirts of Athena. Our destination lay several miles to the west of the city limits, in the gently rolling hills. Diesel stared intently out the window in the backseat, alert to the fact that we were not taking one of our usual routes. He rarely went into the country, so the terrain here was strange to him.

I wondered what lay behind this invitation to River Hill. Miss Dickce hadn't said Diesel and I would be the only guests for tea, so perhaps this was to be an impromptu Friends of the Library board meeting. That thought caused me some anxiety. Would Vera be there? I wasn't sure I wanted to face her again so soon after that scene in my office. Good manners prevailed, however. I had accepted the invitation, and I wasn't going to turn the car around and head home just because Vera might attend.

With a start I realized we were nearing the turn from the highway onto the Ducote estate. The driveway wound through an acre of trees vivid with autumn hues of red, yellow, and orange. After a sharp bend in the road the house came into sight, the last hundred yards or so of the drive was bordered by huge, ancient oak trees. When we cleared the trees, I could see the house more clearly.

The builder of River Hill, Beauregard Ducote, chose the Greek Revival style, much in vogue in the 1830s when the house was erected. Tall columns stretched across the front of the three-story house. Larger than many of its contemporaries, River Hill featured galleries around both upper floors.

The view from there would be stunning, I was sure. The white paint of the house glistened in the late-afternoon sunlight, but shadows from the tall oaks crept ever closer.

Diesel followed closely by my side as I strode up the walk and onto the verandah. In answer to my knock, the door opened almost immediately. Miss Dickce smiled and bade us enter.

The interior of River Hill appeared as elegant as the exterior. A grand staircase led to the upper stories, and the marble floor, where it was bare of antique rugs, gleamed in the light.

"Welcome to River Hill, Charlie, Diesel."

Miss An'gel approached us through a door to my right and extended her hand. I shook it gently, then released it as she switched her attention to my cat.

The preliminaries of petting Diesel out of the way, we followed the elder Ducote sister into the front parlor. The room reminded me somewhat of the parlor at the Delacorte mansion, simply but beautifully furnished with period pieces. Several portraits and small paintings graced the walls. Miss An'gel invited me to sit in an armchair that proved sturdy despite its delicate appearance. The slender, highly polished arms felt smooth and cool to my touch, and the cushioned seat was surprisingly comfortable.

The Ducotes occupied a nearby sofa close to the fireplace, leaving room for Diesel to spread himself between them. He placed his head in Miss An'gel's lap, while his tail flopped across Miss Dickce's legs. The sisters appeared happy with this arrangement, though I winced to think how much cat hair they would have to remove later on from their black dresses.

Miss An'gel pointed to the portrait over the fireplace. "Our ancestor, Beauregard Ducote, who built River Hill."

I gazed with interest at the gentleman. I had heard his name often enough but had never seen an image of him. From what I could discern from the artist's vision, Beauregard Ducote was a man of intelligence. Handsome, with a strong nose and an easy smile. Both the sisters favored their ancestor. "Who was the artist?"

"C. R. Parker," Miss Dickce replied. "He was quite well-known in the antebellum South. He had a studio in New Orleans."

"As I recall he received a commission for some portraits in the Louisiana Capitol in the 1820s." I saw some of Parker's works in an exhibition a few years ago.

"Yes, that is correct." Miss An'gel inclined her head and bestowed a smile upon me, I assumed in approval of my knowledge.

"Here is Clementine with our tea."

At Miss Dickce's words I glanced toward the door to see an elderly woman approaching us pushing a tea cart in front of her. She wore a black maid's uniform complete with frilly white apron and lace cuffs at her wrists. Her head was bare of a cap, however, and her mocha-colored skin made her silvery hair even more striking.

"Thank you, Clementine, I will pour." Miss An'gel nodded at her employee, and Clementine rolled the cart to a stop in front of her. She flashed a quick smile at me, but her gaze appeared riveted on Diesel.

"Is that a bobcat?" she asked, her voice deep and raspy. She sounded like a lifelong heavy smoker.

"No, ma'am. He's a Maine Coon cat, and they can get to be really big. His name is Diesel, and he's large even for a Maine Coon." I smiled up at Clementine. "He's actually a sweet-natured cat and very friendly."

"Yes, sir." Clementine grinned. "That the biggest ol' cat

I ever did see. I reckon I heard about him from Azalea Berry." With that she turned and left the room.

"I believe Clementine was a good friend of Azalea's late mother." Miss An'gel began to pour out the tea, and Miss Dickce prepared a small plate of cookies for me.

I accepted both, worried that I might have one of my clumsy spells and pour tea all over the no-doubt priceless carpet underneath my chair.

Miss Dickce evidently picked up on my anxiety. She pointed to a small table at my elbow that I had overlooked. "There's a table and a coaster all ready for you, Charlie."

"Thank you." I set the cup and saucer down gently. When I focused on the sisters again, I noticed that Miss An'gel had a small plate of what looked like chicken.

"Is it okay to give Diesel a little treat? I thought it would be rude of us not to include him, and Clementine cooked the chicken this afternoon." Miss An'gel cocked her head to one side as she regarded me.

"That's very kind of you." I would have to watch what Diesel cadged from the dinner table tonight, but I figured a little chicken now wouldn't hurt him.

Miss An'gel fed Diesel a couple of small bites of the chicken before passing the plate to her sister. Diesel quickly shifted position to keep the treats in sight.

I sampled one of the cookies, oatmeal raisin, and almost groaned aloud in pleasure. My expression surely communicated my happiness.

The sisters exchanged a smile, and Miss An'gel chuckled. "Yes, Clementine has quite the touch when it comes to baking." She wiped her fingers on a linen napkin, then set it aside. Her tone turned brisk as she continued, "We're delighted you could join us for tea this afternoon, Charlie.

I'm sure you must be wondering, though, why we invited you here on such short notice."

I set my teacup down with extreme care as I answered. "Yes, ma'am, I do admit to being curious."

"My sister and I wanted to express our thanks, privately, of course, for the way you stood up to Vera Cassity yesterday. We know she threatened to retaliate."

My jaw dropped in surprise. How on earth had the Ducote sisters found out about the episode? I hadn't told anyone, and I couldn't imagine even Vera having the gall to take her complaint directly to Miss An'gel or Miss Dickce.

As I struggled to frame a reply, Miss Dickce spoke. "We have our sources for what goes on in Athena. People tend to tell us things, and Vera isn't always as discreet as she should be."

"Especially when she's annoyed with someone." Miss An'gel shook her head. "Even after all this time, she never has learned that it doesn't pay to shoot your mouth off to all and sundry."

I could well imagine. Vera Cassity didn't seem like the type to suffer in silence.

"She did make a couple of threats." I really didn't want to go into specifics and was hoping the sisters would let it rest at that.

"You don't need to have any fears about Diesel," Miss Dickce said with a serene smile. "Vera won't be able to do a thing to harm him." She stroked the cat's head as he sniffed at the now-empty plate, eager for more tidbits. "Not this beautiful boy."

Miss An'gel nodded. "And if she dares to cancel that nice young Wardlaw boy's scholarship, we'll see that she is thoroughly embarrassed for her meanness."

Vera was evidently even more indiscreet than I expected. "Thank you," I said. "I have to admit that her threats had me pretty worked up." I wondered briefly who the informant was.

"Now you can rest easy." Miss An'gel had a sip of tea. "We knew already that you were a man of integrity, Charlie, and your actions in protecting the privacy of our family show that clearly."

As always, any kind of direct praise made me uncomfortable. I mumbled my thanks.

"And you're modest as well." Miss Dickce winked at me, and I relaxed. Somehow that little gesture made me feel more comfortable, less like I was having an audience with the queen.

"We've put up with Vera's little tantrums for years because she does pour a lot of money into worthy causes in Athena." Miss An'gel's expression turned steely. "But there are limits, and lately Vera has been pushing the boundaries of the acceptable in terms of some of her behavior."

"And it has nothing to do with her background," Miss Dickce said. "Despite what she may think." She shook her head. "Good people are good no matter what kind of family they have. Vera is just plain mean."

"That she is." Miss An'gel took back the reins of the conversation. "She thinks we are always thwarting her simply because we think she's socially unacceptable, but that just proves how self-deluded she is." She sighed. "But that's neither here nor there. The problem is, Vera is getting nastier, and she has got to be stopped."

"She's meddling in things that don't concern her," Miss Dickce said. "Not just our family history, though what she expected to find in the family papers, I haven't the faintest idea," she sniffed. "The Ducotes have been boringly respectable for generations."

"Sadly, yes." Miss An'gel laughed. "Dull as ditch water, as the saying goes." Her expression hardened. "All that aside, Vera is headed for trouble, the kind of trouble she may never survive."

SEVEN

Miss Dickce burst into laughter. "Oh, Charlie, your face just now. You'd think An'gel was talking about *strangling* Vera the way you looked."

Diesel tilted his head up at her and warbled.

She laughed again. "See, Diesel thinks it's funny, too."

Miss An'gel frowned at her sister. "I'm sure Charlie thought nothing of the sort. You're entirely too frivolous sometimes." She turned her attention to me, as I was trying valiantly not to laugh.

"There's no need for something so extreme to bring Vera to heel," Miss An'gel said, her tone repressive. "The moment I heard about Vera's attempt to stick her nose into our family papers, I called our lawyer, Q. C. Pendergrast. He knew exactly what to do to put a halt to such nonsense. He simply got on the phone to Mr. Cassity and explained the situation. That was all it took."

Miss Dickce rolled her eyes at her sibling. "Do you truly

think Morty has that kind of control over his wife? You go into the library and pull the dictionary off the shelf. Look under *loose cannon*, and you'll find Vera's picture. That woman is crazy as a betsy bug."

"Very amusing, sister." Miss An'gel cast a venomous glance at Miss Dickce. "I know Vera as well as you do. She has never quite understood the meaning of restraint, but Mr. Cassity holds the purse strings in the family. Without the money to back up her oversized mouth, she can't accomplish much."

There had been no opportunity for me to contribute to the conversation, even had I wanted to. Diesel, however, continued to chirp and purr as the sisters engaged in their verbal sparring match. He appeared to be enjoying the exchange. I found it pretty entertaining myself, but I was afraid it might escalate into something unpleasant. I had heard stories of some of their epic arguments and didn't really want to be witness to one of them.

Miss An'gel must have sensed my concern. "Pay no mind to us, Charlie. This is what comes of two old maids knocking about in a big house like this for decades on end." She cut a sideways glance at her sister.

Miss Dickce took the cue and nodded. "Oh, yes, Sister and I have a fine old time pointing out each other's foibles and follies. But we didn't invite you here to put on a show." She giggled, looking suddenly twenty years younger.

I wasn't quite sure what to say, but Diesel saved me from having to reply right away. His continued vocalizing made the Misses Ducote laugh, and that gave me a few seconds more. "I've seen siblings, um, have differing opinions before. My son and daughter have the occasional disagreement."

"Tactful, too," Miss Dickce murmured.

Her sister ignored her. "We want to assure you, Charlie,

that you don't have to worry about Vera. We still have to deal with her over the gala, of course, but all the arrangements are well in hand. There's not much Vera can do to upset them at this point."

Despite Miss An'gel's assurances, I wasn't convinced that Vera could be dismissed that easily. In the long run, though, I would put my money on the Misses Ducote to triumph in any contest with her.

"I'm relieved to hear that, Miss An'gel," I said. "I'm looking forward to the gala. River Hill is such a lovely setting for an event like that."

The sisters beamed with pride. "Yes, it is. We've been so fortunate to call it home these many years." Miss An'gel paused. "And you'll forgive me if I don't say exactly how many years that is."

We all shared a smile, and I sneaked a glance at my watch. It was nearly four thirty now, and I should head home soon to help with dinner.

"We're so pleased you had time to visit this afternoon." Miss Dickce scratched Diesel's head. "Both of you. And once the gala is over, you two mustn't be strangers here."

"No, indeed." Miss An'gel rubbed down Diesel's spine, and the cat's expression betrayed utter bliss at such attention. I'd have a hard time getting him off that sofa as long as the sisters were petting him.

"Next time you must bring your daughter and son," Miss An'gel continued. "Q.C. tells us Sean is an outstanding young man, and I do believe he thinks there is a faint sound of wedding bells in the air."

Before I could respond, Miss Dickce said, "And I would dearly love to hear about Laura's experiences in Hollywood."

"She'd be delighted to talk to you about them," I said. "Sean is very fond of Alexandra, I know, but if they have

any plans for marriage, they haven't shared them with me."
I smiled. "But I wouldn't be at all surprised if Mr. Pendergrast is right."

The sisters nodded as I continued, "Diesel and I both
have enjoyed this tremendously, and please express my
compliments to Clementine for her wonderful cookies." I
rose. "We mustn't impose on you any longer, though. It's
time we headed home to help with dinner."

Miss An'gel stood, and I tried not to wince at the sight
of a clump of cat hair on her skirt. She appeared serenely
unaware of it. "Of course, Charlie. Thank you again for
sharing tea with us." She stepped forward as her sister gently disengaged herself from Diesel and rose from the sofa.

"Come along, Diesel." I held out my hand, and after a
brief hesitation the cat stepped off the sofa and came to me.
I patted his head before we followed the sisters to the front
door.

"Miss An'gel, telephone." Clementine's voice sounded
from behind us.

"In a moment," Miss An'gel called back. She took my
hand and gave it a firm squeeze. "We'll see you again soon.
Now, please excuse me, I must go answer that call."

I bade her good-bye, and Miss Dickce shook my hand
and added her own farewell. "Don't worry anymore about
Vera."

I assured her I wouldn't. Diesel and I headed for the car
and were soon en route homeward.

The grandfather clock in the front hall was chiming five
as Diesel and I entered the kitchen from the garage. Enticing
aromas eddied through the air, and my nose took notice.
Despite my consumption of several of Clementine's oatmeal
cookies, I felt hungry. The smell of lasagna often did that.

"Hi, Dad." Laura came to greet me with a kiss on the cheek and a hug. "Where have you and Diesel been?"

"Didn't you see the note I left?" I frowned. "I stuck it on the fridge."

Laura laughed, a throaty, infectious sound. "Yes, I did. But all it said was 'Gone to tea. Back around five.' I've been dying of curiosity ever since."

"Sorry, I thought I said where we were going." I loosened my tie and unbuttoned the top button. "Ah, that's better. Diesel and I have been at River Hill having tea with the Misses Ducote."

"Oh, do tell." Laura's eyes lit up. "You'll have to fill me in on it. I can't wait to see the house. All I've seen are pictures of the exterior, and it's gorgeous."

"You'll see inside it soon enough. The gala's only four days away now." I shrugged off my jacket and folded it over my arm. "The house is every bit as beautiful inside as it is outside. At least the areas I saw were, the entryway and the front parlor. Antiques, portraits, and so on. A real showplace."

"The gala will be such a hoot." Laura went back to the oven and peered through the glass. "I think this needs another fifteen or twenty minutes."

"Good. Then I have time to go upstairs and change out of my Sunday-go-to-meeting clothes."

"Aw, you look so handsome and distinguished in that suit, Dad." Laura pouted. "Don't come back looking all scruffy."

I offered her a mock-severe frown. "Young lady, I'll have you know I've never been scruffy in my life. Well, at least not since I was about ten, anyway."

Laura laughed again. "I know, I've seen Aunt Dottie's pictures. You could be quite the dirty little piglet sometimes."

"None of your sass, now." I grinned as I recalled one picture in particular. I was dirt-splattered from making mud pies in Aunt Dottie's backyard. My aunt snorted with laughter, then ran for her camera. Much to my chagrin in later years, she often pulled out that shot to show friends and family.

"I promise to be presentable," I said as I headed for the stairs.

Laura arched an eyebrow. "You'd better be. Don't forget, Helen Louise is coming to dinner."

Hoping against hope that I wasn't blushing, I scooted for the stairs. Behind me I heard Laura talking to Diesel and promising him some tidbits at dinner.

I hadn't forgotten that Helen Louise was coming to dinner, but Laura's reminder prompted me to think more carefully about my change of clothes. I put my suit away, kept the white shirt on, and slipped into dark pants. I added a light cotton sweater, a deep emerald green, which had been a birthday present from Helen Louise. She loved the color, and I knew she'd enjoy seeing me wear her gift.

Downstairs again I found Sean and Diesel with Laura in the kitchen. Sean had his hands in the salad bowl, tearing lettuce. My big helpful kitty kept a close eye on Laura as she put a tray of garlic bread into the oven to warm. He meowed as the bread disappeared and moved anxiously closer as Laura shut the door.

"It will come out all nice and toasty," Laura assured the cat, "and I'll make sure you have a few bites."

I cleared my throat, and Laura started. She flashed me a guilty smile. "That is, if Dad says it's okay."

"He's already had some nice extra treats today, courtesy of the Ducote sisters." I put on a stern expression, then spoiled it with a chuckle. "But you can give him two small—very small—pinches of garlic bread."

"Okay, Dad." Laura came closer and dropped a quick kiss on my cheek.

"You're hobnobbing with the society crowd these days." Sean finished with the salad and moved to the sink to rinse his hands. "Having tea with the Ducote sisters may put you on the A-list in Athena." He grinned as he dried off with a tea towel.

I put on my best aristocratic drawl. "Yes, I'm thinking of hiring a chauffeur to drive the new Rolls I ordered. I can't be seen driving myself around town now."

"Wonderful." Laura clapped her hands. "Does this mean I can have that diamond and emerald tiara I've always wanted? Christmas *is* only a couple weeks away, after all."

"How about a Lamborghini for me?" Sean smirked at me. "I've been a good boy lately."

"Whatever you want," I said airily. "The sky's the limit."

We all had a hearty laugh, and as I watched my two children making merry I felt a deep sense of satisfaction. Having both of them with me these past few months was a great blessing, and I didn't want to think about Laura heading back to California after the holidays. Sean could be moving out also, but perhaps not for a while. He seemed comfortably ensconced here, but if he and Alexandra did get married, they would want their own home.

The ringing of the front doorbell interrupted my journey down Melancholy Lane. "I'll go," I said. "I'm sure it's Helen Louise."

Sean and Laura exchanged a smile, and Diesel, hearing the name of one of his favorite people, loped after me as I headed out of the kitchen.

He reached the front door before me and reared up on his hind legs. With both his front paws he started twisting the knob. He had learned this little trick some time ago, and I suspected Justin had taught him to do it.

"Hang on, boy, there's a dead bolt, too." If he ever learned to open that, I could have real trouble on my hands. With my help at the dead bolt Diesel was able to open the door. We both moved back to admit Helen Louise. She looked lovely tonight in a crimson midlength skirt and jacket over a cream-colored blouse. The crimson suited her dark coloring perfectly.

"Charlie, Diesel, am I glad to see the two of you." Helen Louise slipped off her jacket after giving me a kiss and the cat a scratch of the head. "I've spent the most frustrating hour. I'm about ready to take somebody's head off."

"Uh-oh. What happened?" I took her hand and tucked it into the crook of my arm. I led her toward the kitchen, while Diesel made circles around us on the way.

"Vera Cassity. That's what happened." The venom in Helen Louise's voice didn't surprise me, considering Vera was the cause of her distress.

"What did she do?" I asked as we walked into the kitchen.

"All she's doing," Helen Louise replied, eyes flashing hatred, "is trying to run me out of business."

EIGHT

Helen Louise sank into the chair Sean pulled out for her. Diesel put a paw on her leg and laid his head beside it. He warbled for her, and she sighed and rubbed his head. "Oh, you sweet boy. You're just what I needed." She glanced at me and then at the other two faces regarding her with concern. "All of you."

"How is the Wicked Witch of North Mississippi trying to run you out of business?" Laura handed Helen Louise a glass of iced tea.

Helen Louise took a quick sip before she responded. "Delicious. Vera had the gall to come into the bakery around four thirty this afternoon and inform me—in a voice loud enough for everyone within five miles to hear— that the Friends board was canceling its order for the gala. Do you know how much money I spent on the ingredients for all those pastries and cakes?"

"Why on earth would they cancel? The gala's only a few days away." Laura frowned. "That doesn't make any sense."

"No, it doesn't," I said. "Did Vera give you a reason?"

"She certainly did. She had the colossal nerve to say someone on the board had heard that several people came down with food poisoning after eating some of my food." Helen Louise drained the rest of her tea. "That was an out-and-out lie."

"Of course it was." I squeezed her shoulder, and she put a hand over mine as she smiled up at me.

"How about a refill?" Sean reached for Helen Louise's glass.

"Definitely," she said. "Slip a little bourbon in it while you're at it."

Sean grinned. "If that's what you want, I think Dad's got some stashed away somewhere."

Helen Louise laughed. "No, only kidding. If I start on the bourbon, I'll just get maudlin, and none of you needs to see that."

"What did you say to Mrs. Cassity about the food poisoning?" Laura asked. She bent to peek in the oven. "Time to get this out."

"I lit into her like a wild dog after Jezebel." Helen Louise offered a grim smile. "I told her exactly what I thought of her, and I also told her my lawyer would call her first thing tomorrow and she'd better be prepared for the biggest lawsuit for slander the great state of Mississippi has ever seen."

Sean whistled as he handed her a fresh glass of tea. "I bet you were terrifying. What did Mrs. Cassity have to say then?"

"Not a blessed thing. She turned white as the proverbial driven snow—which she sure isn't—and almost ran out of there." Helen Louise swigged down half her glass with evident satisfaction.

"I'm proud of you for standing up for yourself like that." I bent to drop a kiss on her cheek. "Vera is a nasty piece of work, that's for sure."

Helen Louise frowned. "She did say something odd, though, in the midst of all those lies about the food poisoning. Now, what was it? Oh, I know, she said I ought to be more careful about the company I keep. What do you think she meant by that?"

I felt my blood pressure start to rise, and if Vera had been anywhere near, I think I would have set aside the manners of a lifetime and slapped the pee wadden out of her. It took me a moment to calm myself enough to speak.

"I know exactly what she meant, that vicious harpy. She's angry with me because I wouldn't let her snoop around in the Ducote family papers. She threatened me, but Miss An'gel thwarted her, so she decided to get at me through you."

Helen Louise used a word I had never heard her speak, disconcerting me. Diesel drew back in alarm at her tone, however, and Helen Louise hastened to reassure him. He calmed under her touch.

Laura said, "Amen to that. That woman ought to be put away somewhere. Who does she think she is, anyway?"

"Evidently she thinks she can run roughshod over everyone in town." Sean shoved his hands in his pants pockets as he leaned back against the counter. I could see his hands ball up inside the fabric as his face darkened in anger. "Dad, we can't let her get away with this."

"She won't, I can promise you that," Helen Louise said. "The minute Vera was out the door I got on the phone and called Miss An'gel to tell her about it. She advised me to call my lawyer, as I threatened Vera I'd do. She also said she had plans to give Vera the comeuppance she so richly deserves." She laughed. "She wouldn't tell me what she meant. All she'd say was that I would enjoy this year's gala more than ever and to go ahead and proceed as we'd planned with the pastries."

That must have been the phone call Miss An'gel had to take as I was leaving River Hill, I realized.

"Who is your lawyer, by the way?" Sean asked as he set the heaping bowl of salad on the table.

Helen Louise's expression turned impish. "Why, your future father-in-law, of course. I deal only with the best."

Sean turned bright red, and Laura and I exchanged amused glances. Sean had been remarkably close-mouthed about his relationship with Alexandra Pendergrast since he'd begun working for her father. I could understand his reticence. His abrupt departure from Houston and his job there was connected to a prior romantic relationship.

"How *is* Alexandra? I haven't talked to her in ages." Laura couldn't resist twisting the knife. She loved to rag her big brother; after all, turnabout was fair play when it came to sibling annoyance.

Sean shot a dark look at his sister. I read it easily. Payback would be no fun for Laura.

"If you must know, Alexandra is fine. *We* are fine, but we are *not* talking about marriage." Sean's icy tone boded ill for dinner conversation.

Helen Louise looked contrite. "All in good time. I'm sorry, Sean, sometimes I let my mouth run away from me. Forgive me, please?"

Sean glared for a moment, but his essential good humor quickly reasserted itself. But I didn't trust that glint in his eye as he bent to kiss Helen Louise's cheek. "I'll talk about weddings when I hear you and Dad talking about one, how's that?"

Now it was my turn to blush furiously, and Helen Louise ducked her head, obviously trying not to laugh. "Enough of that," I finally managed to say. "I think it's time we ate dinner."

The quicker we got away from the subject of weddings, the better. Helen Louise and I hadn't looked that far ahead, and frankly, I wasn't ready to just yet. Sean and I were alike in that respect.

At the mention of dinner Diesel meowed loudly and glanced from me to Laura and back again. His expression was so hopeful, and so funny, that we all started laughing, and the tension dissipated.

We busied ourselves with plates and bowls of salad, and the conversation shifted to other topics as we ate. Diesel sat first by Helen Louise, then by Laura, knowing full well they were easier touches than Sean. I would of course be his last resort.

"Where's Stewart tonight?" Sean asked. "Isn't this his lasagna?"

"It is," Laura said. "He has a date tonight, and he was all atwitter." She grinned. "Either it's a first date or the guy must be pretty special. Stewart changed his clothes about seven times before he finally settled on something."

While the others chatted about Stewart and the possible identity of his new flame, I found myself unable to shake Vera Cassity from my thoughts. Her attempts to cause trouble infuriated me, and I wondered what I could possibly do to put a stop to it.

The obvious answer to that was to let her have access to the Ducote archives. But there was no way I was going to compromise my professional ethics and allow that. I'd never be able to look Miss An'gel and Miss Dickce in the face again if I did.

Thoughts of the Ducote sisters reminded me of what Helen Louise had told us earlier—and of my own conversation that afternoon with the sisters. The warlike gleam in Miss An'gel's eyes meant trouble for Vera, but I had no idea what the Ducotes planned to do to neutralize her. Things might come to a head at the gala, according to Helen Louise. I was nervous enough already about that, and the thought of histrionics on a grand, public scale made me push my lasagna away, half eaten.

The biblical adage went around and around in my head: "Pride goeth before destruction, and an haughty spirit before a fall." The language of the King James Version— almost always misquoted, which annoyed me—made it sound more doom laden than the modernized revisions of more recent years.

If anyone seemed hell-bent on destruction, it was Vera Cassity.

NINE

|||||||||||||||||||||||||||||||||||

The Tuesday of the Friends of the Library annual gala dawned cold but clear. The temperature even promised to hit the midfifties by late afternoon. All in all, an auspicious beginning to what would be a long—and stressful—day. We had sold a record hundred and twenty-seven tickets for the event and had raised nearly ten thousand dollars so far. We would get more from the silent auction with prizes like round-trip airfare and a week's stay at a nice hotel in London, signed first editions by Mississippi writers, and gift certificates from local merchants.

The party would overflow with food, probably much more than the attendees could eat. In addition to the pastries and cakes and mini quiches from Helen Louise's bakery, Miss An'gel and Miss Dickce had arranged contributions from two restaurants and a caterer. No one would go hungry tonight.

The board decided early on to make this year's gala

different from previous ones by making it a costumed affair. All attendees were urged to come dressed as their favorite characters from popular fiction. Miss Dickce suggested we have a costume contest, with prizes for the best single and couple costumes, and everyone agreed. Board members wouldn't take part in the contest but would judge instead.

Helen Louise and I, both avid mystery readers, put our heads together several weeks ago and decided we should pick an interesting couple from mystery fiction. As fans of Agatha Christie, we eventually landed on Hercule Poirot and Ariadne Oliver. After a trip to a costume shop and two thrift stores in Memphis, we found what we needed.

Diesel regarded me with what looked like suspicion as I affixed my fake mustache to my upper lip with spirit gum. Once it was in place I looked down at him. "*Bon soir, mon chat.* I am the famous detective Hercule Poirot." Diesel appeared not the least impressed with my attempt to sound like David Suchet, the amazing actor who portrayed Poirot on the small screen so brilliantly.

I surveyed myself in the mirror with a certain amount of satisfaction. Helen Louise had helped me choose the suit, of the type Suchet often wore onscreen. Even if I said so myself, I did look rather dapper. I felt oddly formal, however, and hoped I wouldn't overheat during the gala. The wool of the suit, added to the heavy linen shirt, an undershirt, a silk waistcoat, and a thick cravat were much warmer than I had expected.

It was all for a good cause, I reflected as I preened in the mirror a moment longer. Diesel made snuffling noises, and I wondered if that was a feline attempt at laughter. I rubbed his head, and the noises became rumbling purrs.

"You're not going to be too happy with me in a little

while," I told him. When I left the house without him, he would be annoyed, but there would simply be too many people at the gala. As sociable as he was, he would be freaked out by the noise and the sheer mass of bodies. He would be better off here at home, and Justin had agreed to babysit. He'd had his last final earlier today, and he planned on an evening of relaxation with a good book, an old movie or two, and some quality time with his favorite cat.

The rest of the household would join us at River Hill tonight. Stewart, as a board member, had to be present. Laura would be escorted by her boyfriend, Frank Salisbury, a young professor in the theater department at Athena College, and Sean was going with Alexandra Pendergrast. Neither of my children nor Stewart would tell me what characters they'd chosen to portray. The secretiveness of it all was simply part of the fun, and everyone seemed to have entered into the spirit of the event.

In the back of my mind, however, I couldn't let go of my worries about Vera Cassity and what she might do. Since her attack on Helen Louise a few days ago, she had made no further moves—as far as I was aware—to punish me for not letting her snoop in the archives. Perhaps she was well and truly chastened by orders from Q. C. Pendergrast and her husband to stop meddling. No matter how much money Vera—or rather, her husband, Morty—had, Q. C. Pendergrast would pull out any necessary stops to put Vera in her place.

Maybe I worried over nothing. Maybe the gala would go off without a hitch tonight, and Vera would be on her best behavior. After all, she aimed to be the cynosure of the cream of Athena society, and she wouldn't want to embarrass herself in front of them by doing anything nasty or vindictive.

Right—and the mighty Mississippi might start flowing north any minute now.

Diesel ran down the stairs ahead of me and into the kitchen, where we found Justin eating a sandwich and chips. He had a book propped open beside his plate, but he looked up when I entered.

His eyes widened, and he grinned. "Cool costume, Mr. Charlie. Poirot, right? Love the mustache, too."

"Thanks, and, yes, I'm Hercule Poirot." I glanced at the clock. It was a few minutes past five thirty. "Helen Louise is going as Mrs. Oliver, and I'd better be on my way to pick her up. We're supposed to be at River Hill by six at the latest."

"Don't worry about Diesel," Justin said as he caressed the cat's shoulders and along his spine. Diesel chirped happily in response. "He and I will have a fine old time tonight while y'all enjoy yourselves at the ball. Will someone take pictures? I bet the costumes will be awesome."

"There's supposed to be a photographer from the paper, so I'm sure he'll snap plenty of photos." I grabbed my keys, and Diesel saw me. He started toward me, but Justin called him back. "Not tonight, boy, you have to stay here with Justin."

Distracted by the sudden offer of a bit of ham, Diesel wasn't looking as I slipped out the back door and into the garage.

Helen Louise was ready when I reached her house several blocks away. She lived in her late parents' home, a lovely two-story brick house that dated from the early twentieth century.

"You look terrific," she said as I stepped into the entryway. *"Très formidable."* She kissed me, then stood back so I could get the full effect of her ensemble.

She had decided to model herself on Zoë Wanamaker's portrayal of Ariadne Oliver in the television series. Her below-the-knee-length dress sported a multitude of colors in an abstract pattern. Three long necklaces with beads of varying sizes circled her neck and dangled down her chest. Her hat—well, her hat sported enough flowers to fill three or four bouquets. She carried a handbag, and she opened it to show me several apples inside it. "So what do you think?"

"Magnificent, and beautiful as always."

That earned me another, longer kiss, and when we drew apart her cheeks glowed pink. Mine probably did as well.

"We should get going," I said, a little out of breath. "Too bad we can't enter the contest, because I think we could win." I opened the door.

"I'm sure we could," Helen Louise said as she stepped outside. I waited while she locked the door, then escorted her down the walk and to my car.

"I hope everything goes smoothly tonight," I said as I fastened my seat belt.

"It will," Helen Louise replied, her tone firm. "Miss An'gel and Miss Dickce wouldn't have it any other way."

"It's not them I'm worried about."

"Stop scowling, Charlie. Your mustache will fall off." Helen Louise laughed. "Vera wouldn't dare pull anything tonight of all nights. It's a perfect chance for her to be the grande dame, so she'll be on good behavior, just you wait and see."

The sun had been setting the past few days at just about five o'clock, but the twilight would persist awhile yet. Traffic was sparse on the way to River Hill. Most of the guests wouldn't arrive for a good half hour or more, and by then it would be dark.

Lanterns lit the driveway to the estate, and Morty Cassity's valet-parking staff—employees from his car dealerships dragooned into service—stood ready to go into action as I pulled the car up in front of the house. I handed my keys over to a uniformed young man and received a plastic disk in return. He nodded as I thanked him, and one of his coworkers held the door for Helen Louise. As we climbed the steps to the verandah, I glanced back to see my car disappear down a gravel road to the east of the house.

A butler in Edwardian dress greeted us at the door and, in the posh tones of an Oxbridge graduate, informed us we would find the Misses Ducote in the kitchen and ushered us there.

The sounds of clinking china and utensils greeted us, along with the voices of the catering and serving staff who swarmed like bees under the basilisk gazes of the elder Ducote sister and her housekeeper, Clementine.

"Good evening, my dears." Miss An'gel motioned for us to precede her back into the hallway. "Everything is under control here. Clementine is in charge, and I think we'd probably better get out of the way."

We stood aside to let Miss An'gel lead us to the front parlor. The house glowed with light, and the mingled scents of vanilla and lavender emanated from the candles.

"This is going to be such a wonderful night, don't you think?" Miss An'gel turned to smile at us, and now I had time to take in her costume.

I should have guessed that Miss An'gel would choose to portray one of the most indomitable females in all of mystery fiction. "Amelia Peabody Emerson. You look marvelous."

Indeed, the elder Ducote sister made a splendid Amelia. She had the outfit down to the smallest detail, except for the umbrella the intrepid Egyptologist usually brandished.

The split skirt, the pith helmet, the belt of tools, the sturdy boots—all perfect.

"Thank you, M'sieur Poirot. And how clever of you to bring Mrs. Oliver with you." Miss An'gel's aristocratic Mississippi drawl didn't fit, but that didn't matter. She had the grand manner down pat.

"Hello, everyone." Miss Dickce spoke from behind us, and I did my best not to gawk when I turned to greet her. Beside me I heard Helen Louise turn a startled gasp into a more polite and genteel cough.

Red hair piled into a bun on the top of her head, a pencil sticking out of it, an overlarge handbag on her arm, and a pantsuit in neon shades of green and blue—the only thing missing was a cigarette. Miss Dickce was every bit as big a fan of Elizabeth Peters as her sister, and her portrayal of Jacqueline Kirby revealed an impish side to her character that I'd not suspected before now.

I bowed over her extended hand and brushed the knuckles with a light kiss. *"Enchanté, madame."*

Miss Dickce giggled as I released her hand. *"Merci, Hercule."* She clapped her hands, the handbag wobbling on her arm. "Isn't this a hoot? We're going to have a blast tonight. I can just feel it."

"And no one is going to spoil the fun." Miss An'gel regarded Helen Louise and me with a grim smile. "Vera won't dare. She won't bother either of you, I promise you that."

"Thank you," Helen Louise said. "I was doing my best to reassure Charlie of that on the way here."

Miss Dickce moved to stand beside her sister. They exchanged a glance that seemed laden with meaning before she spoke. "An'gel and I have taken care of everything. After tonight, Vera won't be in a position to bother anyone ever again."

TEN

All my earlier worries about tonight returned. Miss Dickce spoke lightly, but the import of her words chilled me. What on earth were the sisters planning to do to Vera?

Helen Louise squeezed my arm as she whispered, "Don't look so alarmed, Charlie."

I gave her a weak grin. "I'll do my best," I responded in an undertone.

The attention of the sisters shifted toward the parlor door, and Helen Louise and I turned to see the new arrivals.

"Sissy, dear, and Hank. Don't you both look wonderful." Miss An'gel stepped forward and held out both hands as the Beauchamp siblings neared her.

Sissy grasped one hand and Hank the other as they murmured their responses. I speculated on the identities of the fictional characters they represented. Sissy's was easy to discern, but Hank's puzzled me. They certainly presented sharp contrasts, one to the other.

Sissy wore a tight red dress that left little to the imagination, and her high-spiked heels caused her to thrust her two major assets forward at a dangerous angle. A black and red shawl that looked like cashmere draped her shoulders. One hand clutched a red silk purse, the small kind that women brought to parties. She had a stuffed dog, a Yorkie, by the look of it, attached to her other wrist, like a corsage. The dog's head was near her hand, and its tail almost to her elbow. It looked awkward to me, but I supposed it was easier than carrying it around all evening.

The Yorkie, Chablis, offered the telling clue. Sissy had to be none other than Tinkie Bellcase Richmond, sidekick to Carolyn Haines's heroine Sarah Booth Delaney. If anyone was ever reared to be a "daddy's girl," it was Sissy.

Her brother surely wasn't dressed as Oscar Richmond, Tinkie's husband. That would be creepy. No, Hank's dark suit looked severely Victorian rather than contemporary and bankerish, but his appearance was on the untidy side. His hair was not as carefully groomed as usual, and his pants pockets bulged under the contours of his jacket. His handkerchief straggled out of the breast pocket, and surely that was a pencil beside it. If he was going for messy, he'd achieved it. The suit looked like he had been wearing it for days.

"Good evening." Hank turned to me and Helen Louise and inclined his head. "Thomas Pitt, at your service."

The untidiness should have tipped me off because Anne Perry's policeman hero went about in such fashion. Hank's face, however, made me think more of Mr. Rochester, the tortured love interest of Jane Eyre. The skin beneath his eyes appeared bruised, and his eyes themselves were bloodshot. His handshake lacked firmness, and his whole demeanor betokened weariness, if not utter exhaustion.

Sissy, however, sparkled with energy and gaiety. "This is going to be *the* event of the year, Miss An'gel. Oh, Miss Dickce, you look absolutely fabulous. You, too, Miss An'gel."

Hank smiled at the sisters, but it seemed an effort for him. "If I'm correct, you must be Amelia Peabody and Jacqueline Kirby. Right?"

"Right." Miss Dickce nodded approvingly. "You're so clever, Hank." She batted her eyes in an overtly flirtatious manner, and Hank forced his lips into the ghost of another smile.

If I read him properly, I'd say Hank Beauchamp was near the breaking point. Was it merely physical exhaustion? Or was it emotional strain? I recalled the odd episode at Helen Louise's bakery just last week. Helen Louise explained to me later that Hank evidently suffered from financial problems—due, she suspected, to a gambling habit—and that his law practice was in trouble, too. That was certainly more than enough to make a man look tired and perhaps desperate.

Two of the catering staff entered the room, bearing trays with drinks and finger food. Miss An'gel insisted that we all eat and drink. "Because things will start getting hectic soon, and we all have to be on our toes tonight. Remember, we want to get pockets open and money into our hands."

We all nodded at that. I wasn't looking forward to gladhanding people and urging them to donate even more money to the library. I believed in the cause, certainly, but I didn't like feeling pushy, and that was the way fundraising made me feel.

But the Ducote sisters would not be denied. The library was probably their favorite charity, and they worked hard to support it and literacy efforts in Athena and surrounding counties. So I'd have to suck it up, as the saying went, and do my best to solicit more donations.

If ever I could have used Diesel at my side, tonight was the time. He was a terrific icebreaker, and he charmed most everyone except the most hardened antifeline contingent. He made people feel good, and when they felt good, they were more open to giving money.

For a moment I wished I were at home with Diesel and Justin, but then I chastised myself for being such an old fogy. Tonight *would* be fun, and I should stop being silly and enjoy myself. I sipped at my champagne and nibbled on canapés and listened to the small talk.

Stewart came bopping—not a word I often used, but one that seemed appropriate at the moment—into the parlor right then. His breezy "How ya doin', peeps? Ain't we gonna have fun tonight!" put Miss An'gel at a temporary loss. Her expression went utterly blank.

Stewart had that effect on people sometimes.

Helen Louise and I exchanged glances, and that did it. We both burst into laughter, and Miss Dickce joined in. Miss An'gel's face had taken on a slightly pained look. Neither Sissy nor Hank reacted that I could see. Sissy was too absorbed in staring into a mirror on the wall, and Hank seemed wrapped in apathy.

"I haven't the foggiest notion what a *peep* is in this context, Stewart, but I presume you're not talking about those absurd marshmallow candy things I see all over the place at Easter." Miss An'gel reminded me of one of my high school English teachers, Mrs. Leverette, who abhorred any use of slang.

"No, ma'am," Stewart replied. "It means *comrades*, I suppose, in this context, or perhaps *fellows at arms*. We *are* going into battle tonight, aren't we? Fighting for dollars, so to speak."

"We sure are," Miss Dickce said. "I'll be your peep, Stewart, even if An'gel won't. She's so *proper* sometimes." For a moment I thought she might stick her tongue out at her sister.

Miss An'gel ignored her. "Money is the object of the gala, naturally, but I hope you're planning to be a tad more *genteel* in pursuit of it tonight, Stewart."

Stewart bowed. "I shall display every ounce of gentility I possess, dear lady, which is considerable." He smirked.

"Get over yourself, Stewart. You're such a poser." Hank Beauchamp's comment startled me because I thought he was oblivious to what was going on around him.

"Hank, darling, you are so utterly and divinely predictable." Stewart's cool tone didn't fool me. I could see the color rising in his face. "I thought surely you'd be over me by now, but could it be you're still pining?"

"Gentlemen, cease this at once." Miss An'gel's voice struck like the lash of a whip. "If neither of you can behave in a civil fashion, then you will leave right now."

Both Hank and Stewart blanched. Hank apologized first with a muttered, "Sorry, Miss An'gel," before turning away.

"I will be on my best behavior from now on," Stewart said. The rigid set of his back and shoulders led me to think he was still angry but embarrassed enough by his outburst to comply with Miss An'gel's orders.

"Very well." Miss An'gel summoned one of the waiters to bring her champagne. Glass in hand, she turned to Helen Louise. "The canapés you provided are delightful. I don't know what we'd do without your contributions every year."

"Yes, they are nummy," Sissy said.

"Thank you," Helen Louise said. "I'm happy to do what I can."

Their conversation continued from there, with Miss Dickce joining in. Hank remained aloof and quiet, however, wandering into a corner of the room away from the rest of us.

By this time I felt almost ill from all the tension. I hated confrontations, but I'd had little choice with this one. More than ever I longed to be home with Diesel and a good book, but if I tried to bolt now, Miss An'gel would have my hide. Plus Helen Louise would be sorely disappointed in me, and I didn't want that.

So suck it up, Charlie, I told myself.

"I bet you're wondering who I am." Stewart sidled up to me and turned his back. "Maybe these will help you figure it out."

By *these* I assumed he meant the small wings attached to the back of his vest. His tight pants and shirt showed off his physique, and I couldn't reconcile that with the wings.

"Maybe if I told you I'm a *fairy fairy*?" Stewart grinned.

That gave me the answer. "Claude Crane. Of course." I knew Stewart loved the Sookie Stackhouse books, and one of the characters was a gay fairy. Stewart obviously couldn't resist the joke, and I laughed appreciatively.

"No sign yet of Cruella de Vil, I take it?" Stewart snagged champagne from one of the waiters, a handsome young man of about twenty who offered Stewart an engaging grin along with the bubbly. Stewart winked and smiled back. The waiter lingered a moment, then moved on as Miss Dickce beckoned him.

"No Vera yet," I said. "I suppose it's too much to hope that she came down with something and is staying home."

"No such luck." Stewart downed half his champagne at one go. "Vera wouldn't miss this, even if she had to drag herself out of her sickbed to get here. One of my former students."

The abrupt change of subject threw me for a moment. "You mean the waiter."

Stewart nodded. "Took my freshman chemistry course last year. Bright young man, but very flirtatious. Even if he weren't a student, he's much too young." He sounded depressed.

"You're so old, after all." I couldn't resist teasing him, because I had close to a decade on him.

"Ha, ha." Stewart drained his glass and motioned the waiter back for another. "End-of-semester blues, I guess. Pay no attention to me. A few days of no papers to grade and no lectures to prepare, and I'll be fine."

"I'm looking forward to the holidays myself. We can all relax and stuff ourselves with good food."

"And spend extra time in the gym to work off the million extra calories." Stewart quirked an eyebrow at me. "The invitation still stands, Charlie. If you decide you want to join, I'll be happy to help you get started on your workouts."

He would have to choose this moment to remind me, I thought as I suppressed a grimace. Between Azalea's Southern cooking and Helen Louise's amazing desserts, I watched my waistline enlarging—almost on a daily basis, it seemed. The walking I did helped, but I had the sad suspicion it was not nearly enough.

"After the first of the year." I suppressed a sigh. "I promise." It was a necessary evil, and for the sake of my health, I knew I couldn't put it off any longer.

"I'll hold you to that," Stewart said. "Trust me, you'll feel better once you get into it."

"And I'll hold *you* to *that*." I grimaced.

Further discussion of the merits of exercise would have to wait. Vera and Morty Cassity arrived, evidently in the middle of an argument.

". . . and why you had to wear that damn big skirt I don't know." Morty's deep voice cut easily through the hum of conversation. "I've nearly tripped on it five times already."

"Then don't walk so close. You are the clumsiest man alive." Vera's hissing response echoed through the sudden hush. Belatedly she appeared to notice that the rest of the room was silent, and her face colored to match the scarlet of her hoop skirt and bodice. Though she was decades too old, and had nothing close to a seventeen-inch waist, Vera had to be Scarlett O'Hara. Her wig mimicked Vivien Leigh's hair, and the extravagant hat with its long velvet bow called to mind the one Miss Leigh wore in the film.

Sadly for her, Vera's Rhett Butler looked much better in his getup than she did in hers. Morty Cassity stood an inch or so taller than his wife. His hairline had receded a couple of inches, but his broad shoulders, handsome face, and general air of confidence more than compensated for his lack of height.

"Good evening, Morty, Vera." Miss An'gel was equal to any occasion, and she greeted her guests as if there had been no unpleasantness between Vera and Morty just now.

Morty bent over Miss An'gel's hand and brushed it with a kiss. "You're looking mighty fine, Miss An'gel, though I've got no idea who or what you're supposed to be. Vera's the reader in our family."

Vera grimaced. "Evening, An'gel." She nodded in the direction of everyone else. "Sorry we're late, but Morty had a meeting he couldn't postpone."

"No matter," Miss An'gel said. She motioned the wait-

ers forward. "The guests won't be arriving for a few more minutes yet. In the meantime, help yourselves to the champagne and nibbles. They're delicious."

Morty reached eagerly for the champagne, I thought. And his eyes fastened just as avidly on Sissy Beauchamp. I couldn't blame him. She was stunning in her Tinkie costume, and she knew it. She preened for him, but from my vantage point, it looked like she was staring right at Vera. Hank, at Sissy's side as always, gazed straight ahead, as if he didn't see either Vera or Morty.

The babble of conversation resumed, but for the moment I stood alone. Helen Louise had gone off to use the ladies' room, while Stewart sauntered over to talk to his former student. Morty sidled closer to Sissy, and Miss An'gel joined them. Probably a good idea, I reckoned, if the fire in Vera's eye was anything to go by. If we made it through the night without an eruption from her, we'd be extremely lucky.

Miss Dickce approached me, and we chatted happily about our joint favorite, Elizabeth Peters. Miss Dickce, while she loved Amelia Peabody, absolutely adored Jacqueline Kirby and lamented the fact that there weren't more Kirby novels.

"I know, but it's a shame. Jacqueline is such a hoot. I'd love to be her when I grow up." Miss Dickce giggled, and I felt a sudden rush of empathy and affection for her. She was truly endearing, and behind the humor I sensed a certain yearning, perhaps for the adventurous life of her chosen character.

"Jacqueline has nothing on you, Miss Dickce," I said.

"You're so gallant, Charlie." She smiled up at me. "A true Southern gentleman. It's a shame that Diesel couldn't be here. He's a gentleman, too."

We chatted further about my cat and soon shifted into discussion of plans for the money to be raised from the gala. Miss Dickce wanted to ensure adequate funding for the literacy programs, which I supported, but I also hoped to see some money spent on materials for the library, like children's books.

A shriek of rage accompanied by a resounding slap interrupted us, and conversation ceased immediately. Startled, Miss Dickce and I turned to see what was going on.

ELEVEN

||||||||||||||||||||||||||||||||||||||||||||||

All eyes focused on the area near the parlor door. Vera and Sissy stood barely a foot apart, chests heaving in anger. Vera had one hand cupped to her cheek.

Vera uttered a nasty word in a low, vicious tone. Sissy drew back as if to strike Vera again, but Hank rushed forward to get between them. Morty darted toward Vera. They dragged the women apart.

"An'gel's going to have a cow," Miss Dickce confided to me in an undertone. "Not that I can blame her. I wonder what on earth Vera said to Sissy." Without waiting for a response from me, she approached her sister and spoke to her.

My stomach knotted up. I frankly didn't care what Vera had said to Sissy. I hated the intense feeling of hostility in the room.

Helen Louise moved closer and slipped her arm around me. "This is awful," she said in an undertone. "You'd think

Vera had more sense than to provoke Sissy publicly like this."

"If I never see that woman again after tonight," I said, "I will be really and truly happy. She is pure poison."

"Well, Sissy's not entirely blameless, you know." Helen Louise shook her head. "She and Morty haven't been very discreet with their rendezvous from what I've heard. I can't blame Vera for being angry over the infidelity, but still. . . ." Her voice trailed off.

Miss An'gel strode purposefully to the corner of the room where Morty had pulled a furious Vera. Miss Dickce went to talk to Hank and Sissy.

Stewart, Helen Louise, and I stared at one another. "I've never seen Miss An'gel so angry," Stewart said after a moment. We continued to watch uneasily. I couldn't hear either of the low-voiced discussions going on, and I wondered whether Vera or Sissy—or perhaps both of them—would be sent home in disgrace.

Teresa Farmer and Cathy Williams, the final two board members, walked into the parlor then. They paused after only a few steps and glanced uncertainly around the room. Stewart hurried over to them and urged them forward to where Helen Louise and I waited.

We all exchanged greetings, and Stewart explained quickly that there had been an argument between Vera and Sissy. He didn't elaborate, but apparently he didn't have to. From what I could see, as they both shook their heads, Teresa and Cathy seemed aware of the reasons that Vera and Sissy were at odds. The grapevine in Athena had sturdy roots and long tendrils. There were probably few people in town who weren't part of it.

As we waited in silence to see what would happen next, I took a moment to identify the characters Cathy and Teresa had chosen to portray. That was certainly better than dwelling on the unpleasantness.

Cathy wore a caftan in a colorful print, with a scarf wound around her head, and long earrings dangled from her earlobes. I knew she was a huge fan of Alexander McCall Smith, so it took little imagination to peg her as Mma Precious Ramotswe of the No. 1 Ladies' Detective Agency in Botswana.

Teresa, wearing a long black wig, her torso encased in leather and a metal bra, sported a costume like the one Lucy Lawless wore as Xena, Warrior Princess. Armbands, knee-high boots, dagger at her belt—she looked fierce and ready for combat. Since public librarians often had to campaign hard for their funding, I had to admire her choice. I also knew that, behind Teresa's normally modest and easygoing demeanor, there lurked a strong and determined will.

Miss An'gel turned away from Vera and Morty, and Vera scuttled from the room. Morty glanced over at Sissy and Hank. The naked yearning in his face unnerved me. Sissy ignored him, though Hank stared back at him. Morty trailed off after his wife.

"There will be no more such incidents tonight." Miss An'gel's implacable tone made me want to squirm, as if I were somehow at fault. "Vera will remain, but I trust that you will all stay out of her way until the gala is over. I will not have this event ruined by sordid personal matters." She glared hard at Sissy and Hank as she uttered that last sentence.

Sissy and Hank both reddened, but they nodded.

"Our guests will be arriving any minute now," Miss An'gel continued. "I suggest you all station yourselves in the hallway to greet them. I am going to check with the caterer but will return shortly." Without waiting for a response, she moved in stately fashion from the room.

"I'd better go with her," Miss Dickce said after a moment, and she, too, went out.

"All right, kiddies," Stewart said, "time to get to work." He began to herd us all into the hallway.

Helen Louise and I took up position near the grand staircase while the others ranged themselves around the entranceway. The butler waited by the front door, and I wondered how much of the brouhaha in the parlor he had heard. The door stood open the entire time, so if he had been in the hall he'd probably heard most of it. More grist for the gossip mill, but there was nothing any of us could do about it now.

I hoped the hordes were advancing up the walk right this minute. The sooner the house filled with people, the better. Plus, the less likely—or so I hoped—that we would witness further histrionics from the board members.

The doorbell rang, and the butler went into action. The first arrivals came into the hallway, and others quickly followed. Soon there were at least thirty people milling about, and Helen Louise and I did our duty and greeted as many of them as possible and complimented them on their costumes.

The crowd parted for a moment, and I saw three people admitted, two of whom I recognized. Kanesha Berry, chief deputy of the Athena County Sheriff's Department, strode in, accompanied by her mother, Azalea. Behind them came a tall, striking black man. He appeared to acompany Kanesha, and that intrigued me. I knew almost nothing about Kanesha's private life, other than the fact that she was unmarried and had no children. Azalea complained about these two lamentable states from time to time.

Azalea didn't appear to be in costume, unless her sensible

print dress, short jacket, and comfortable shoes were clues to a character I didn't recognize. Frankly, I wasn't surprised because somehow I couldn't see Azalea consenting to dress up as someone else.

Kanesha, on the other hand, was dressed in far different fashion from the manner in which I usually encountered her. No uniform tonight—instead she wore a sleek, bright orange pantsuit, and large bangles in her ears. Her hair was pulled severely back with a large bun jutting upward. A purple and orange scarf cinched her waist, and her high-heeled purple pumps completed the outfit. I knew she was a mystery fan, but I hadn't a clue whether she was dressed in costume or simply as herself.

Her companion, who looked to be at least six foot six, towered over her. His clothing was in stark contrast to Kanesha's because he looked like he'd bought the cheapest things he could find and put them on without washing and ironing them first. Khakis with a sharp crease and a drab flannel shirt with the collar of a T-shirt just visible at his neckline. Except for his height, he would blend into the woodwork, but perhaps that was the intention.

It took me a moment—because I hadn't yet read any of the books—but I figured it out. Jack Reacher, the hero of Lee Child's series. Teresa was a big fan, I knew, and we had talked about the series several times.

Kanesha spotted Helen Louise and me and looked up at her companion. They spoke briefly, then approached us along with Azalea.

"Good evening, Azalea." Helen Louise extended a hand, and my housekeeper grasped it briefly. "How lovely to see you here tonight."

"Somebody insisted I had to tag along." Azalea glowered at her daughter. "Ain't got much use for dressing up and carrying on. Especially knowing who's going to be here."

That was probably a reference to Vera Cassity, and I sent up a quick but fervent prayer that Vera stayed out of Azalea's way.

"Mama, I'm sure you'd enjoy yourself if you tried." Kanesha's long-suffering tone elicited another hard glance from her mother.

"I understand, Azalea, believe me." I smiled. "I'd much rather be home right now. All these people milling around make me feel tired."

"You a homebody like me, Mr. Charlie." Azalea nodded in approval. "Although you do get to gadding about sometimes and being nosy."

"Mama." Kanesha invested the word with years of wrangling with her parent. I sympathized with her, especially given my recent experience with Azalea.

"Evening, folks." Kanesha's friend spoke, probably tired of waiting for his companion to recall her manners and introduce him. He stuck out a hand. "Robert Sharp. Nice to meet you."

I quickly introduced myself and Helen Louise.

"You've been in my bakery a couple of times," she said. "As I recall you're pretty fond of my bacon and onion quiche."

"Yes, ma'am, I surely am." Sharp's slow drawl marked him as a fellow Southerner, and I wondered whether he'd grown up in Athena. "I can't eat it too often, though, have to watch my cholesterol."

"Robert is a cardiologist," Kanesha said. She appeared a bit fidgety. "He moved here from Atlanta about six months ago."

"I hope you're not finding Athena too slow paced, compared to Atlanta." I noticed that Kanesha continued to act ill at ease, but I couldn't imagine why.

"I grew up in a small town south of Atlanta," Sharp responded. "Couldn't wait to get out of the big city, and I'm sure glad I found Athena." He gazed down at Kanesha with what I interpreted as a doting look.

Kanesha squirmed a bit, and I finally realized that she was uncomfortable being in public with her boyfriend. She was an intensely private person—exactly like her mother in that respect—and she probably didn't want anyone who wasn't a close connection knowing too much about her life outside the job.

"Going to find Clementine, see if she needs help." Azalea nodded at us before she disappeared into the increasing throng crowding the hallway.

"Mama, you come back here." Kanesha entreated her mother in vain.

"Let her be, babe," Sharp said, placing a large hand on Kanesha's shoulder. "You know she's going to do exactly what she wants. Relax and enjoy yourself."

The understated note of humor in his voice convinced me that he already knew the Berry women pretty well.

"Yes, help yourselves to the food and drink." Helen Louise looked about for a waiter. "You might want to escape into one of the other rooms, though. It's getting pretty cramped in here."

"Great idea." Sharp took Kanesha by the arm and drew her toward the parlor. "Talk to you later."

"How wonderful," Helen Louise said in an undertone. "I'm so glad she's found such a delightful man. Gorgeous, and a cardiologist, too. I'm sure Azalea must be thrilled."

"She will be if she can get Kanesha married off with a houseful of grandchildren." Privately I thought Azalea was right. I hoped Dr. Sharp was just what she needed, and vice versa.

People finally began to move into other rooms and made some space in the hallway. More arrivals, however, soon added to the crush. By this time my feet ached, I needed desperately to find the bathroom, and I wanted something besides champagne.

Helen Louise asked me to bring her water, too, when I shared my needs with her. Then I threaded my way through the crowd in the direction of the kitchen. Muttering *excuse me* over and over, I dodged bodies until I finally made it down the hall to the back of the house.

I opened a door and stepped into the room beyond. Instead of the hive of activity I expected, I found myself in a small room with two women—Azalea and Vera—in the midst of a yelling match.

". . . pure evil. The Lord gonna strike you down one day for all your lies, and I'm gonna be there to sing His praises."

TWELVE

|||||||||||||||||||||||||||||||||||||||||||

Should I intervene?

Azalea looked like the wrath of God about to strike, fists clenched at her sides, her breathing labored.

Vera, on the other hand, eyed my housekeeper with cold contempt. "My conscience is clear. If the Lord strikes anyone down for lies, it will be you. And if you spread any of your lies in public, my lawyer will take care of it." She turned in my direction, started in surprise, but then brushed past me as if I had turned invisible.

As the door shut behind me, I regarded Azalea with concern. She drew shuddering breaths, and I feared she might have a stroke. I scuttled over to her and put an arm around her shoulders. She leaned against me for a moment, her eyes closed.

"Do you need a doctor?" I asked. "Why don't you sit down and let me get you something?"

She let me lead her a few feet to a chair, and she sank

down. Her eyes opened, and she stared at me as I knelt before her. Her breathing slowed and returned to normal. When she spoke, her voice came out in a hoarse whisper. "No, Mr. Charlie, I'll be fine. Just need a minute to catch my breath."

"Would you like me to find Kanesha and Dr. Sharp?" She should have her daughter with her, and a cardiologist on hand wouldn't hurt, either.

"No." The sharp blast of the word startled me, and I rocked back on my heels. Azalea's gaze was fierce. "Don't be telling her about this. No point to it."

"If that's what you want." I burned with curiosity, even as my concern for her well-being mounted. She didn't look good at all, and I still feared she might suffer a stroke or a mild heart attack. "Let me get you something to drink."

"I told you I'll be fine." Azalea scowled at me. She pushed herself up out of the chair, and I hastened to get to my feet and out of her way.

"Thank you, Mr. Charlie. You're a good-hearted man, but you got no cause to be worrying about me." She moved toward the door. "I'm gonna find Clementine." She left the room.

I hesitated, debating whether I should talk to Kanesha despite Azalea's request that I not. Whatever caused the bitter hatred Azalea had for Vera, Kanesha surely knew about it. Did she also need to know about this confrontation?

It really wasn't any of my business, as Azalea had already informed me. I squirmed at the memory. Best to stay out of it, then.

I remembered why I'd left Helen Louise in the hall and decided I'd better attend to my needs, find some water for us both, and get back to my duties as a board member.

There was no sign of Azalea or Clementine in the

kitchen when I finally remembered the correct door. Glasses of water in hand, I found Helen Louise where I'd left her about ten minutes before. She accepted the water gratefully. I would keep mum on the scene I'd witnessed, at least for now.

The influx of guests slowed after another twenty minutes, and Helen Louise and I moved into the parlor where Miss An'gel and Miss Dickce held court by the fireplace underneath their ancestor's portrait. I spotted Vera in one corner, talking to Cathy Williams and Robert Sharp—no doubt giving them a rundown on all the things she had done to benefit the Athena hospital.

Sissy and Hank occupied another corner, heads together, seemingly oblivious to the party going on around them.

Helen Louise found two empty chairs and occupied one of them with a sigh of relief. "My feet are killing me. I'm not used to wearing high-heeled pumps like these." She rubbed her right calf, and I admired the shapely curve. She caught me looking and grinned, and I grinned back.

Miss An'gel addressed the room in a loud voice. "Good evening, everyone. Could I have your attention, please?" She waited a moment for the hubbub to die down, then issued her appeal for quiet again. The buzz subsided, and Miss An'gel regarded the assembled company with a gracious smile.

"Thank you all. On behalf of my fellow Friends of the Library board members, I thank you for your support of tonight's event. Your generous sponsorship of the library's programs makes a huge difference to literacy efforts in our town and the surrounding area." She beckoned for Teresa Farmer to join her.

Teresa stepped up and added a few words of thanks, then moved aside.

Miss An'gel spoke again. "Tonight we have a special presentation to make, and I'm delighted to introduce our mayor, who will do the honors. Please, everyone, welcome the Honorable Lucinda Beckwith Long."

The mayor joined Miss An'gel beneath the portrait, a large plaque in her hands. Lucinda Long, daughter of another of the first families of Athena, was the product of several generations of well-known Mississippi politicians. She was rumored to be contemplating a run for governor, while her son currently served in the state legislature. Dressed impeccably in a rose wool suit and high heels, she was every inch the public figure.

I leaned over to whisper in Helen Louise's ear. "This is the first I've heard about the presentation of an award. Is this something the board does at every gala?"

Helen Louise frowned and shook her head. "No, this is something new. Strange that you didn't know about it."

I shrugged. Perhaps the board had discussed it before I joined and the subject hadn't come up again. I would ask Miss An'gel or Miss Dickce about it later. I settled back to listen to the mayor.

"Good evening, everyone." Lucinda Long offered her standard mayoral smile, one that never seemed to reach her eyes. She had always struck me as rather a cold person, but she was an efficient and energetic mayor, at least. "As Miss An'gel said, this is a wonderful event, and I'm proud to see my fellow citizens here supporting a truly worthy cause. I'm also delighted to be asked to present a special award tonight to a citizen of Athena who has worked tirelessly over the years to promote the well-being of our town in so many areas. At the same time, however, I am saddened to know that this highly esteemed person has decided to retire from public life for personal reasons. Everyone in Athena will miss her helping hands, but we will remain forever grateful for all she has done in the past, and I know we all will wish her well in her retirement."

The mayor paused, and I had the impression everyone in the room held their breath waiting for this paragon to be named. I figured I knew who was going to receive the award, and I admired the masterstroke that Miss An'gel had obviously engineered. Machiavelli had nothing on her. I glanced at Helen Louise, and I could see her suppressing a grin. She'd figured it out as well.

The mayor spoke again. "It is my great pleasure to present the first Beauregard Ducote Award for Distinguished Public Service to Mrs. Morton Cassity. Vera, would you please come forward to accept the award?"

There was a moment of silence before the applause broke out, and I could have sworn I heard a gasp. I was watching Vera when the mayor made the announcement, and her jaw dropped open, even as her face flooded with color to match her over-the-top costume. Fury flashed in Vera's eyes as she made her way forward.

Would she accept her defeat graciously? I wondered. If she didn't, she risked huge public embarrassment. She would become a laughingstock if she made a scene, and somehow I couldn't see Vera exposing herself to open public ridicule.

Vera's hoop skirt snagged on the spurs worn by one man in cowboy garb. As she jerked the fabric loose with a vicious tug, she nearly pulled the man off his feet. He managed to stay upright, but Vera never paused to apologize. She made it the last three feet to where the mayor and Miss An'gel waited and turned to face the room.

Miss An'gel preempted her. "Vera, my dear, I'm so delighted you were chosen for this award, and my sister and I are thrilled to support it. You have done *so much* for the community, and we wanted to be sure you got the kind of award you so *richly* deserve. We regret that you have decided to retire from your charitable work, but we understand that sometimes private life must come before public duty. We will surely miss your work with the Friends of Athena Public Library." She bestowed a beaming smile upon her adversary.

Vera's shoulders slumped as she accepted the plaque from Lucinda Long. She struggled for a smile but never quite managed it. When she spoke her voice was unsteady. "I can't tell you all how surprised I am to receive this. I never expected anything like it." Her mouth closed, and she stood there awkwardly, clasping the award to her bosom.

I almost felt sorry for her. The Ducote sisters had managed to spike her guns but good.

I was also relieved that she appeared to accept the inevitable. There had been enough unpleasant scenes tonight.

Morty Cassity joined his wife, and Miss An'gel stepped aside. "Thank you all. I know Vera is touched and honored by this gesture." He frowned, no doubt puzzled by all this, since I was sure it was as much a surprise to him as it was to his wife. "I think this calls for some more of that fine champagne." He led Vera away, and conversation slowly resumed as the waiters spread through the room dispensing more of the bubbly.

Helen Louise and I looked at each other. "Can you beat that?" I said.

She grinned. "Remind me never to get on Miss An'gel's bad side. That was absolutely brilliant."

"You have to hand it to her. She said she and Miss Dickce were going to neutralize Vera, and they did it."

I felt a hand on my shoulder and glanced up to see my daughter, suddenly blond, smiling down at me. "Hi, Dad, Helen Louise. Frank and I ran late, I'm afraid. What did we miss?"

Frank, a husky, bearded young man a few years older than Laura, greeted us. "My fault. Had a student having a postexam meltdown that I had to take care of." Frank taught lighting and set design at the college.

"We only caught the tail end of it." Laura sipped her champagne. "Mrs. Cassity looked like a thundercloud when she passed us on the way out of the room."

I quickly explained, and Frank and Laura shared a glance of amusement.

"Think that will really shut her up?" Frank shook his head. "In my experience nothing except the grave will stop that harpy from meddling in things."

"After what Miss An'gel just pulled off," Helen Louise said, "Vera will look like a fool if she doesn't go quietly."

"Enough of that," I said. "Let's forget about Vera and try to enjoy the party." I examined my daughter. The fake hair, along with a demure wool dress, gloves, sensible shoes, and cloche hat, reminded me of illustrations from one of my favorite series of children's books. She also clutched a magnifying glass in one hand. When I matched that with Frank's getup—gray flannel trousers, white shirt with bow tie, and letterman's sweater emblazoned with a large *E*—I figured I knew who they were supposed to be.

Helen Louise spoke first, however. "Well, Miss Nancy Drew, how nice to see you with your favorite escort, Ned Nickerson. How are things at Emerson College, Ned?"

Frank laughed. "Peachy keen, ma'am. I hope you don't mind that I didn't shave tonight."

"I think Ned looks rather fetching with a beard, don't you?" Laura's eyes sparkled with humor as she regarded her boyfriend.

"Definitely," Helen Louise said.

"Have you seen Sean and Alexandra?" I asked. "I'm curious to see how they're dressed."

"They're here somewhere," Frank said as he glanced about. He waved. "Here they come now."

Sean and Alexandra Pendergrast loomed into view, and they made a particularly striking couple. Sean was six-three, and in her heels Alexandra was only a couple of inches shorter. Sean had his hair slicked back in a severe style, and he sported a monocle in his left eye. His Edwardian-style evening wear flattered his muscular figure, and Alexandra's frock, a straight flapper dress with sheer beaded overdress, complimented his attire nicely.

"Good evening, all. What an absolutely frightful crush." Sean's attempt at an aristocratic English accent was excellent. His sister must have coached him.

"I think there's another actor in the Harris family," Alexandra said with a fond glance at my son.

Laura grinned. "I know. I've been telling Dad that Diesel would be a natural for cat food commercials."

"So frightfully unamusing, sister dear." Sean's tone was frosty, but his eyes twinkled.

"My dear Lord Peter," I said, addressing my son, "it doesn't do to insult one's sister in public." I turned to Alexandra, who was as big a fan of Dorothy L. Sayers as my son was. "Miss Vane, you are looking particularly lovely tonight."

"Merci beaucoup, M'sieur Poirot." Alexandra's French accent was flawless, as were the teeth she flashed in a broad smile.

We continued to chat for a while, and I enjoyed myself.

Nothing pleased me more than having those I loved so close by. If only Diesel and Justin were here with us, I thought.

The party wore on, but by nine thirty people began to leave. Tomorrow was a workday for many of those in attendance, including Helen Louise and me, and I was ready to go home. As a board member, however, I needed to hang on for a while yet. Laura, Frank, Sean, and Alexandra had departed about twenty minutes prior, and only five other people were still in the parlor. Even the waiters had left the room.

Neither of the Ducote sisters was present, nor did I see Sissy, Hank, or Stewart. I thankfully hadn't seen Vera since she had received her award. Perhaps she and Morty had left already.

"Let's go find Miss An'gel," I said to Helen Louise, "and let them know we're going."

"Good idea." Helen Louise covered her mouth as she yawned. "I have to be up at four."

"Poor baby. You'll be exhausted at work all day." I tucked her hand in my left arm as we headed for the parlor door.

In the hallway we encountered Kanesha and Robert Sharp. Kanesha appeared worried. "Charlie, have you seen my mother recently? We can't find her anywhere. She's not in the kitchen, and Miss Clementine hasn't seen her in half an hour, at least."

"I'm sure she's fine, honey," Sharp said, a protective arm sliding around Kanesha's shoulders.

"Who're you looking for?" Morty Cassity walked up to us. "I can't find Vera, neither. Any of you seen her lately?"

THIRTEEN

||||||||||||||||||||||||||||||||||||||||||||||||||||

Azalea and Vera both unaccounted for—that earlier ugly scene between them reran in my head. What if they had confronted each other again?

"We need to find them," I said. "Quickly."

Kanesha's eyes narrowed as they bored into me. I knew that look of suspicion all too well. "Right. Robert and I will take the third floor. We've already been through this floor. Helen Louise, you and Mr. Cassity take the second. Charlie, would you find Miss An'gel or Miss Dickce? They're probably down here somewhere."

She didn't wait to see if we obeyed, simply took that as a given. Dr. Sharp followed her as she ran up the grand staircase, his long legs allowing him to keep up easily.

"Come on, Morty," Helen Louise said, taking hold of his arm. "Get moving."

I started checking each room on the first floor. I knew the Ducotes weren't in the parlor, so I started with the room across the hall, the dining room. No sign of them there.

No sign of either sister in any of the rooms. I came at last to the kitchen. I'd expected to find the catering staff at work cleaning up, but the room was empty. They couldn't have left yet, because there was still equipment on the counters. The back door stood slightly ajar, and I strode over to it. As I neared I could smell the cigarette smoke and hear the sound of laughter and conversation. Evidently the workers had stepped outside for a smoke break before finishing up.

I was about to stick my head out the door to ask if they'd seen the Ducote sisters when I heard a muffled thumping nearby. I moved away from the back door and scanned that side of the room. There were two doors on the wall near me. The first one turned out to be the entry to the pantry, but it was empty of people.

The next door was five feet further down the wall. As I came closer I could hear the thumping again, and this time I heard the faint sound of a voice. I grabbed the knob and pulled, but the door wouldn't open. I glanced down and saw a doorstop jammed under the bottom of the door.

"Hold on, gotta get the door loose." I raised my voice to be heard over the thumping as I kicked at the doorstop. My feet failed to dislodge it, so I bent down to wrest it away with my hands.

The darn thing was really wedged in there, but I managed to loosen it and get it out of the way. I twisted the knob, and the door burst open. Azalea Berry stumbled into my arms. "Thank the Lord. I been beating on that door for ten minutes." She pulled away to stand on her own. Then she started trembling. "Oh, Mr. Charlie. It's terrible."

"What is?" I said, afraid she was going to pass out. I

reached toward her, but she turned and pointed toward the open door.

"In there."

I stepped around her and peered into the dim light of what turned out to be a narrow staircase leading up. I gasped when I saw a body sprawled headfirst and prone about halfway up the stairs. A hoop skirt was canted forward with the crinolines revealed, and the red silk of the gown covered the head. One arm extended beyond the cloth.

Inching forward to the foot of the stairs, I reached out to touch the one visible wrist. I felt for a pulse, but there was none.

Vera Cassity was dead.

I withdrew my hand and backed away. As I did the door at the top of the stairs opened, and more light streamed in.

"Who's there?" a voice called down to me. I looked up to see Kanesha on the landing, peering down.

"It's me, Charlie," I said. "Your mother is down here in the kitchen with me, Kanesha. She's okay."

"Is that Mrs. Cassity on the stairs?" Kanesha asked.

"Yes, and she's dead. Don't try to come down the stairs." She couldn't come down at all, I realized, as I took in more of the scene in front of me. Vera's hoops blocked the narrow stairs completely. That made me wonder whether she had simply stumbled and fallen and had the bad luck to break her neck.

Maybe it wasn't murder after all. That was my first assumption, but I hoped like anything I was wrong.

The catering staff began to come in through the back door, and I wasn't sure what to do. It was cold outside, and I didn't think they would pay any attention to me if I told them they shouldn't come back into the kitchen.

"Listen, everyone, please listen."

They stilled and stared at me curiously, and in some cases, with hostility. I was sure they were tired and ready to finish up, but they probably wouldn't be going home for a couple of hours yet. Neither would I, I realized as a wave of exhaustion washed over me.

"Thank you. There's been an accident, and I'm afraid you'll have to wait on packing up and leaving."

The grumbling started, but Kanesha's voice cut through it. She must have run through the mansion at top speed to get to us so quickly.

She strode forward to where I stood, pushing her way through the milling group of workers. She identified herself as she moved closer.

"Mr. Harris is right. I need you all to move out of the kitchen for now. Please make your way to the front parlor and wait there. The sheriff's department is on the way, and someone will be talking to you soon. We'll let you go as soon as we can."

There was more grumbling as they complied with Kanesha's orders, but no outright rebellion.

Kanesha turned to her mother, who had slumped into a nearby chair. "Mama, are you okay?"

Azalea nodded wearily. "She be dead, Kanesha, but she that way when I found her."

"Okay, Mama," Kanesha said gently. She turned to me. "Charlie, will you find Robert and send him in here? I want him to check my mother. He's in the front parlor with the others."

"Sure." I was glad to get out of there.

Dr. Sharp stood at the door of the parlor, and as I reached him I heard the drone of sirens approaching the house. I explained what Kanesha wanted. He hurried off.

I was about to enter the parlor when the front door opened. Men in uniform streamed in, including the sheriff himself. Gerald Tidwell was a massive man, about six-three and probably two hundred and fifty solidly muscled pounds. He barked out orders to his men. Obviously familiar with the layout of the house, he sent two men ahead of him to the kitchen. He turned to another, an officer I recognized as the man who often accompanied Kanesha, Deputy Bates. After a brief conferral Bates nodded and headed toward me. Sheriff Tidwell strode off toward the kitchen.

"Evening, Mr. Harris." Bates paused in front of me. "Why don't you go on in, sir? I need to speak to everyone."

"Certainly." I walked into the parlor, and all eyes focused on me and the man entering behind me.

Miss An'gel and Miss Dickce occupied one sofa, and Helen Louise shared it with them. Stewart sat on the arm of the sofa next to Miss An'gel. Hank and Sissy Beauchamp sat in chairs nearby, while Morty Cassity stood staring out a window opposite the door. Teresa Farmer, now wigless and looking exhausted, sat with Clementine on another sofa. Cathy Williams must have left already—probably had to go to the hospital to deal with some emergency among her nursing staff, I speculated. Then I realized the catering staff wasn't in the room, and I wondered where they were. Someone, perhaps Dr. Sharp, had probably sent them to another room where there were enough chairs for them all. There wouldn't have been in here.

"Evening, folks." Deputy Bates took up a stance in the middle of the room as I moved to sit on the arm of the sofa by Helen Louise. I put my hand on her shoulder and gave it a gentle squeeze. Her hand brushed mine gently as she gazed into my eyes. I wished there were room on the sofa so I could put my arm around her and draw her close. I could certainly use the comfort, and no doubt she could, too.

The officer continued. "I'm sorry to have to tell y'all this, but there's been an accident involving Mrs. Cassity. Sheriff Tidwell is here and will be investigating. I have to ask y'all to remain here until the sheriff can talk to you. In the meantime I also have to ask you not to talk about anything to do with the accident until the sheriff has interviewed you."

"Certainly, Officer Bates." Miss An'gel spoke for us all. "We will do whatever we can to assist the sheriff."

As we waited for the sheriff to appear, I finally felt my head clear enough to think about what I had seen in the kitchen. My forebodings of disaster for the evening had come true, and I wondered whether I had some sort of affinity for dire happenings.

Another murder. This made the fourth time I'd encountered a dead body, a potential homicide.

I chided myself. It could have been an accident. Vera might have been in a hurry, trying to rush down the stairs, when her hoops stuck. In trying to wrench them free she could have fallen and broken her neck.

I prayed again that it would turn out to be an accident. Tragic, but an accident.

But what was Azalea doing locked in the back stairway with Vera?

Could they have argued again? Did Azalea's temper get the better of her? Could she have pushed Vera down the stairs in anger?

The arrival of Kanesha and Dr. Sharp cut my speculations short. Kanesha's normally impassive countenance was gone, replaced by an expression of sheer fury.

She made a beeline for me, shrugging away her companion's restraining hand and ignoring Bates's command to halt.

Kanesha looked so angry I thought she was going to strike me, and I jerked myself up from the arm of the sofa and braced myself for an attack.

Instead of hitting me, however, she halted mere inches from me and glared at me. "I'm going to need your help. My idiot boss thinks Mama killed Vera Cassity."

FOURTEEN

|||||||||||||||||||||||||||||||||||||||||||||||||||||||||||

"Deputy Berry."

Bates's voice rang out, and Kanesha turned to face him as he strode toward her. He did not look happy.

"I know you're upset, but it's not gonna do you any good if you piss off the sheriff." Bates spoke in a low voice, but he was close enough that I heard every word.

Kanesha sighed. "I know, Bates, I know. Thanks for the reminder. But he's telling me I can't work this case. He's crazy if he thinks my mama killed that woman."

Bates realized that both Dr. Sharp and I were listening avidly to his conversation with his superior officer, and he motioned for her to follow him to the area near the door.

"This is nuts," Dr. Sharp muttered as he shoved his hands in his pants pockets.

I nodded in sympathy, but since Bates kept glancing my way, I didn't dare speak. The doctor nodded back in understanding.

Azalea as the chief suspect in a murder. How bizarre.
Then it hit me.

If the sheriff considered Azalea a suspect, that had to
mean he thought he was dealing with a murder, not an acci-
dental death.

I wondered what evidence of homicide the sheriff might
have found. I also wondered how competent he was at
investigating murder. Usually that duty fell to Kanesha, as
chief deputy, or in special cases the Mississippi Bureau of
Investigation.

Considering the identity of the victim, I thought it
highly possible the MBI could be brought in to handle this.

No matter what the sheriff thought, I couldn't see Azalea as a murderer. I knew she hated Vera with a passion,
although I didn't know why. But Azalea was a woman of
strong faith and ironclad principles. She wouldn't kill a
person simply because she hated her.

But I also recalled those words I'd heard not that long
ago, from Azalea herself—she hoped the Lord would
strike Vera down. Had Azalea considered herself an instru-
ment of God and pushed Vera down the stairs?

Down the stairs.

There was something wrong with that picture. I frowned,
forcing my tired brain to recall the scene in that dimly lit
staircase.

The door was blocked from the outside, and it opened
outward. Azalea was stuck inside because she couldn't get
the door open. She might have been able to get out if she
went up to the next floor, however.

She couldn't do that, I realized, because Vera's body and
her big hoops blocked the narrow stairwell effectively. Azalea would have had to climb over Vera's body to go either up
or down the stairs, and I couldn't see her doing that.

The crime-scene investigators would surely find some sign if Azalea—or anyone else—had climbed the stairs over Vera's body. That could be why the sheriff was convinced Azalea had done it. He'd found evidence to that effect.

No, I simply couldn't see it. Azalea had to have been at the bottom of the stairs when Vera fell—or was pushed.

In that case, maybe Azalea knew who the killer was because she'd seen the person behind Vera on the stairs. This could all be over quickly if she had witnessed the attack.

I perched on the sofa arm again, and Helen Louise's hand sought mine. I squeezed it, and she leaned against me. I knew if I was tired, she must be exhausted. She had put in a pretty full day at the bakery—a day that started at four a.m.—even before we came to the gala.

At least another quarter of an hour passed before the sheriff finally came to the parlor. He called Kanesha out into the hall, but they reappeared a couple of minutes later. Kanesha beckoned for Dr. Sharp to join her. After a brief conversation, he returned to his former position near me while Kanesha departed.

Where was Azalea? I wondered. I hoped that the sheriff had allowed Kanesha to take her home and that she wasn't sitting in a cell at the county jail right now.

Sheriff Tidwell addressed the room. His attention seemed focused on Miss An'gel, however. "Thanks for your cooperation, folks. I know y'all must be mighty tired by now, but I'm sure y'all understand that we've got a serious situation we're dealing with here. I'm going to need to talk to each and every one of you, and then you'll be able to go home. I promise to make it as quick as possible. Miss An'gel, I'd like to start with you."

Miss An'gel rose. "Sheriff, since I am in my own home

and don't have anywhere else to go, I suggest you leave my sister and me to the last, and take my guests first."

Considering the tone Miss An'gel used, she did more than suggest. The sheriff knew when he was outmatched, I was sure, and he didn't argue. He simply nodded.

"All right, then," he said. He surveyed the room. "Mr. Cassity, I'll start with you. Come with me, please."

Morty and the sheriff left the room, and Bates resumed his position at the door.

Ten minutes dragged by, then the door opened again. Another officer, whom I didn't recognize, summoned Dr. Sharp.

First Stewart, then Sissy, then Hank, then Helen Louise, until only the Ducote sisters, Clementine, and I were left.

Finally my turn came, and I drooped with fatigue as I bade my hostesses and their housekeeper good night. I followed the deputy across the hall, where he motioned for me to enter the library.

Sheriff Tidwell sat behind a massive desk. He pointed to a chair facing the desk and indicated that I should sit. I glanced at my watch as I did and noticed dully that it was about twenty minutes to midnight.

Before the sheriff said anything, I had a question for him. "Where is Ms. Brady, Sheriff? She came with me, and I'd like to see her home."

"No need to worry about that, Mr. Harris. One of my men is driving her home right now."

"Thank you." I was glad Helen Louise would soon be in bed and hopefully asleep, but at the same time I was irked that I hadn't had a chance to say good night.

"Mr. Harris, you seem to have a knack for turning up where dead bodies are present."

I couldn't tell whether Tidwell was amused or irritated. I, however, was definitely the latter.

"Simply a coincidence, Sheriff. I was looking for Mrs. Berry and happened to be the first one to find her. With the body." Waves of tiredness washed over me, and all I wanted was to get home to my bed. I surely didn't feel like sparring with the sheriff.

"How well did you know the deceased?"

"Not particularly well. She often came into the library on Friday afternoons when I volunteer there. I had some dealings with her in the past couple of months as a fellow member of the board of the library's Friends group. That's about it." At this stage I wasn't going to mention the unpleasant scene I'd had with Vera in the archives office.

Tidwell hardly waited until I finished answering one question before he was on to the next. "What about Miz Berry? How long have you known her?"

I thought back. Azalea had started working for my late aunt about twenty-five years ago, and I had met her several times when my family and I visited Aunt Dottie. I explained this to the sheriff.

"And she's worked for you how long?"

"Since I moved back to Athena four years ago," I said. With a slight smile I continued, "I inherited Azalea along with the house. I had little say in the matter."

Tidwell smiled also. "She's a strong-minded woman." The smile faded. "Tell me what you saw when you found Miz Berry."

I took a moment to collect my thoughts. My brain felt fuzzy. I focused on the door in the kitchen and the sounds I heard. Then I gave the sheriff a summary of what I saw.

"The door was definitely blocked from the outside?" Tidwell asked when I finished.

"Yes, the doorstop was wedged very firmly under it, and I actually had to bend down and pull it out with both hands. I tried kicking it aside, but it was embedded too deeply."

Tidwell frowned. "So in your opinion, was Miz Berry unable to get out of that stairwell on her own?"

"Yes." I didn't elaborate further.

"Describe for me again Miz Berry's demeanor when you found her."

"She was obviously upset. She seemed frantic to get out of the stairwell, and frankly I couldn't blame her."

"What did she say?"

"That she had been banging on the door for ten minutes. Then she said it was terrible. That's it, really."

Tidwell stared hard at me. "You're sure that's all she said?"

His tone irritated me. "Yes, I'm sure."

"What was Miz Berry's relationship to Miz Cassity?"

"None that I know of."

I thought he would press me on that, and when he didn't, I found it strange. He was no dummy, despite Kanesha's earlier comment when she referred to him as an idiot. That was only her anger talking. Tidwell was a sharp, politically savvy man, and he might be perfectly aware of Azalea's antipathy toward Vera.

My mind flashed back to the scene I'd witnessed between the two women earlier tonight. I hoped I wouldn't have to tell the sheriff about that, at least not until I'd had a chance to talk to Azalea about it—and Kanesha, too.

"I reckon that's all for now, Mr. Harris. If I have more questions, I'll let you know."

I rose gratefully. "Certainly, Sheriff." His deputy showed me out and escorted me to the front door.

I found my car, keys in the ignition, in the driveway. A

deputy waited nearby, and I figured they had sent the valets home earlier. I climbed in and headed for home, yawning the whole way.

The house was quiet when I reached it, with lights burning in the kitchen and the hallway. I made my way slowly up the stairs to my bedroom, and within five minutes I was in bed. I barely had time to wonder where Diesel was before I dropped off to sleep.

Having failed to set the alarm before I stumbled into bed, I woke two hours later than usual, around eight thirty. As I began to stir, I felt a paw on my arm. I turned to see Diesel sitting on the bed beside me. He meowed at me, and I scooped an arm around him and pulled him closer. He warbled for me as I rubbed up and down his back, then concentrated on his head. There was no standoff kitty routine this morning. He was as happy to see me as I was to see him.

Twenty minutes later, showered and dressed for work, I caught the scents of fresh coffee and bacon as Diesel and I headed downstairs. My stomach rumbled. Either Stewart or Laura must be cooking breakfast, and I was grateful. Even though I was running late, I was so hungry I wasn't going to skip this meal. I needed energy for the day ahead.

When I walked into the kitchen, Azalea turned away from the stove to glare at me. "I didn't murder nobody. Not even that hateful woman."

FIFTEEN

||||||||||||||||||||||||||||||||||||||||||

I hadn't expected to see Azalea at her usual place at the stove this morning. For one thing, she had to be even more exhausted than I was last night. But here she was. The woman was indomitable.

"Of course you didn't." I put every ounce of conviction I could muster into those four words.

The rigid set of my housekeeper's shoulders relaxed a fraction. "Thank you, Mr. Charlie. I appreciate that." She turned back to the stove.

At a loss as to what I should say next, I sat down. Diesel walked around me and over to where Azalea stood. He sat by her feet, looked up at her, and chirped several times.

Startled, she glanced down at him. "He be trying to tell me something." Uncertainly she faced me again. "He upset with me?"

Smiling, I shook my head. "No, in his way, he's trying

to tell you he knows you're upset and he wants you to feel better."

"Well, don't that just beat all?" Bemused, she watched the cat for a moment, then reached with a trembling hand to touch his head. Diesel, smart boy that he was, simply sat there and let her stroke him tentatively.

"You maybe ain't so bad after all, cat." Azalea went to the sink and washed her hands, and Diesel moved to sit beside me.

I never thought I'd see the day. My mouth probably hung open in astonishment. Diesel appeared to be smirking. He could be quite a self-satisfied puss on occasion, but he more than deserved to be this time.

"I was about to forget your coffee, Mr. Charlie." Azalea muttered to herself as she brought the coffeepot and filled my cup.

"Thank you."

"Breakfast is almost ready. Let me just check on the biscuits." She bent to peer in the oven door.

"Morning, Dad, Azalea. Isn't it a gorgeous day?" Laura breezed into the kitchen. "The semester is done, I've turned in all my grades, and now I'm a free woman. I could eat a horse."

Talk about strange. Laura and Sean and their dates had left the party before Vera's body was discovered, and obviously she hadn't heard the story from anyone yet this morning. Stewart must still be in bed. Otherwise the whole house would be buzzing with the news.

What could I say? I didn't want to bring the subject up in front of Azalea, but my housekeeper solved my dilemma for me as she set my plate of scrambled eggs, bacon, and biscuits on the table.

"Something bad happened last night, Miss Laura. I reckon you was gone by the time it happened." She set down Laura's plate and then disappeared into the laundry room.

Wide-eyed, Laura left off stroking Diesel and gazed at me. "What on earth happened, Dad?"

"Happened where?" Sean startled me. He wandered over to the stove and filled a plate. "Want coffee, bug breath?"

"No, thanks, snot brain." Laura glared at her brother. "Go on, what went on after we left last night?" She sneaked Diesel a bite of bacon when she thought I wasn't looking.

Maybe one of these days my darling children would stop referring to each other by those silly nicknames. "Vera Cassity died, and it looks like she might have been murdered."

Sean paused, fork halfway to his mouth, and the eggs plopped back onto the plate.

Laura groaned. "Don't tell me. You found the body, didn't you?" She and her brother shared a glance—of commiseration, I assumed.

"Not exactly." I had a sip of my coffee. "Kanesha was worried because she couldn't find her mother, and Morty Cassity mentioned he hadn't seen Vera. So we started looking for them." I gave them a brief account of my discovery of Azalea and Vera's body in the stairwell.

Laura shivered, her breakfast forgotten. "How terrible for Azalea. Locked in with a corpse."

"Sounds like the title of a Golden Age detective story." Sean scooped up the fallen egg and popped it into his mouth. Not much interfered with his appetite.

"Don't be facetious, son."

Sean shrugged. "Sorry."

I suppressed a sigh of irritation. "Azalea was terrified,

and Kanesha was pretty upset, too. She seemed to think Sheriff Tidwell was considering her mother as a suspect in Vera's death."

"Azalea? You've got to be kidding me." Sean set his fork aside. "No way she'd kill someone. Did she even know Mrs. Cassity?"

"She knew her." I hadn't confided in either Sean or Laura about my set-down from Azalea or the reason for it. I would explain that to them later. I didn't want Azalea to come back into the room and catch me talking about it.

"To know her was to loathe her, evidently." Laura broke off another bit of bacon and gazed innocently at me as it disappeared under the table. Smug purring followed.

"That's putting it mildly. Vera made enemies all too easily." I had some bacon and biscuit and a forkful of eggs.

"Maybe one of the Ducote sisters caught her snooping and pushed her down the stairs. Maybe Ducote is French for 'ruthless.' " Sean was being particularly smart-mouthed this morning.

My temper flared. "I'm not too happy with you right this minute, Sean. Your flippancy is totally out of place. What happened last night was horrible, and you ought to have more respect for Azalea and what she went through than to carry on like this."

Diesel appeared at my side, meowing anxiously. He got agitated anytime he thought I was upset. In taking a moment to reassure him I began to calm down myself. I almost—almost, mind you—regretted my outburst.

"Sorry, Dad." Sean looked suitably abashed. "I guess it seems a little unreal. I didn't know Mrs. Cassity."

"Neither did I, but I do know Azalea." Laura seemed to withdraw for a moment, and I realized she must be thinking of the events of three months before when a friend of hers was murdered and she found the body. "I'm sorry she had to go through all that."

Sean reached over and squeezed her shoulder. His voice was gruff when he spoke. "Sorry, Laura, I was really insensitive."

"It's okay." Laura offered the ghost of a smile. "Dad, is there anything we can do for Azalea?"

"Just let her be," I said. "She's a strong woman, and if she needs us to lean on, we'll be here."

"What about her being a suspect?" Sean poked at his eggs. "Do you think the sheriff is really serious?"

Before I could respond, Laura asked, "Is the sheriff investigating this? And not Kanesha?"

"Yes, the sheriff is in charge. It wouldn't be ethical for Kanesha to investigate, I suppose, because her mother was found with the body." I sighed. "Kanesha's not going to be happy having to sit this one out."

Sean reminded me I hadn't answered his question.

"I know from my own experience that they tend to be suspicious of the person who finds the body. But I think once the sheriff and his team have had time to evaluate the evidence, they'll have to conclude that Azalea couldn't have pushed Vera down the stairs." I paused. "If that's what caused her death."

"You sound awfully sure," Laura said.

I explained my reasoning, keeping an eye out for Azalea. She'd been in the laundry room for a good ten minutes or more, and she might pop back in any minute now.

She hadn't reappeared by the time I finished my explanation. Sean looked particularly thoughtful. "How wide is that stairwell?"

I thought for a moment. "Maybe an inch or so wider than my shoulders. It really is a tight squeeze."

"Then I don't see how Azalea could have done it, unless she's a world-class gymnast." Sean rolled his eyes. "I thought the sheriff was smarter than that."

"I'm sure he is," I said. "I don't know him personally, but I know he's highly regarded. He seems to run the department effectively—and honestly, from all I've heard."

Laura pushed her plate aside. "Then by now he's surely realized that Azalea is innocent. Just unlucky enough to be in the wrong place at the wrong time."

"For her sake," Sean said, his tone grim, "let's hope the murderer didn't know she was there, or she could be next on the list."

"That thought had occurred to me." I got up to refill my coffee. "I'm sure it's occurred to Kanesha, too. Frankly I'm surprised she's let her mother out of her sight."

"Do you really think Azalea is going to let Kanesha tell her what to do?" Laura grinned.

"That girl don't need to be minding my business." Azalea walked into the room with a basket of laundry. "I been taking care of myself just fine on my own." She disappeared in the direction of the stairs, and seconds later we heard her going up to the second floor.

Diesel meowed, and we three humans shared a smile. Azalea truly was indomitable. The sheriff was no match for her.

SIXTEEN

|||||||||||||||||||||||||||||||||||||||||||||

On the walk to work at the college library I pulled out my cell phone and called Helen Louise. I figured by now the morning rush had subsided and she might have a moment to chat. She answered after two rings.

"Good morning," I said. "Are you totally exhausted?"

"Pretty wrung out," she responded, and I could hear it in her voice. "I think I managed about four hours' sleep, if that much."

"Any chance you can sneak in the back and have a nap in your office? Or take the afternoon off to get some rest?"

"Not today." Helen Louise sighed heavily. "I have a huge order of petits fours for a garden club tea this afternoon and three dozen quiches for a bridge party this evening."

"Poor baby. I'm glad business is so good, but I wish you had some time to rest."

"That will have to wait until tonight. I'm planning to

leave around seven and go home and drop in the bed straightaway."

"No dinner tonight, then." I was disappointed, but she needed the rest.

Diesel could hear her voice emanating from the cell phone, and he meowed and chirped. I told her that, and she chuckled. "Give him a kiss from me," she said. "Afraid I have got to go now, sweetie."

"Talk to you later, then."

By now Diesel and I had reached the steps of the antebellum house that housed the library's administration offices and the rare book room and archives.

Diesel scurried up the steps as soon as I released him from his halter, and moments later I heard him warbling away. I trotted up the stairs after him to see what had him so excited.

As I stepped onto the second-floor landing and glanced down the hall toward the door of my office, I saw two figures, their backs to me, bending down to pet the cat.

"Good morning, Miss An'gel, Miss Dickce. How are you?"

"Tired, Charlie, but otherwise tolerable." Miss An'gel straightened. "You're running a bit late today."

"Goodness, An'gel, the poor man probably overslept after such a terrible night." Miss Dickce scowled at her sister. "I know I would have if you'd left me alone."

Miss An'gel shot her sibling a look of withering contempt, and I had to suppress a smile as I responded. "I'm afraid I did oversleep this morning, ladies. Forgot to set the alarm, and my backup didn't try to rouse me the way he usually does." I begged their pardon as I stepped around them to unlock the door.

"Diesel, I'm surprised at you." Miss Dickce chuckled.

"Sometimes he takes pity on me," I said as I switched

on the lights. "Please come in." I strode ahead to find a second chair to add to the one in front of my desk.

The Ducotes seated themselves, Diesel between their chairs, and I faced them from behind my desk. "Can I offer you something to drink? Coffee, tea, or water? It won't take a moment."

Miss Dickce opened her mouth to speak, but Miss An'gel cut her off. "No, thank you, Charlie, we've just come from breakfast at home." Miss Dickce looked decidedly grumpy now. She stroked Diesel's head, and her frown eased into a smile.

"What can I do for you?" I couldn't think what brought them to my office so soon after the events of the previous night.

"You've been involved in other murders." Miss An'gel got straight to the point. "We want you to help us figure out who murdered Vera. The sooner this is resolved, the better for all of us."

"We can't believe someone had the audacity to commit murder at River Hill," Miss Dickce said. "Vera will probably haunt us for the rest of our lives now."

"Beauregard will take care of that," Miss An'gel sniffed. "She wouldn't dare. The point is, Charlie, I will not have it said in Athena that Dickce and I had anything to do with Vera's death. We had no reason whatsoever to want the wretched woman dead. We had already taken steps to remove the thorn from our side, and it didn't involve anything to do with murder."

"I have to say, it certainly was a masterstroke how you maneuvered Vera into retiring from active charitable works." Despite the gravity of the situation I was hard-pressed not to grin as I recalled the presentation of the award.

"Thank you," Miss An'gel responded with a prim smile.

"But that's just the point, you see. Vera had to accept that award or become a laughingstock by making a scene and refusing it. Arranging it that way, so she would have to resign from all her committees, was the worst thing we could have done to her. We didn't need to push her down the stairs."

"Not at River Hill," Miss Dickce said, eyes flashing. "We would never desecrate our own home like that. There have been enough deaths there over the years."

"I do see your point." I glanced over at Diesel, who appeared slightly antsy, thanks to the sudden tension in the room. He moved away from the Ducotes and clambered behind me into his usual spot in the window. "Besides, as much as we all disliked Vera, the person who killed her had to hate her to the point of desperation."

"Exactly." Miss An'gel nodded vigorously. "We want you to figure out who that person was. He or she had to have a motive far stronger than any one that my sister or I could have. We pitied Vera and—I must admit—disliked her heartily, but she didn't deserve to be killed."

"I appreciate your confidence in me, ladies, but the sheriff wouldn't be too happy to have me poke my nose into this." I had poked my nose into things in the past, despite Kanesha's best efforts, but I had done my best not to interfere in her investigations. Of course, Kanesha was on the sidelines this time, I remembered.

"Don't you worry about Gerald Tidwell." Miss Dickce waved a hand in a dismissive gesture. "If he gives you any trouble, An'gel will have a little talk with him. He's coming up for reelection next year, and without a good word from An'gel he'll have a hard time winning."

"Dickce, you shouldn't say such things." Miss An'gel scowled at her sibling. "Even if it's true. People will get entirely the wrong idea." She turned to me. "I don't think

Gerald will be a problem, really. Besides, he has the notion stuck in his head that Azalea Berry killed Vera. That's the biggest load of bull hockey I've ever heard."

That was probably the closest to swearing that Miss An'gel would come in mixed company, and once again I had to resist the urge to grin.

"Azalea Berry is a fine Christian woman," Miss Dickce said. "She would never strike another person in anger. She does have a temper, the good Lord only knows, but she would never turn violent."

"Even though she did have plenty of reasons to despise Vera." Miss An'gel sighed. "Now, think about your aunt Dottie, Charlie. Wouldn't she have wanted you to do your best for Azalea?"

That was hitting below the belt, and from the gleam in Miss An'gel's eye, I saw she knew exactly what she was doing and was daring me to deny her.

I'd rather take on Attila and a battalion of his Huns before I'd hold out against Miss An'gel. "Very well, I'll do what I can."

"Good man." Miss An'gel beamed, and Miss Dickce nodded. They both rose. Miss An'gel continued, "Now you must excuse us, Charlie. We have an appointment with Q. C. Pendergrast. If you need anything at all, let us know." After calling good-bye to Diesel and receiving meows in return, they departed.

Too late I realized I hadn't asked them about Azalea's possible motive for killing Vera. If I was going to help exonerate Azalea completely and identify the real killer, I needed to know the source of Azalea's loathing for Vera. Otherwise I'd just be spinning my wheels and not accomplishing much.

I turned to look at my cat lounging in the window. "I have

my marching orders, boy, but I'm not too thrilled about it." I reached forward to rub his head, and his expression of blissful contentment tickled me. I wouldn't mind trading places with him for a week or two, though the litter box might not be that much fun. "All that will have to wait, though. Right now I need to get back to the work I'm actually paid to do."

"I always figured you talked to that cat. What I want to know is, does he talk back?"

I whirled around to see Kanesha Berry standing in the doorway. Her expression enigmatic as ever, I couldn't tell whether she was amused or annoyed. I felt my face redden.

"Please, come in." I stood and beckoned her forward.

We both sat, and I watched her warily. Was this an official visit? I presumed it was, since she was in uniform.

"I'm not part of the investigation into Mrs. Cassity's murder." Kanesha stared right at me. "So this is all off the record, all right?"

Surprised, I nodded. "Fine with me."

"Despite the evidence to the contrary, the sheriff is insisting on treating my mother as the chief suspect." Kanesha's nostrils flared, a slight crack in the facade. "It's absolutely ridiculous because it would have been physically impossible for Mama to push that woman down the stairs."

"I know," I said, and Kanesha's eyes gleamed. "She was locked in at the bottom of the stairs—the *narrow* stairs—and there was no way she could have pushed Vera down from above and then gotten herself to the bottom without trampling all over the body."

"Exactly."

"Is the sheriff that dumb, that he can't see the obvious?"

"No, but he's using Mama to get at me."

"I thought he was the one who promoted you in the first

place. Why would he want to get at you?" I couldn't figure that one out.

"Because I'm too good at my job." Kanesha shrugged. "Next year he's up for reelection, and he has this crazy idea that I'm going to run against him."

"Are you?"

"Not yet."

Neatly, coolly said. I admired the woman's sangfroid. "Even so, he's not going to be able to railroad Azalea on this. When it comes to court, he'd be a laughingstock."

"Yes, but that doesn't mean he's not going to push it as far as he can, do his best to humiliate me and my family. I am not going to let that happen."

Tidwell had better watch his back. He'd made an enemy now, an implacable one.

"It won't. Your mother has some powerful allies, you know." I told her about the Ducotes' visit, and she relaxed, almost imperceptibly.

"That's good to know. And I appreciate the fact that you are willing to stand up for Mama, too."

"I am," I said and decided it was time to get everything out in the open. "One thing puzzles me, though. I know your mother despised Vera, but I don't know why. I can't imagine Azalea has a strong enough motive to want to kill Vera."

"That's just the problem." Kanesha's tone was cool. "Mama and I both have reason to want that witch dead. Vera Cassity as good as murdered my cousin."

SEVENTEEN

||||||||||||||||||||||||||||||||||||||||||||||||||||||||

"Murdered your *cousin*? How horrible." That was the last thing I expected to hear. I felt a paw on my shoulder—the tone of my voice made Diesel anxious. "It's okay, boy, I'm all right." I patted his paw, and he settled back down.

"He didn't die by her hand," Kanesha said. "But he might as well have."

"What happened? I'm sorry. I know it must be painful for you to talk about." I hated to make her dredge up sorrow-laden memories, but I needed to understand the situation.

Kanesha shrugged, but her gaze hardened. "Johnny Golliday was my mother's sister's only son. Her only child, as a matter of fact. He started getting in trouble when he was thirteen or fourteen, nothing too serious. At least, no felonies. But my aunt was always there to bail him out. He was in his twenties when he got mixed up with a rougher

crowd, started getting into bigger trouble. Spent some time
in jail."

Suddenly Kanesha got up from the chair and began to
pace. "Johnny going to prison like to've killed my aunt. My
mother, too. They're both proud women, and Johnny was
the first one in the family who ever spent time behind
bars." She came back to the chair and gripped the back of
it with both hands as she looked at me. "But he was doing
better, had a job, was living at home, helping his mother
take care of his father who was a quadriplegic." Her voice
cracked slightly.

She let go of the chair and turned away a moment. When
she faced me again she seemed to have regained her com-
posure. Behind me, Diesel moved restlessly on the windowsill. He muttered in that peculiar way of his, and I knew he
was unsettled by the tension emanating from Kanesha.

I felt at a loss, because I had never seen her this vulner-
able. In my way I was as uncomfortable as Diesel. My normal response would have been to go to her, give her a hug
or at least a friendly shoulder squeeze, but Kanesha and
I didn't have that kind of relationship. My heart went out
to her, because I could imagine how painful all this was
for her.

Kanesha resumed her seat. "One day nearly ten years
ago, Johnny went to the bank with a couple of his so-called
friends. What they didn't tell him was they were planning
to rob the bank."

"Oh, no." The words slipped out before I could stop
myself. I could see the scene unfolding in my mind, and I
didn't like the picture.

Kanesha didn't appear to have heard my comment.
"When they reached the bank, one of the men pulled a gun
and told Johnny he was going to help them. Johnny tried to

get away, but he was terrified they would shoot him. So he went into the bank with friend number one while number two waited in the car." She paused for a couple of deep breaths. "Johnny wasn't too coordinated, always dropping things, stumbling, and the idiot with him made him take a gun. He was terrified of them. Johnny said he was shaking so hard he dropped the gun three times."

"What happened when they made it into the bank?"

"Stupidity, that's what happened." Kanesha's tone turned vicious. "Idiot number one was trigger-happy and ended up shooting one of the tellers and pistol-whipping a customer."

"Oh, my Lord," I said, appalled. "Did the teller die?"

"No, thankfully," Kanesha replied. "It could have been worse in so many ways, if Johnny's so-called friend wasn't so inept. Johnny stumbled all over the place, and it was his bad luck he tripped and fell onto another customer. Vera Cassity. Knocked her down and she banged her head on the floor. At the trial she claimed he threatened her with his gun. Said he'd kill her if she made a sound."

Kanesha slumped back in the chair, eyes closed. "The police arrived in less than two minutes. Caught them still inside the bank. Johnny was sentenced to thirty years in the state pen. Wasn't eligible for parole because he was convicted for armed robbery. Might have received a lighter sentence—not that it mattered in the long run—but Vera Cassity, egged on by the prosecutor, made it sound like the only reason she wasn't killed was because the police arrived so quickly." She opened her eyes and stared at me, though I wasn't sure she actually saw me. "Johnny insisted he dropped the gun right after he entered the bank, but nobody could attest to that. With Vera swearing he threatened her with it, nobody believed him."

"Except his family," I said softly. I had to consider that

Kanesha was prejudiced in her cousin's favor, but if he was truly uncoordinated *and* afraid of guns, I could see him dropping the thing and not bothering to pick it up again.

Kanesha nodded. "I knew my cousin, Mr. Harris, and I believed him. I knew what a klutz he was and how scared he would have been. If he said he dropped the gun and only stumbled into Vera Cassity, then that's what happened."

"Where does murder come into it, then?"

"Two and a half years after Johnny went to the state pen, he was killed by a couple of the other inmates."

"I'm so sorry," I said, knowing the words were completely inadequate.

"Aunt Lily was devastated, and so was my mother. They blamed Vera Cassity—mainly because she was so nasty in the courtroom. He would have gone to prison regardless, but the way Vera talked him down, well, they just couldn't forgive her." She threw up her hands. "The whole thing was so freakin' stupid, from beginning to end."

I waited a moment before I spoke, trying to marshal my thoughts. I could understand why Azalea and her sister Lily had taken against Vera so harshly, but I honestly couldn't see that their feelings translated into an active motive for murder.

I voiced that to Kanesha, and she nodded. "I agree with you. Mama and Aunt Lily hated Vera like you wouldn't believe, but neither one of them would ever have laid a hand on her."

"But the sheriff obviously disagrees," I said.

"Up to a point." Kanesha shook her head. "Once he thinks he's done me enough damage, he'll ease off my mother."

"What are you going to do about it in the meantime?"

"Do my best to figure out who really killed Vera," Kanesha said. "But it can't look like I'm doing it. That's where you come in."

I wasn't completely flabbergasted. I had helped her on previous cases, pretty sub rosa as well, but her words sounded more like an order than a request. "I'll do what I can to help, naturally."

"Good. The first thing I want you to do is to talk to my mother. She won't talk to me about it, no matter what I say to her." I could hear the frustration in her voice.

"What makes you think she'll talk to me?" I quailed at the thought of cornering Azalea and persuading her to talk to me.

"I'm not sure she will," Kanesha admitted. "But you've got to try. I know she likes and respects you."

"Really?" With Azalea I had never been able to tell what she thought of me. Most of the time I felt like an inept schoolboy when she was around.

Kanesha nodded. "Oh, I know what she's like, believe me. Makes you feel like you can't even tie your own shoes without someone helping you. But that's just her way. She doesn't tolerate fools, and to her a lot of the world is filled with fools. But she doesn't think you're one of them." She graced me with a brief smile.

There was no point in holding out. The moment I'd agreed to do what the Ducote sisters wanted, I knew I'd have to talk to Azalea. "Okay, I'll talk to her."

"How about now?" Kanesha stood. "The sooner, the better. We need to find out whether Mama saw anything. That's the thing that really puzzles me. She had to be in that stairwell when Vera fell down the stairs, so surely she must've seen whoever pushed Vera."

"But why isn't she saying anything?"

"Exactly my point." She stared hard at me. "So when are you going to talk to her?"

"I'm at work," I said. "I can't just walk out and go play detective." Actually I could probably have the time off, but I really dreaded confronting Azalea.

"You couldn't get some time off today? Surely they'd understand, after what happened."

I sighed. "You're right. I'll see if I can't take the rest of the day off. The sooner I talk to Azalea and get it over with, the better."

"Thanks. I appreciate this." She handed me a card. "My private cell phone number is on the back. Call me if you turn up anything significant."

"I will." I stuffed the card in my shirt pocket.

Kanesha headed out the door, and I turned in my chair to regard my cat. "Well, boy, looks like we're going home early today. Time to get your harness back on."

Diesel meowed, then stood and stretched. He knew what *home* meant.

Five minutes later, we headed out the front door. I explained to Melba Gilley, the director's secretary and an old friend, that I didn't feel well and was going home for the day. I knew Melba was dying to quiz me over what had happened at the gala, and I promised to tell her all about it later.

On the brief walk home, I pondered where to talk to Azalea. I figured the kitchen might be best, because I tended to think of it as her domain. I was pretty sure she did, too.

The house was quiet when Diesel and I entered through the back door. I hoped everyone besides Azalea was out, because it could be awkward if someone walked in on us.

"Hello, anyone home?" I released Diesel from his harness, and off he trotted to the utility room.

When there was no response to my question, I walked

into the front hall and repeated it, aiming my voice up the stairs. About ten seconds passed, and Azalea appeared at the top of the stairs, dust cloth and furniture polish in hand.

"You need something, Mr. Charlie?" She frowned. "You sick? What you doing home so early?"

"I came home early because I need to discuss something with you. Would you mind coming downstairs? It's important," I added when she hesitated.

Her frown deepened, but she came down the stairs and followed me into the kitchen.

"Want some coffee?" she asked as she laid the dust rag and polish on the counter. "They's still some left from the pot Miss Laura made a while ago."

"No, thank you," I said. Diesel wandered into the kitchen. He paused to warble at Azalea, and she gazed at him blankly. "Please, Azalea, sit down. I really need to talk to you."

She complied, but her expression threatened mutiny, to judge by the set of her lips. "What is it?"

"It's about last night," I said. I held up a hand as she started to rise, mutiny turning swiftly to outrage. "Azalea, please. I'm serious. For your own sake, sit down and talk to me. You're in trouble, whether you want to believe it or not." She hesitated, and I played what I considered my trump card. "Aunt Dottie will haunt me to the end of my days if I don't do everything I can to help you. She might just haunt you, too, if you don't listen to reason."

I braced myself for the lightning strike that I figured was about to hit, but to my great surprise, Azalea burst into tears instead.

EIGHTEEN

|||||||||||||||||||||||||||||||||||||||||||||||||||||||

I froze. Maybe I shouldn't have mentioned Aunt Dottie. I'd never expected Azalea to react like this. What should I do?

Diesel acted while I hesitated. He went to my house-keeper and placed a paw on her thigh. Startled, she glanced down at him, still sobbing. "What's he doing?" she finally managed to choke out.

"He's showing you that he's concerned. He knows you're upset, and I'm sorry about that. The last thing I meant to do was upset you." I started to get up, but she indicated that I should stay where I was.

"I be okay in a minute, Mr. Charlie." Azalea blew her nose into a handkerchief that suddenly appeared in her right hand. She looked at Diesel again, still sitting be-side her and watching her closely. "Don't you worry no more, cat."

Diesel meowed twice before he left Azalea and came to

sit next to my chair. I rubbed his head, and he butted against my hand.

"Are you sure I can't get you something? Water, iced tea?"

She shook her head. "No, thank you. Guess I'm just tired. Can't remember when I slept so bad. Hardly closed my eyes all night."

Thinking guiltily of how soundly I had slept, I nodded. "It's no wonder you couldn't sleep. After everything that happened last night."

Azalea regarded me warily, her momentary breakdown finished. "What you want to talk about?"

"Last night," I said. "But first I need to tell you something. Miss An'gel and Miss Dickce came to see me at the library this morning. They're concerned about you, too, and they want me to help make sure the real killer is identified. They know you couldn't have had anything to do with Mrs. Cassity's death."

"That's mighty nice of them, to be concerned like that." Her expression hadn't changed.

I decided I'd better not mention that Kanesha also wanted me to help. That would put her back up straightaway.

"Now, about last night," I said. "I know it's not pleasant, but I need you to tell me about everything that happened in that stairway. Let's start with how you came to be there."

From the set of her mouth—I knew that stubborn line from compressed lips all too well—I thought she was going to balk. I decided that starting with a specific question would probably work better.

"It was strange about the door at the bottom of the stairs being blocked that way. Do you know if it was blocked earlier in the evening?"

"Expect it was," Azalea said after a moment's thought.

"Think they keeps it like that. Them stairs is old and in bad shape. It's real dark in there, too. That light don't do much good."

"Where did you enter the staircase? On the second floor or the third?"

"Second. Ain't much call to go up to the third floor, and them stairs even worse than the ones down from the second floor."

This reminded me of questioning my children during their teenage years—not much volunteered, so I had to keep coming up with the right things to ask. "Why did you come down those stairs? Why not use the main staircase at the front of the house?"

"Back stairs was closer," Azalea said. She paused, then all at once the floodgates burst. "Reason I went upstairs, some lady come in the kitchen with her skirt about falling off. Needed it sewn up or she was gonna be parading around showing what the good Lord never intended the rest of the world to see. I said I'd sew it up for her, and Clementine said to go up to the second floor. They's a little room at the back, right across from them stairs. Miss Dickce turned it into a sewing room."

That spate of information ceased as suddenly as it started.

"You went up by the front stairs, surely?"

Azalea nodded.

"How long were you in the sewing room with the lady and her skirt?"

"Ten minutes, maybe. Lady got dressed again and went back downstairs." She glanced down at her hands, pleating and unpleating her handkerchief. She'd been doing it for several minutes.

"But you stayed up there. Why?"

"Had some personal business to take care of."

It took me a moment, but I suddenly realized what she meant and was evidently too embarrassed to say openly. She'd needed to use the bathroom.

I nodded. "Okay. What happened after you took care of your personal business?" I was getting a headache from the tension I felt. I wasn't enjoying this, and I'm sure Azalea wasn't, either.

"I's about to go back downstairs, but when I opened the door I heard some people arguing right there in the hall. So I stayed where I was. Hoping they'd go away."

"Could you tell who the people were? And how many?"

Azalea grimaced. "I could tell just fine. They was two of them, Mr. Cassity and Miz Cassity. They wasn't yelling or anything, but you could tell they wasn't happy with each other."

An argument between Vera and her husband—could it be as simple as that? Morty pushed Vera down the stairs in a fit of anger?

But then I realized at this point in Azalea's story, she was still in the bathroom, and the Cassitys were out in the hall.

"How long did this go on?" I asked.

Azalea considered that. "Few minutes, I reckon. Kept opening the door just enough to peek out, but there they was, still fussing."

"Could you hear what they were saying to each other?"

She nodded, reluctantly, I could tell. "Some of it. Never heard such words before in my life. Miz Cassity had an ugly way of talking when she be angry. Miss An'gel wouldn't ever talk like that."

"No, I'm sure she wouldn't. Now, could you tell what they were arguing about?"

"About him tomcatting around on her. That ain't a Christian way to behave. You marry somebody, you don't run around like that." She shook her head. "But when you married to poison like her, well, can't say as I blame him too much."

"Did you hear any threats from either of them?"

"No, 'cepting him saying he was going to divorce her, and she telling him he could try, but she'd take ever' bit of his money."

That was a powerful motive. Vera's refusal to give Morty a divorce, along with the monetary threat, might have goaded him past endurance—and then he pushed her down the stairs as a solution to his problems.

"Anything else you hear that sounded bad?"

"No, sir. They both got real quiet then, and when I looked out I saw them going into a room down the hall." She paused. "Well, I know I saw her. That big ol' skirt she was wearing, you couldn't miss. I reckon I thought he was in front of her, but I can't be sure."

"Do you think he had time to reach the stairs and head down?" If my scenario were to hold together, then Morty probably would have gone into that room with Vera.

"Maybe." Azalea didn't appear too certain.

I'd come back to that.

"What did you do after they went into the other room?"

"I was gonna go down the stairs, but I heard her talking. The door was open about halfway, and I didn't want them seeing me if I went past."

"Was that when you remembered the back stairs?"

Diesel was getting restless. I felt his head butt against my thigh twice, and I stilled him by scratching his head. He purred in response. As long as he received some attention he would be okay, and I could continue questioning Azalea.

Azalea nodded. "I ducked back down the hall and opened the door. Had to find the light switch, and when I did, it didn't do a whole lot of good. I was gonna go back and try to get down the front stairs, but then I heard her out in the hall again. So I started down. Had to go kinda slow. Them stairs is so old I was afraid some of 'em might be rotten."

Now we were getting to the critical part. I tried to keep my tone calm as I asked my next question.

"Think carefully now, and tell me what happened next."

"I got all the way down. Reckon they's about twenty-five steps, something like that. Got to the door and tried to open it, but it was dark down there and I couldn't see much. Light's back up near the top. Kept twisting the knob and pushing, but couldn't get the door to move, not one bit." She shuddered. "I don't like being shut up like that in the dark. I's about to go back up when I heard the door up there open."

I didn't prompt her when she stopped. I could tell she was reliving the experience.

After a moment she continued. "Saw somebody step inside. Had to be her, because the skirt was so wide. That was about all I could see. Then she said something like 'Why you wanna go in here?' I didn't hear nothing right after that, then she said, 'Well, if this is the best way to catch them at it, okay.' She took a couple steps down, and then . . ." She stopped and shuddered again.

I waited and nodded encouragingly when she looked at me. She took a deep breath to steady herself. I could sympathize with her, because I was seeing that scene play out in my mind, and I knew what was coming next.

"She came down a couple steps, I guess, then all of a sudden, I heard her grunt real loud, and she came flying down the stairs. Groaned when she landed, and then she was quiet." She rubbed her hands up and down her arms. "Reckon I could use some water, Mr. Charlie."

"Right away." I jumped up to get it for her.

When I brought it to her, she had her eyes closed. I touched her gently on the shoulder as I set the glass in front of her. She nodded, then took the glass and drained two-thirds of it. "Thank you."

"Do you feel like telling me the rest of it now?" I asked gently.

She drew another deep breath. "I couldn't move, I was so scared. Then I figured I'd better get to her to see if they was something I could do. But when I touched her I knew the spirit had done left her. They wasn't a thing I could do for her. After that all I wanted was to get out of there. Couldn't go up. Her and her skirt blocked the stairs, so I started banging on the door till somebody heard me and let me out. Thank the Lord you come along when you did." She drank the rest of her water.

"What do you think happened? Do you think she tripped, maybe caught her foot on her skirt and fell?"

"No." I barely heard her.

"So somebody pushed her?"

Azalea nodded, eyes averted.

"Could you tell who was on the stairs behind her?"

After a nearly imperceptible pause, she whispered, "No."

Had it not been for that slight hesitation—so slight I might easily have imagined it—I would have believed her. As it was, I was convinced she wasn't telling me the truth.

Why?

NINETEEN
||||||||||||||||||||||||||||||||||||||||||||||||||||||||

The obvious answer—Azalea was protecting someone.

Or maybe she saw something and wasn't certain what to think, how to interpret it.

I decided to take a slightly different tack.

"Could the person who pushed Vera have seen you?"

Azalea shook her head. "Don't think so. It was dark down where I was, and I scrunched up against that door. Didn't want nobody to know I be there."

No hesitation there. Good. "After you heard Vera fall, what did you do? Take me through it again."

She frowned at me. I thought she was going to protest, but she complied after a brief hesitation. "Like I done said, I went up to her to see if they's anything I could do, but she was dead."

"Did you look up at the top of the stairs at all?"

She nodded. I waited for her to elaborate, but she didn't.

"When did you look? Before you went to check on her?"

"I don't rightly remember," Azalea said slowly. She glanced away.

Again it didn't feel right. I pressed her. "Was the door at the top of the stairs open or closed when you looked?"

"Closed."

"So whoever it was got out of the stairwell before you looked up?" I felt like I was leading the witness, so to speak, but I had to wring whatever information I could from her.

"Reckon so." Suddenly she pushed back in her chair and stood. "Ain't nothing more I can tell you, Mr. Charlie. I need to get back to finishing my dusting."

"Okay, Azalea. You go on ahead." There was no point in my insisting that she stay. Frankly I was surprised I'd managed to keep her talking this long.

Diesel butted my leg with his head again. Evidently he had gone too long without attention, and he was letting me know. My mind remained elsewhere as I rubbed his head and down his spine.

Despite what Azalea had told me—that the upper door was closed when she looked—I was convinced she was holding something back. She must have seen something. But what? Or whom?

Then again, maybe I had simply misread her body language. Was I too anxious for a simple solution to this mess?

A simple solution would be that Morty Cassity pushed Vera down the stairs, angry because she refused to divorce him.

I needed a drink. My throat felt dry after my interrogation of Azalea, so I got up and poured myself a glass of water and downed it.

That was better. I leaned against the counter and stared down at Diesel. He sat at my feet and stared up at me as if to ask, "Okay, what now?"

"I'm not sure, boy."

He meowed and thrust out a paw to touch my leg. I had to smile. I wasn't sure what he was trying to convey, but the fact that he always seemed to respond when I talked to him made me feel like we were having a conversation.

My cell phone rang, and I peered at the number that came up on the screen. I frowned. Why was Melba Gilley calling me?

I answered the call and before I could do more than utter hello, Melba was off and running.

"Charlie, the weirdest thing. One of the work-study students just walked over from the main building with a letter for you. Apparently it got delivered by mistake over there and was sitting on somebody's desk since Monday. Anyway, you'll never guess who it's from."

I suppressed a sigh of irritation. I loved Melba dearly, but she could be exasperating—especially when she thought there was gossip involved. "No, you're right, I'll never guess. So who's the letter from?"

"Vera Cassity."

I nearly dropped the phone.

"Charlie, you still there?"

"Yes, I'm here." Shaken, but here. Why would Vera write to me?

"Don't you think you ought to come and see what's in the letter? Or I could bring it to you in a little bit, when I go out to lunch."

"I'll come get it," I said. "I'm feeling a bit better now, and the walk will do me and Diesel good. We'll see you in about fifteen minutes." I ended the call.

A letter from Vera—that was distinctly creepy. Obviously she had written and posted it late last week, probably after she came to see me at the archives. It might not be anything more than another attempt to coerce me into letting her nose around in the Ducote papers.

Too late for that, I thought grimly.

"Come on, boy, we're going back to work." Diesel waited for me by the door as I scribbled a quick note for Azalea and left it on the table. I wanted to let her know that I would be back for lunch later on. If I didn't turn up as usual, I would mess up her routine, and I had upset her enough already today.

When Diesel and I walked into the library director's suite, Melba's face lit up with excitement. She bobbed up out of her chair and came to greet us. She and Diesel were great pals, and she squatted to put herself on face level with him. They rubbed noses, and she scratched his head and talked nonsense to him while I stood patiently by.

At last Melba stood, brushed some hair from her bright turquoise pants, and said, "Charlie, I know you're tired, but you have to tell me all about what happened last night." She pointed to a chair by her desk. "Now, sit and spill."

I'd known Melba since elementary school, when she was a gap-toothed, pigtailed nuisance who could talk the hind legs off a mule. Forty-odd years later she was an attractive, stylish woman, but her mouth hadn't slowed down. I had to be careful what I told her, because it would be all over town ten minutes after I left her.

I started out with a carefully edited account of the gala, but Melba interrupted with questions.

"How was Vera dressed? The article in the paper didn't say anything about it, and they haven't run any photos from the gala yet."

"She came as Scarlett O'Hara, and her husband was Rhett Butler."

Melba snorted with laughter. "You have got to be kidding me. Vera Cassity as Scarlett O'Hara? That must have been a sight."

I winced, thinking of Vera's corpse on the stairwell, with that hoop skirt billowing up, stuck in place. I wasn't going to share that detail with Melba, however.

"Sorry." Melba looked almost contrite. "I know it's terrible of me to make fun of her like that, but a woman her age dressing like that. She should have gone as Scarlett's grandmother, Lord have mercy. She was seventy-five at least."

That surprised me. "I thought she was about sixty. She sure didn't look seventy-five."

"Well, she was." Melba's tone brooked no argument. She was invariably right about these things. "Don't forget, honey, she had the money for plastic surgery. She'd had everything that sagged tucked up so many times it's a wonder her toes weren't on top of her knees."

"Then her husband must have had surgery, too, because he doesn't look much more than sixty himself."

"That's because he's only about ten years older than you and me, honey." Melba shook her head at my obvious denseness. "Vera was at least a dozen years older than Morty. I thought you knew that."

"I had no idea," I said. "Why did he marry a woman that much older?"

"Money."

"I thought Vera came from a poor family." This wasn't adding up.

"She did," Melba said. "Dirt-poor. But Vera's mama inherited some money from some old aunt in Georgia, or maybe it was Florida, around the time Vera was almost thirty. Then her mama died and left it all to Vera. Morty came calling soon after, and he used Vera's money to get started in business."

"He couldn't have been more than eighteen or nineteen at that point."

"He wasn't," Melba said. "But they got married, and within ten years Morty had three car dealerships. He's got seven now, I think. Loaded, and it all started with Vera's mama's money."

Diesel, tired of being ignored, crawled into Melba's lap, and she laughed. "Sweetie, I'm sorry I've been neglecting you." She loved on him as she continued, "I got you side-tracked, Charlie. Go on, tell me the rest of it."

I spent another fifteen minutes talking, until I got to the point where I found Azalea and Vera's body in the stairwell.

"That's the end of it," I said, my throat dry. "After that we all had to wait to talk to the sheriff, and then we were able to get home."

Melba's eyes narrowed. "I know you're leaving out a lot. You can't fool me."

"I've told you all I can," I said. "I'll have to leave it at that, but I promise to tell you, as soon as I am able, anything else that I might have left out. Deal?"

Melba sighed and nodded. "You're going to be nosing around again, aren't you?" She didn't wait for an answer as she reached into a drawer and pulled out an envelope. "Here's your letter."

The envelope was made of thick, quality paper, and Vera's name and address were embossed in silver on it. My name and address were handwritten in block capitals.

I debated whether to open it in front of Melba, but I could always claim the contents were private. She might badger me, but I could handle that. Curiosity was eating at me, and I couldn't wait any longer.

"Can I borrow your letter opener?"

Melba handed it across to me, and I slit the envelope. There was a single sheet inside, and I pulled it out.

I unfolded it to reveal the scanned image of a photograph. An old photograph, judging by the clothing of the woman in the picture. The words "Essie Mae Hobson" were printed underneath the photo. I had no idea who she was.

I showed it to Melba, and her eyes widened as she spoke. "Why would Vera send you a picture of her mother?"

TWENTY

|||||||||||||||||||||||||||||||||||||||||||||||||

I stared at the face of the woman in the picture. The photograph was cracked and faded, probably taken in the mid-1920s, to judge by the subject's clothing. Essie Mae Hobson looked young here, perhaps no more than twenty. She sat in profile, her head bent shyly, so it was difficult to get a full impression of her.

I couldn't see much of Vera in her, except perhaps the shape of her nose. Vera must have taken more after her father—unless the plastic surgery Melba told me about had altered her features significantly.

There was something elusively familiar, however, about Essie Mae's face. Maybe Vera looked more like her mother than I realized.

"What do you know about Vera's mother?" Melba knew most every family in Athena and the surrounding county, so she ought to be able to tell me something.

"Not much," Melba said in a grudging tone. "She was

married to Jedediah Hobson, who was a drunk and a fool, according to my grandma on my daddy's side. She knew the family. About as redneck as they came, she said, and mean and stupid with it. Jedediah ran shine until he was killed in a car wreck when Vera was probably about twelve or thirteen, I think. Amory, Vera's brother, would have been eight or nine. They didn't have any money to speak of, until Essie Mae got her inheritance."

Sounded like Vera had grown up in an unpleasant, if not sordid, environment, with a father like that. I looked at Essie Mae again, and my heart went out to her. Such a gentle, sweet-looking girl to end up with an ignorant moonshiner.

"Why on earth did Vera send me this picture?"

"Maybe she wanted you to help her do some research on her family," Melba said. She frowned. "You know, come to think of it, I never heard anybody say where Essie Mae came from or even who her people were. That's odd." She cooed at Diesel, and he chirped for her.

I paid them scant attention, lost in my thoughts.

Could Essie Mae Hobson have anything to do with Vera's death? The chances seemed remote, but I was definitely intrigued. Sending me this copy of a photograph was a bizarre thing to do—unless Melba was right about Vera's wanting help to find out more about her mother and her family.

I wouldn't accomplish anything by sitting here at Melba's desk. Time to go back to my office upstairs and get busy.

"Come on, Diesel, let's go." I stood and motioned for the cat to get out of Melba's lap.

Melba scowled at me. "Can't he stay down here with me for a bit? I'll bring him up later."

"If he wants to, I reckon it's okay." I trusted Melba to take good care of him. From time to time he visited with her down here while I worked upstairs.

Diesel jumped down and ambled toward the door. "Not today, I guess." Melba sighed. "Men are so fickle, even the feline ones."

I gave that the answer it deserved by ignoring it. "See you later," I said. "And thanks for letting me know about the letter."

Upstairs Diesel wasted no time in settling down in his napping spot in the window. I figured he was ready to snooze for a while; otherwise he would have stayed with Melba. Wished I could catch a few winks myself, even after the sound sleep I'd had last night.

I switched on the computer and checked my phone for voice mail from yesterday when I was out of the office. I hadn't thought about it this morning, and I saw now that the message light was blinking. I turned the speaker on so I could listen while I checked e-mail.

The first two calls were basic reference questions, people looking for genealogical information. I'd get back to them later today or tomorrow.

The third call startled the heck out of me. I heard Vera Cassity's strident voice. Talk about unnerving. Diesel sat up and meowed, just as disturbed by it as I was.

I missed the first part of Vera's message, so I had to replay it.

"By now you ought to've received a letter I sent you. It's a photograph of my mother. I know diddly-squat about her life before she married my father, because she never talked about those years. I want to know, and I figured you could help me. I think there was some kind of connection with the Ducotes, though, and if you won't let me look in those papers, maybe you can do it for me. I'll see you at River Hill tonight."

That was the final message. More final than Vera could have known, I realized, and that creeped me out again.

I thought about the message. Did Vera really not know anything about her mother's early life? Or had she intended to use her mother as a ploy to get into the Ducote papers?

As the archivist, I had access to the papers, and Vera had probably figured that out. But whether I could justify snooping in them on another person's behalf was questionable.

I didn't entirely trust Vera, even in death. If I complied with her request, I could waste a lot of time on something that was a complete dead end.

What should I do? Ignore this and focus on other aspects of the case?

What other aspects did I have to focus on?

Morty Cassity and his desire for a divorce, for one.

Sissy Beauchamp's alleged desire to marry Morty, for another.

I couldn't rule out Hank Beauchamp, either. He might be just as interested in Morty's money as his sister. I recalled the unpleasant little scene at Helen Louise's bakery, when Hank's credit card was declined.

Then there was Azalea, and potentially her sister Lily. Both of them despised Vera because of what had happened to Lily's son, Johnny. But Lily wasn't at River Hill last night, so far as I knew, and Azalea couldn't have pushed Vera down the stairs.

That let Azalea out, but I couldn't forget my feeling that she'd seen more than she'd been willing to admit to me this morning.

Kanesha. I needed to talk to Kanesha, let her know what

her mother had told me and share with her the photograph and phone message from Vera.

I found the card with her private cell number and called it. Voice mail. I left a hasty message, stressing that it was urgent she call me back.

Within two minutes my phone rang—Kanesha returning my call.

"Are you where you can talk?" I asked.

"No. Where are you? I can meet you." She sounded angry—not at me, I hoped.

"The archives. Come as soon as you can."

"Right." She ended the call.

I tried to settle down to work while I waited for her, but to no avail. My brain simply couldn't focus on regular tasks. I kept hearing Vera's voice in my head, and that wasn't pleasant. The sooner I told Kanesha about this, the better. Maybe then Vera's voice would go away.

Either Kanesha broke the speed limit or she wasn't far away when she called me back, because she walked in my office door within ten minutes.

"Shut the door," I said. "I don't want to be overheard."

Diesel sat up and warbled a greeting at her, but she was so focused on me she didn't appear to notice. Diesel resumed his nap, no doubt affronted at the slight.

"You talked to my mother," she said as she slid into a chair.

"Yes, I did." I launched into a full summary of Azalea's story, and Kanesha did not speak until I finished. While I talked I tried to read her expression, but it was no use. She had the consummate poker face.

"Did she tell the sheriff everything she told you?"

I felt like an idiot. "I don't know. I didn't think to ask."

Kanesha's lips tightened. "You've got to ask her that. I

tried to get a look at the statements they took last night, but the sheriff is making sure I can't."

"I will. That aside, what is your impression of her story?"

"It all sounds like the way she'd behave in those situations. Overhearing the argument, then getting stuck in the dark at the bottom of those stairs." She paused. "One thing at least. I'm more convinced than ever that Mama didn't kill Mrs. Cassity."

"I don't see how she could have, unless, like Sean said earlier, she's an Olympic-level gymnast."

Kanesha ignored that. "The sheriff ought to be focusing on Morty Cassity. Surely Mama told Tidwell about the argument she overheard." Her eyes flashed. "But of course he could always say she was making that up to divert suspicion from herself."

"He can't keep this up for long, surely."

"He'd better not," Kanesha said. "And for all I know he's grilled Morty Cassity about all this. I can't get any real info on what's going on. Even Bates can't find out, because no one will talk to him, either. He's actually gotten to where he likes me, and right now that's not a good thing in the department."

I couldn't blame Kanesha for feeling frustrated. The whole thing was petty and stupid, but it was all too human and believable.

"There's one thing I haven't told you about your mother's story." I paused for a breath, and Kanesha's eyes narrowed. "I think Azalea might have seen something that she didn't tell me. I may be totally off base on this, because it was simply an impression I had that she hesitated the tiniest fraction of a second before she answered my question.

About whether she saw anyone or anything at the top of the stairs after Vera fell."

"Why would she do that?" Kanesha didn't sound angry, and that relieved me.

"I don't know. Like I said, I could have imagined it, because Azalea is always such a straight shooter."

"Yeah, right between the eyes." Kanesha shrugged. "You could be right. If Mama saw something and she's not talking about it, she has her reasons. They might not make sense to anybody else, but they will to her. Getting her to tell you, well, I don't know."

"I'll try talking to her again when I go home for lunch," I said. I glanced at the clock, surprised to see that it was nearly eleven. "There's more I need to tell you."

Kanesha leaned back in her chair and nodded. I handed her Vera's letter and explained who the woman in the photograph was.

"What has her mother got to do with anything?" Kanesha stared down at Essie Mae Hobson.

"I don't have a clue. Wait, though, I want to play you a message from Vera that came in yesterday. I don't work here on Tuesdays, so I didn't hear this until a little while ago." I skipped to Vera's message on my voice mail and played it for her.

When it ended I saved it and waited for Kanesha to comment.

"What did she mean about looking in the Ducote papers?"

"Sorry, I should have explained that. Vera came in here last week and demanded access to the Ducote archives, and I had to tell her she couldn't have it. The papers are sealed, and no one can look at them without permission from the family or their legal representatives." I paused. "She even threatened me because I denied her." I shared the threats with Kanesha, but I did not mention what Vera had tried to do to Helen Louise. I didn't see any point in bringing Helen Louise into this.

Kanesha handed back the photograph. "Are you allowed to look through the papers?"

I nodded. "As archivist, I can, basically to conserve and catalog them."

"I think you should."

"Why? How could Vera's mother be connected to any of this?"

"I don't know," Kanesha said. "There's something about that woman's face. I get the feeling that there's an interesting story there. Could be a false lead, but I don't want to take a chance on missing anything important." She stood. "Anything else to tell me?"

"That's it for now."

She headed for the door but paused before she opened it. She glanced back at me. "Thank you." Then she was gone.

I felt a paw on my shoulder and turned to see Diesel yawning and stretching. "Looks like I'm going to be pretty busy, boy. I can count on you to help, can't I?"

Diesel warbled, as if to say, "Of course," and I grinned. The paw retracted, and Diesel stretched some more before settling down again.

I picked up the photograph and studied it. Kanesha was right. There was something about Essie Mae's face. If only I could find a better picture of her I could figure out what was haunting me.

Then another thought struck me. What if this was the only photograph Vera had of her mother?

TWENTY-ONE

▏▏▏

I managed to focus on regular work long enough to put in about forty-five minutes, but by then my stomach started rumbling. Time for lunch. I shut down the computer and roused Diesel from his nap.

On the walk home I thought more about Azalea's story. Surely she must have told the sheriff what she'd told me. Otherwise why was the sheriff treating Vera's death as murder? Without Azalea's evidence of a third person in that stairwell, it could easily be considered an accident.

As Kanesha said earlier, though, the sheriff seemed to be using the case for his own personal and political ends.

My head ached from all the ideas bouncing around in my brain. I needed time to let the bouncing ideas subside. A good lunch would help.

There was no sign of Azalea when Diesel and I walked into the kitchen. I found a note on the table that informed me she had gone to the grocery store. My lunch was in the fridge.

Diesel sat by my chair and watched hopefully as I enjoyed my ham and potato salad. I picked out a few small bits of ham as a treat for Diesel, and that seemed to satisfy him. As long as he got even a small quantity of something from the table, he was happy. I supposed he didn't want to feel left out.

Besides, I'm sure Azalea's and Stewart's cooking tasted far better than his cat food.

For dessert I had a nice big wedge of Azalea's lemon icebox pie. I treated Diesel to a couple of licks of the pie from my finger, and he warbled happily. I agreed. This was my favorite dessert, and I'd never had better than Azalea's recipe.

I wondered idly where everyone was. Sean was at work at the Pendergrast law offices. Until he could take the Mississippi bar exam in February, he was serving as an assistant—for that read gopher and researcher—for Alexandra and her famous father. Laura and Stewart were done for the semester, and I'd thought I might find one or both of them here.

Foolish hope in Laura's case—she seemed to spend most of her spare time with Frank Salisbury. Since I liked Frank and thought he was good to my daughter, I didn't quibble too much over the hours Laura was with him.

I was anxious for Azalea to return from shopping so I could pose my question to her. While I was at it, I might as well ask her if she knew anything about Essie Mae Hobson. Azalea knew as much, if not more, about the families of Athena as Melba did. There was a domestics network that rivaled anything Melba and her cronies operated.

Dirty dishes put away in the sink, I checked my watch.

Nearly twelve thirty. I should be back at the library by one, but frankly my heart wasn't in it. As long as I was preoccupied by the mystery of Vera's death and its implications, I wouldn't be able to focus all that well on regular work.

I was reaching for the phone to call Melba and tell her I wasn't coming back this afternoon when the front doorbell rang. Diesel shot off toward the front door. I'd call Melba later.

"Twice in one day." Miss Dickce flashed a bright smile when I opened the door. "I hope you won't get sick at the sight of us, Charlie. Hello, Diesel."

I invited the Ducote sisters in, and Miss An'gel apologized for bothering me again so soon. She carried a large shopping bag, and she showed me its contents—the award plaque from the previous night—as I ushered them into the living room.

"We feel rather awkward about this," Miss An'gel said as she took her seat on the sofa. Diesel jumped up between her and Miss Dickce and settled in for some serious attention.

"Clementine found it a little while ago, stuck behind a potted plant in the library," Miss Dickce said. "We think Morty Cassity should have it."

Miss An'gel interposed, "But we think it might be better if someone else took it to him. Morty is aware of the ill feelings Vera had toward us, and it might be more tactful if we kept ourselves out of it."

I thought they were being overly sensitive, but far be it from me to tell them that. "Would you like me to deliver it to Mr. Cassity?"

"Thank you, Charlie. Yes, we would." Miss An'gel exchanged a glance with her sister. "We also thought it would give you a good opportunity to have a little chat with Morty. As part of your investigation."

"I see."

And I did see—the Ducote sisters were intent on making sure that I didn't slack off on my *investigation*.

They were a trip, as Sean might say. But a delightful one.

"I'll do my best. I'll see if I can talk to him this afternoon."

"Excellent." Miss An'gel beamed at me. Miss Dickce was busy cooing and petting Diesel. "Come along, Dickce. We mustn't take up more of Charlie's valuable time." She took a moment to stroke Diesel's back before she rose, and the purring doubled in volume.

"So lovable." Miss Dickce sighed before she kissed Diesel's nose. "All right, Sister. I'm coming."

Diesel and I escorted them to the front door and bade them good-bye. Instead of closing the door, however, I stood in the doorway, suddenly curious to see what kind of car they had and who did the driving.

They strolled at a sedate pace down the walk to a late-model Lexus parked at the curb. Miss Dickce got in on the driver's side, and moments later the Lexus took off. Miss Dickce floored it, and it's a wonder Miss An'gel's head wasn't in the backseat somewhere. I sent up a quick prayer for anyone who happened to cross their path, thankful that I was safe inside.

Chuckling, I went back to the living room and retrieved the plaque. Though I'd promised the sisters I would try to talk to Morty Cassity today, I certainly wasn't looking forward to it. He might not be a grieving widower, but he might have been the one who pushed Vera down the stairs. I didn't relish the idea of confronting him on my own, with only Diesel as backup.

I grinned. Diesel could be pretty fierce on occasion,

though. His size sometimes intimidated people, and when he growled he sounded scary to those who didn't know him.

Back to the phone to call Melba. Luckily for me she was out, and I left a message. Otherwise I might have been on the phone with her for ten minutes.

Azalea still hadn't returned from shopping, and it was now a few minutes past one. While I waited for her to return, I looked up the number of Morty Cassity's car dealership here in Athena. Might as well try to reach him, see if I could make an appointment.

I spoke to a man who put me through to Morty's secretary.

"I'm sorry, but Mr. Cassity is not here today. His wife passed away yesterday, and he probably won't be in for a few days. Can someone else help you?"

I thanked her but said that I would try again next week.

If Morty wasn't at work today, then he would probably be at home. I debated whether to call him there but decided that he could easily put me off. Whereas if I showed up on his doorstep with the plaque, he would be more likely to let me in the house.

I waited another fifteen minutes for Azalea, but to no avail. I might as well go talk to Morty Cassity and get it over with.

"Come on, Diesel, we're going for a ride." I scooped up the plaque, and we headed for the car.

Ranelagh, the antebellum house the Cassitys had purchased some years ago, was in the same neighborhood as the Delacorte mansion. The drive there didn't take long, and soon I pulled the car into the oak-lined driveway.

Ranelagh was smaller than River Hill, but just as lovely, with the same Greek Revival architecture. I'd never been inside, but I'd heard the Cassitys spent a fortune restoring it and filling it with period furniture. The drive wound about fifty yards into the property and curved in front of the house. A leg of the driveway veered off behind the house, and as I rounded the curve I caught a flash of bubble-gum pink from a car parked near the back of the house.

The only person in Athena I knew who had a car that color was Sissy Beauchamp.

How interesting.

TWENTY-TWO

|||||||||||||||||||||||||||||||||||||||||||||||||||||||||||||||||||||||||||||||||||||||

I hesitated as I stopped the car near the front door. Perhaps I should come back another time. Things could be awkward if Sissy was really here.

Diesel chirped at me, no doubt wondering why we still sat in the car. That decided me. Forge ahead.

"Come on, boy." I grabbed the bag with the plaque and held the door open for the cat.

I clanged the ornate door knocker three times and waited. Diesel sat at my feet and stared up at me. This was a new place, and he was curious.

No response. I knocked again, three times.

Moments later the door opened, and an unshaven, tired-looking Morty Cassity stared out at me. He wore a rumpled suit jacket with a pair of ragged gym shorts. He looked like I'd gotten him out of bed and he'd thrown on the first thing he could find.

"Good morning, Mr. Cassity. I'm Charlie Harris. We

met last night," I said with an apologetic smile. "I'm sorry to intrude on you at a time like this, but I have something for you."

He glanced down at the shopping bag, then at Diesel. I expected him to reach out for the bag and slam the door in my face, but for whatever reason, he stood aside and motioned me to enter.

"I've heard about your cat," he said once the door shut behind us. He held out a hand to Diesel, and the cat sniffed it, then butted his head against it. "I've always liked cats, but Vera didn't. Wouldn't have one in the house."

Good thing I'd brought Diesel with me; otherwise he might really have slammed the door in my face.

"This is Diesel. He's a Maine Coon."

"He's a big, beautiful boy," Cassity said. His face looked less drawn as he continued petting the cat. He straightened. "No point standing around here in the hall. Come on into my study."

He strode away to a door halfway down the hall. I glanced about as Diesel and I followed him. The hallway at Ranelagh wasn't that different from the one at River Hill. Beautiful Oriental rugs, antique furniture, and paintings adorned the space. The effect was gracious and elegant.

The study was more of a library, I thought, as I gazed at a couple of book-lined walls. A large desk occupied one quadrant of the room, but a leather sofa and two chairs sat before a fireplace. Morty Cassity motioned for me to have a seat on the sofa while he took one of the chairs. I expected Diesel to sit with me, but he took up position beside our host's chair instead. Morty seemed pleased with the attention. Thank goodness for a smart cat, I thought.

"Again, my apologies for intruding, Mr. Cassity," I began.

"Morty, please. Charlie, right?" He didn't pause in his attentions to the cat.

"Right. Well, Morty, I'm really sorry about the loss of your wife. She was, um, she did a lot for the community." I winced inwardly at the awkwardness of that, but I couldn't bring myself to heap fulsome praise on the dead woman.

Morty cast me a sharp glance. "Vera was a giant pain in the ass to everybody, me included. She spent a lot of money trying to get people to like her and think she was a Somebody with a capital *S*." He grimaced. "I'm not saying that the money didn't do good. Of course it did, but she didn't do it out of the generosity of her heart."

I wasn't prepared for such bitterness, even though I knew he hadn't been happy with his marriage. I couldn't think of any way to respond to him that wouldn't sound hypocritical or idiotic. No point in trying to defend Vera, even if I had wanted to.

My host left off his attentions to Diesel and leaned back in his chair, arms across his chest. "Sorry if I'm shocking you, but I'm too tired right now to give a horse's patoot what anybody thinks."

"I understand," I said. "It was all a great shock."

He snorted. "Only that it didn't happen years ago. Vera made enemies the way rabbits reproduce. Somebody'd finally had enough, I guess. It wasn't me that knocked her down the stairs, though."

"Glad to hear it," I said, though it sounded fatuous to me.

"What have you got in the bag?"

I extracted the plaque and stood to hand it to him. "The award that the mayor presented last night. The Ducotes' housekeeper found it this morning."

Morty accepted the plaque and stared at it for a moment.

Then he reached and stuck it on the seat of the other chair near him. "Vera was livid. You have to give it to those two old busybodies, though. They figured out a way to get Vera off their backs publicly."

Someone else figured out how to do it permanently, I added to myself. *Was it you, Morty?*

I didn't quite buy this let-it-all-hang-out routine. Was he really this careless and uncaring, to talk this way to someone he'd met once? Or was it calculated? How could he know I was investigating Vera's death?

He could have seen my name in the local paper in connection with the previous murders. In the past six months or so I'd been approached twice by people who thought I was some kind of private detective. Morty Cassity could suspect me of ulterior motives, then.

"Miss An'gel and Miss Dickce ought to be running a major corporation," I said. "They definitely know how to get people to do what they want."

Morty's expression hardened as he spoke. "They're completely ruthless when it comes to getting what they want. They're also devious enough to double-bluff their way out of murder."

That second statement shocked me. "What do you mean? Are you accusing them of murdering Vera?"

He shrugged. "I'm just saying it's entirely possible. First they stage this elaborate public display, which on the surface of it looks all nice and wonderful. But that's only a cover-up so nobody would ever think they'd put Vera out of the way permanently."

I had to admit—but only to myself—that the Ducote sisters probably *were* devious enough to think of a scheme like that. But did they despise Vera enough to go to such lengths?

I put the question to the widower.

He gazed at me through slitted eyelids. "Vera hated those two old biddies with a passion. I never could figure out why and couldn't have cared less. But the past couple of weeks she seemed more intent than ever on digging up something to humiliate them. She couldn't stand how high-and-mighty they were."

I debated whether to mention Vera's letter and her phone message. Perhaps Morty would know something about that.

I quickly decided against it, however. I didn't want to tip my hand in any way with him. I would probe indirectly instead.

"The Ducotes are a proud family," I said. "With a pretty distinguished history in this town, too. They probably have a few skeletons in the family closet, like everybody else, but I can't see them wanting to kill anybody."

"Maybe they didn't." Morty shrugged again. "Just saying. All I know is, it wasn't me." He checked his watch. "Sorry, but I've got to hit the shower. Places to go, people to see, you know how it is."

I took the hint and rose. "Of course. Thank you for your time. Come on, Diesel, time to go."

Diesel meowed as he left Morty's side.

"He sure is beautiful," Morty said as he followed the cat and me to the front door. "What did you say he is again? I might get one now."

"Maine Coon. They're wonderful companions."

Morty nodded and opened the front door. I was about to step out when I realized a man stood there, hand raised to knock. I moved back. "Excuse me."

"Gerry. Come on in." Morty extended a hand to Sheriff Tidwell.

"Sorry to bother you, Morty, but you know how it is."
Tidwell's gaze swept Diesel and me. "Afternoon, Mr. Harris. Didn't expect to see you here. And with your pet mountain lion. I've heard plenty about it." He guffawed. He held a hand out to Diesel, but the cat moved away, his ears laid back. Tidwell shrugged.

"I was delivering something to Mr. Cassity," I said coolly. "At the request of Miss An'gel Ducote. Diesel and I will get out of your way, Sheriff. Good to see you. Goodbye, Morty."

Tidwell mumbled something, and Morty snickered before the door closed behind us. "Jerk," I muttered. As usual, Diesel was an excellent judge of character. I would certainly be voting for Kanesha when she decided to run against that oaf.

As we drove away, I wondered how official the sheriff's call on Morty Cassity was intended to be. He came alone, and I found that odd, if he planned to question Morty about the previous night.

This kind of speculation wouldn't get me anywhere, I realized. I would mention it to Kanesha, though, to get her take on it. She knew Tidwell far better than I ever would, or wanted to.

Diesel chirped away from his spot in the backseat of the car. I remembered that he seemed quite taken with Morty Cassity, and that was a good sign. Especially contrasted with his reaction to the sheriff. I wasn't going to exculpate Morty in his wife's death simply because my cat liked him, of course, but it was a definite mark in Morty's favor.

I pondered my next move as we neared my house. What would Hercule Poirot or Miss Jane Marple do?

If Azalea was in the house, I would talk to her. After that, I wasn't sure.

No signs of life as Diesel and I entered the kitchen. I checked the laundry room. No Azalea. I looked in the fridge, and it was fuller than it was at lunchtime, so she had at least come back from grocery shopping.

I went to the bottom of the stairs and called out her name.

No response.

Up to the second-floor landing, then, Diesel right alongside me. I called out again.

"What you need, Mr. Charlie?"

I glanced up to see Azalea's head sticking over the railing on the third-floor landing.

"I need to talk to you for a minute. I'll come up there," I said.

"I done finished up here. Be right down." Azalea brought the vacuum cleaner with her, puffing slightly from the weight of it.

I knew better than to try to take it from her, however. I'd made that mistake a couple of times before, right after I moved back to Athena, and my housekeeper had let me know in no uncertain terms that she didn't need any help from me.

Perhaps today I should have risked it. Her face looked gray from tiredness, and she moved more slowly than usual. I remembered her saying how poorly she'd slept last night.

She stowed the vacuum cleaner in the closet where she kept extra cleaning supplies and then finally joined Diesel and me on the landing. "Yes, sir?"

"Just a quick question," I said in a reassuring tone. "I forgot something when we talked this morning."

Her lips tightened, but she nodded.

"I wanted to check. Did you tell the sheriff everything you told me? When he questioned you last night?"

"Yes, sir, I told that fool what he wanted to know."

I noticed that she didn't answer the exact question I'd posed, but I decided not to press her on it. Then I remembered there was something else I wanted to ask her.

"Sorry, Azalea, I just thought of one more thing. Do you know anything about the Hobson family? In particular Essie Mae Hobson? She was Vera Cassity's mother."

"No-account white trash," Azalea sniffed. "Miss Essie Mae was a nice lady, but she sure married into a bad group of folks."

"Do you know anything more about Essie Mae? Like who her people were, anything like that?"

Again, that fleeting second of hesitation before she responded. "No, sir, I sure don't. Now, I got to get supper started." She headed down the stairs.

TWENTY-THREE

||||||||||||||||||||||||||||||||||||||||||||||||||||||||||||||||||||||||||||||||||

Slightly stunned, I stood at the top of the stairs and watched Azalea go down. Why did I get the feeling that she was holding something back? Was my imagination working overtime?

"Come on, Diesel." I went into my bedroom and closed the door after the cat walked in. He hopped up on the bed and settled down for a snooze. Right about now a nap would be nice, but I didn't have the time.

I sat on the edge of the bed and pulled out my cell phone. Maybe Kanesha could dig up some information on Essie Mae Hobson. Once again I got voice mail. I let her know her mother's response to the question of whether she had told the sheriff what she'd told me about Vera's last moments. Then I related the incident just now and ended the call.

There was no point in my going back to the archives for the rest of the afternoon, but I felt at a loss over what to do next. I'd start looking in the Ducote papers for some mention of Essie Mae tomorrow.

I looked down at Diesel, comfortably stretched out and already asleep. All of a sudden I felt really tired. *What the heck,* I thought. I kicked off my shoes and stretched out right alongside the cat.

The ringing of my cell phone roused me sometime later. I checked my watch as I sat up and reached for the phone. I'd napped for nearly ninety minutes—it was almost four thirty. My brain felt a little foggy as I answered the call.

"Hello, honey," Helen Louise said. "How about dinner tonight at my house? Diesel, too, of course. I feel like spending some time with my two favorite guys. I decided I can catch up on my sleep later."

"Sounds good to me, although Diesel might have to check his social calendar."

Helen Louise laughed. "See if he can manage to squeeze me in. About six thirty?"

"We'll be there, as long as you're sure you're not going to be too tired."

After reassuring me she'd be fine, Helen Louise rang off. I realized I needed to let Azalea know there would be one less for supper tonight.

When Diesel and I reached the kitchen, I discovered Azalea had left for the day. Supper was done, according to the tersely worded note I found. Everything was either in the oven or in the fridge.

Diesel suddenly shot off into the hall. He probably heard someone at the front door. I followed at a more leisurely pace, and Laura walked through the door moments later. "Hello, you sweet boy," she said as she patted his head. "Hi, Dad. Isn't it adorable how he always comes to meet me?" She came forward to kiss my cheek.

"You look familiar, young lady. Where have I seen you before?" I gazed at her sternly.

Laura giggled. "I haven't been gone that much lately, have I? Sorry, Dad, all this business of grading exams and turning in the final grades for the semester has kept me hopping. But it's all finally over." She walked toward the kitchen, Diesel right by her side.

"Not to mention all the time making sure poor Frank isn't too lonely." I sighed. "It's okay, I'm merely a father, and I'm used to my only daughter abandoning me. I'm much too dull, I know, whereas Frank . . ."

Laura punched me playfully on the shoulder. "Oh, you poor thing. So neglected. Well, you'll be happy to know that I am yours for the whole evening."

"Not this evening," I said. "Diesel and I will be dining with Helen Louise."

"You cad. Deserting me for the Other Woman." Laura giggled again. "Two nights in a row with Helen Louise. What will the neighbors think?"

"The neighbors can mind their own business," I said dryly, well aware of the irony of that statement.

Laura shot me a look that said she was aware of it, too. She fetched a can of diet soda from the fridge. "Want anything while I'm in here?"

"I'll take one of those," I said. Diesel chirped. "No," I told him. "I draw the line at letting you drink anything with caffeine. You go have some water."

After giving me an affronted look, he turned away, tail in the air, and headed for his water bowl in the utility room.

Laura and I laughed as we sat down at the table.

"I still can't fully believe what happened at River Hill last night. How awful. Vera being killed so violently and poor Azalea, being locked in with the body like that. I hope she doesn't have nightmares." Laura shivered and a shadow crossed her face. I knew she was again reliving her own discovery of a dead body only a couple of months before. I also knew that while Laura and Sean had both inherited my love of mysteries, this last one hit far too close to home because Azalea was involved.

I brought her up to speed on all that had happened earlier in the day, and when I finished, she posed a question.

"Do you really think Azalea is holding out on you?"

"I think so, but it's simply an impression."

"Want me to try talking to her? I might be able to wheedle it out of her, whatever she's not telling." Laura looked eager. Her choice of Nancy Drew as a character for the gala was truly heartfelt, and as an actor, she could probably see herself in the role. Even though Azalea definitely had a soft spot for my beautiful daughter, I thought it best that Laura left this to me.

"I'd rather you didn't," I said. "I'm sure she's feeling upset enough at the thought of me being in her business, you might say, without having another member of my family getting into it too."

"You're probably right." Laura sighed, obviously disappointed. "But if you need me for anything, I'm there for you."

I thanked her. We talked about more mundane matters for a while, including plans for the rapidly approaching holidays. Laura said she still had some Christmas shopping to do, and I told her smugly that mine was all done.

Diesel head-butted my leg, and automatically I reached down to rub his head. "I didn't forget you, boy, never fear. You'll have a present or two to play with." He warbled. An empty box was as good as anything to him. Like most cats he liked to stuff himself into them, and the smaller they were, the better he appeared to like them. He also loved ribbon, but we had to watch him to make sure he didn't try to eat any.

I broached the subject of Laura's postholiday plans with some caution. She had been remarkably uninformative on the subject whenever I mentioned it recently, and I secretly hoped it meant she might stay in Athena for another semester at the very least. I knew Frank wouldn't be any happier to see her leave for California than I would.

"No firm plans yet," Laura said with a shrug. She avoided my eyes as she continued. "I talked to my agent yesterday, and she's working on some auditions in January. Two movies and one TV sitcom thing. Just minor parts, but you never know when they can lead to something bigger."

"I see." I felt deflated. I knew it was selfish of me to want my daughter to give up her career in Hollywood to live here in Athena, but since I'd had her and her brother with me for months now, I was reluctant to see either one of them move too far from home. "Well, I'm sure you'll knock their socks off in those auditions and get the parts. They'd be idiots not to hire you."

"Thanks, Dad. My biggest fan." She beamed at me.

"Always." I finished my drink and got up to dispose of the can. "I'd better start getting ready for dinner. See you later, sweetheart."

Diesel remained with Laura while I went upstairs to shower and change clothes. I checked my face in the mirror and decided that it wouldn't hurt to shave again. My five o'clock shadow looked more like seven thirty.

The cat wandered into my bedroom as I finished tying my shoes. "Are you ready to go, boy? We're going to have dinner with Helen Louise."

His ears perked up at the mention of Helen Louise, and

he meowed. It was very sweet, the way those two adored each other. And a good thing as well, since I could never care for anyone who didn't love my cat as much as I did.

Helen Louise lived only a few blocks away, so Diesel and I walked over. It was a fine, clear night, though chilly, but not too cold to be uncomfortable for a cat walking on the pavement. I rang the doorbell right on the dot of six thirty. Helen Louise knew I always turned up on time, so she would be ready for us.

The door swung open, and she greeted me with a kiss and Diesel with head rubs. We followed her to the kitchen, led as much by the enticing aromas as by our hostess.

Helen Louise had inherited the house from her parents, and Bradys had lived in it since the early twentieth century. Though not as large as Aunt Dottie's place, it nevertheless had the same sense of warmth and welcome, the aura created by a loving family.

The one room Helen Louise had changed was the kitchen, remodeling it to serve her needs as a baker and chef with more up-to-date ovens and refrigerator. I had no idea what the appliances cost, but her fridge alone was twice the size of mine. She was proud of her kitchen, and with her culinary skills, she deserved a first-class one.

"Do I smell coq au vin?" I sniffed appreciatively.

"*Mais oui, mon petit chou.* I know how much you love it. We also have *haricots verts Lyonnaise* and *gratin Dauphinoise.*" Helen Louise grinned wickedly as she continued, "And there just might be a special *gâteau au chocolat* for dessert."

I still wasn't quite used to being referred to as a *little cabbage*, but I knew it was a classic French term of endearment.

I pulled her into my arms, and we spent several satisfying minutes before I released her. "What happened to that early night you planned on? You must be exhausted, and here you are cooking dinner for us."

"I've caught my second wind," she said with an impish smile. "You just recharged my batteries."

I laughed and pulled her close again.

Diesel warbled indignantly at being ignored so long, and we were both grinning as we separated and reached at the same time to stroke his head.

"This is what I needed," Helen Louise said softly.

"Me, too."

She tapped me playfully on the chest as I attempted to kiss her again. "Time for more of that later. I don't know about you, but I'm starving. Sit yourself down and prepare to feast." She pointed to my chair.

The old oaken table was covered by a beautiful white linen cloth that made the cobalt Fiestaware stand out nicely. Helen Louise's set was vintage, lovingly cared for by her grandmother Brady and then her own mother.

"Why don't you pour the wine?" Helen Louise said as she took my plate to fill it.

She'd chosen a Nuits-St.-Georges Chardonnay, a favorite of both of ours. Helen Louise would never settle for cheap wine, and, having benefited from her expertise on numerous occasions now, I had to agree.

Over the delicious dinner we chatted about ordinary things, neither of us wishing to let the events of the previous night intrude. We ate dessert in her living room in front of the fireplace, all nice and cozy. The dark chocolate cake, paired with a delicious tawny port, had me groaning with a combination of pleasure and guilt.

Diesel desperately wanted to taste the chocolate, but Helen Louise fended him off with a couple of bites of chicken instead. Chocolate was dangerous for cats and dogs, no matter how much they might beg for a taste.

When we set our plates aside, the cat took it as his signal to jump onto the sofa with us. He spread himself across our laps, with Helen Louise getting his head. His tail thumped against my chest, and I only narrowly avoided receiving a mouthful of hair. He settled down after a moment, and then we were able to talk about the subject we had avoided thus far.

"Was it only last night?" Helen Louise shook her head. "Hard to believe."

"I know. I feel like I've aged a couple of months already."

"Tell me what you've been up to. I have a feeling you haven't been able to keep out of this." Helen Louise grinned.

"True," I said, "but not exactly by choice." I shared with her the visits from the Ducote sisters and Kanesha Berry, then went on to relate the rest of my day.

"You have been busy," she said when I finished. She filled my glass with more of the delicious tawny port, and I had a few sips. "Any conclusions?"

"Not really, though I still figure Morty Cassity had the best motive for pushing Vera down the stairs."

"He's the most likely one," Helen Louise agreed. "I can't believe he and Sissy are brazen enough to be carrying on in Vera's house less than twenty-four hours after the woman died. That's cold."

"Isn't it?" I recalled Morty's attitude when I talked to him that afternoon. "He certainly didn't hold back his feelings. No grief there, for sure. How long have he and Sissy been having an affair?"

"A couple of years, maybe three," Helen Louise said. "It's hard to know. First I heard of it was two years ago, I think." She frowned. "Before that there was always talk that Morty was seeing other women, but no one could ever come up with a name that I recall."

"He's at least twenty or twenty-five years older than she is, right? What do you think she sees in him?"

Helen Louise shrugged. "He's actually rather attractive, but for Sissy I imagine the main attraction is money. She's like Morty in that respect, and maybe the two of them deserve each other."

"Is she really that mercenary?" I didn't know Sissy well at all, but she hadn't come across that way to me.

"Not for her sake, no, but she'd do anything to help Hank."

"I know you mentioned that he's been having financial issues and could lose his law firm." I also remembered something about Hank having a gambling problem, too.

She looked troubled as she nodded in agreement. "From what I've heard recently, Hank's on the verge of bankruptcy. There are even rumors that he's going to sell Beauchamp House. That must mean they're both pretty desperate."

TWENTY-FOUR

I pondered what Helen Louise told me. Holding on to the ancestral home was a powerful incentive indeed, especially for a family as proud as the Beauchamps.

"So add both Sissy and Hank to the list of potential murderers," I said.

"I hate to think of either Sissy or Hank as a killer," Helen Louise said. "But money—or the lack of it—makes people do terrible things."

"I wouldn't want to marry a murderer," I said. "Or be the sibling of one."

Helen Louise arched an eyebrow at me. "They may be the best suspects, but they're not the only ones."

"The Ducote sisters, you mean." I sighed. "I suppose you're right, but I can't take them seriously as cold-blooded killers. Besides, we don't know that they have a compelling motive. Intense dislike of Vera isn't enough."

"They *are* ruthless in their own way; cold-blooded is an

apt description really." Helen Louise stroked Diesel's head. "Otherwise they wouldn't have dreamed up that award business last night. That was a killing in its own way. They killed Vera's career as a prominent public figure in one neat gesture."

"True. They achieved their goal, though, so why would they go even further and eliminate her completely?" I shook my head. "I simply don't see it. There's no motive strong enough."

"That you know of," Helen Louise pointed out. "What about this business of that old photograph? What if Essie Mae Hobson is the key to it all?"

I had the sudden urge to yawn. The warmth of the fire, the delicious meal, and the two glasses of port all hit me at once, and I felt sleepy. I shook my head in an attempt to make myself more alert.

"I'm going to dig into the Ducote papers tomorrow," I said. Then the yawn escaped me after all. "Sorry, it's not the company. Too much good food, I guess." I yawned again.

Helen Louise started to smile but then had to yawn herself. "I know what you mean. I think I'm starting to fade, too." She glanced down. "Even Diesel is asleep, or at least looks like he is."

"Time to wake him up and get him home," I said, rousing Diesel gently. "Come on, boy, time to go."

Diesel yawned as he gazed at me reproachfully for disturbing him. He stretched in a graceful, languorous movement before he climbed off our laps.

"You could stay here tonight." Helen Louise smiled shyly.

I was truly tempted. Helen Louise had never looked more lovely, but now was not the time to move our relationship into a more intimate phase. I think she realized that, too, as I gently declined.

She escorted us to the door, and we shared a satisfying kiss before Diesel and I headed home. "Talk to you tomorrow. Sleep well."

"Good night. You sleep well, too."

I felt like whistling as we walked, but I've never been able to carry much of a tune. Instead I smiled a lot.

As Diesel and I neared our house an unfamiliar car pulled up to the sidewalk ahead of us. I slowed my pace and kept a wary eye on it as the driver's door opened and a dark figure stepped out.

The moment she turned to face me I recognized Kanesha Berry, and I relaxed.

"Good evening, Mr. Harris. You two out for a stroll? Seems a little chilly for it." She stepped onto the sidewalk a few feet away as I paused.

"Coming home from dinner with a friend."

I heard the faintest trace of humor in her voice as she replied, "And I reckon the cat was invited, too."

"Naturally," I said. I gestured toward the house. "Won't you come in? I'm assuming that you're here to talk to me."

"Thanks. I'm sorry I couldn't call you back sooner, but we had a couple of emergencies to deal with." She preceded me up the walk to the front door. "I was on my way home and thought I'd stop by on the off chance you had a moment to talk."

"You're always welcome," I said as I inserted my key in the lock. Diesel chirped at her, but she was still wary of him. She had her mother's mistrust of cats, but I think Diesel was gradually winning her over.

"Come on in the kitchen. Can I offer you something to drink?"

"No, thanks, I'm fine," she said. "I won't keep you long, just wanted to follow up on the message you left me. Plus I have a bit of news for you." She took the chair I pulled out for her, and I sat down across from her. Diesel padded off into the utility room.

"You go first," I said.

She shrugged. "Okay. I managed to get hold of one important piece of information about Vera Cassity's death from a source I have. It was definitely murder because she didn't fall. She had two big bruises on her back. Looks like the killer hit her pretty hard to knock her down the stairs. The rest of the bruising could be accounted for by the fall, but not the ones on her back, because of the way she fell forward."

I felt sick at my stomach. I had seen the body on the stairs—only dimly because of the poor light—but it had a certain air of unreality about it.

Until now.

The mental image of the killer striking Vera that hard brought home the viciousness of the attack and the cold, heartless intent behind it.

Kanesha regarded me almost sympathetically. "Nasty, isn't it?"

I nodded. "Nasty and sad. You know, I don't think there's a single person who will mourn her passing."

"Probably not. She didn't work too hard on getting people to like her." She paused. "One more thing, and this is good news. My same source tells me the sheriff is backing down on treating my mother as the only suspect."

"That *is* good news. Maybe now he'll get somewhere." I recalled Tidwell's visit to Morty Cassity this afternoon, and I told Kanesha about it. "Shouldn't the sheriff have had another officer with him if he was going to question Morty?"

In my peripheral vision I noticed Diesel return from the utility room. Instead of coming over to sit by me, however, he left the kitchen and, I presumed, headed upstairs. He was ready for bed.

"He should have, to make it formal, but Tidwell likes to play the 'good ole boy' routine. Thinks it'll get him what he wants faster, at least with some people. Like Morty Cassity, I reckon. They go hunting and fishing together a few times a year, so they're buddies." Kanesha didn't sound too pleased about that.

"Tidwell wouldn't look the other way if he found evidence that Morty was the killer, would he?" The whole good-ole-boy thing irritated the heck out of me, and it made me angry to think the sheriff was guilty of cronyism.

"He can't afford to. He knows if he pushes things too far, the MBI will step in. I'll see to that. I have a good contact there." Kanesha smiled, and if Tidwell knew what was good for him, he'd better watch his back.

"What do you think of Morty's attitude?"

"His whole image as a businessman is based on that kind of no-bull, down-to-earth talk. Haven't you ever seen one of his commercials?"

"Probably." I shrugged. "Frankly I don't pay much attention to ads like that. I usually turn the sound off."

"There isn't any point to him acting grief stricken over Vera's death. Everybody in town knows it wasn't a happy marriage. Now, about my mother. Tell me again about the second talk you had with her."

I did as she asked, and she listened, her eyes intent on my face.

"You think she knows something about Vera's mother that she's not telling? In addition to something she's not telling about what she saw on the stairs last night?"

"Yes. It isn't anything concrete, like I may have said to you before. I simply can't shake the feeling that she's holding back. In both instances."

Kanesha shook her head. "And if she doesn't want to tell you, she won't. My mother could out-stubborn the stubbornest mule you ever met."

"Laura wanted to try talking to her, but I discouraged her. One more person putting pressure on her to talk wouldn't do any good, I think. It might make things worse."

"I know Mama is pretty fond of your daughter, but the more you try to get Mama to do something, the less she's inclined to do it. It's best that Laura stays out of it." Kanesha rose. "It's bad enough that I had to involve you. I need to get home, so I won't keep you any longer. Let me know anything you find out."

"I will," I said as I showed her to the front door. "I need to check the county and city records for anything regarding Essie Mae Hobson. But maybe it would be better if you did it."

She paused on the doorstep. "No, it's better if you do it. I need to keep my fingerprints off this investigation as much as possible, at least for now. The woman in the records office will help you. They get people looking in the records all the time, and she's not going to think anything about your poking your nose in. Good night." With that she turned and headed down the walk.

I waited until she reached her car before I closed the door and locked it.

The house was quiet as I climbed the stairs. It was only a quarter past nine, but I was more than ready for bed. There was no cat on the bed when I entered my room. Diesel was most likely with Laura. I left the door cracked so he could get in, whenever he deigned to join me for the night.

I dropped off to sleep quickly, too tired even to think much about the events of the past twenty-four hours. I awoke the next morning when the alarm went off. Diesel purred in my ear to make sure I didn't try to roll over and go back to sleep.

Fat chance of that happening, not with a thirty-six-pound alarm clock always ready to pounce into action.

On the way downstairs about twenty minutes later I was surprised not to smell the usual odors of fresh biscuits and bacon or sausage wafting through the house. Surely Azalea was here. She had never missed a day since the day I moved in.

I found a note on the kitchen table. It informed me—in Azalea's hand—that Azalea was unwell and couldn't work today. Not a surprise, really. I thought she should have stayed home the day before, too, but she was too stubborn to give in. Today, though, it had all caught up with her. I hoped she took it easy and actually did rest at home, but I wouldn't count on it.

Though I had the time, I didn't feel like cooking a full breakfast. Instead I contented myself with cereal, toast, and some apple juice. It wouldn't hurt me to miss one cholesterol-laden breakfast, that was for sure. I enjoyed the quiet as I read the paper, sipped my coffee, and finished my simple meal.

Diesel didn't pester me for anything, once he realized there were no pancakes, bacon, or sausage to be had. He turned up his nose at mere wheat toast and bites of cereal.

As I was rinsing my dishes in the sink, Stewart bounced into the kitchen with a cheery "Good morning, Charlie. How's my favorite landlord today?" He poured himself coffee, then leaned against the counter near me. His eyes sparkled with morning energy, and he grinned broadly between sips of coffee.

He could be annoyingly like Tigger on occasion, a little too perky and awake in the mornings, but I tried not to hold that against him. "Doing fine, I guess. How about you?" I dried my hands on a towel before I faced him.

"Excellent," he replied. He set his coffee cup down on the counter in order to rub Diesel's head with both hands. The cat rewarded him with happy chirps, and Stewart talked nonsense to him for a moment. Then he regarded me again as Diesel rubbed against his jean-clad legs. "No Azalea today? If I'd known that, I could have made breakfast for us."

"No, she won't be here," I said. "I couldn't believe she was here yesterday, after all the stress of the night before. But I guess it finally caught up with her, and she decided she'd better take it easy today."

Stewart grimaced as he topped up his coffee. "I still can't believe that someone finally did Vera in. It's amazing to me that she lasted this long, frankly, but why now? What did she do to push someone over the edge?"

I frowned at his poor choice of words, and he shrugged. "You know what I mean."

"Unfortunately, I do." I sighed. "You're right, though. Whoever pushed Vera down those stairs must have reached the point of desperation. But who was it?"

"I can think of several candidates, but I can't imagine which of them would actually hit the breaking point and kill." Stewart set his coffee down and moved to the fridge where he extracted eggs, milk, and cheese. "How about a little more breakfast?"

"Thanks, but I've had enough," I said. "Time to get ready for work. What are you up to today?"

"Not much of anything," he replied with evident satisfaction. "The semester is over, and Stewart is going to be a bum."

Diesel and I left him to his breakfast preparations and headed up the stairs.

By the time I was ready to leave for the library, Stewart had disappeared, and no one else had come downstairs. Laura and Justin were probably sleeping in, now that the semester was officially finished. I wondered idly where Sean was, because I'd expected him to be down for breakfast. I had a sneaking suspicion his bed hadn't been slept in. He was spending more and more time with Alexandra at her house, including a few nights.

The weather had turned colder overnight, but was still bearable. Diesel seemed unaffected by it, though I feared his feet might get too cold. Today was my last in the office, because the library would be closed the next two weeks for the holidays and the semester break. I was looking forward to the time off.

Diesel settled down happily in his window aerie, and I put away my things before firing up the computer. I'd barely sat down and begun to check e-mail, however, when I heard a knock on my open door.

I turned to see Miss An'gel and Miss Dickce standing there. I rose. "Good morning, ladies. What a pleasant surprise." *What do they want now?* I wondered. Were they going to drop by every day until the case was solved? Not that I minded seeing them, of course, but they did require a high level of mental energy.

"Morning, Charlie." Miss An'gel beamed at me as she approached the desk and took the same seat she'd sat in the previous morning. Miss Dickce smiled and sat down beside her.

Before they even had time to make themselves comfortable, Diesel stood between them, looking back and forth to see which of them would pay attention to him first.

I allowed them a few moments to adore the cat before I spoke. "What can I do for you? I should have let you know yesterday afternoon, but I'm afraid I forgot. I did return the plaque to Morty Cassity as you requested."

"No matter," Miss An'gel said, dismissing my apology with a wave of one elegant, beringed hand. "We knew we could rely on you."

"How did you find the grieving widower?" Miss Dickce asked. "Not grieving too deeply, I'm sure." She kept one hand on Diesel's head as we talked, and Diesel purred, adding his rumbling voice to the conversation.

"No, he wasn't, I have to say." I gave them a brief account of my interview with Cassity. I did not mention, though, that I'd seen Sissy Beauchamp's car parked behind the house.

The sisters shared a look, one I couldn't interpret, then Miss An'gel turned back to me. "We have another little favor to ask you, Charlie. We know you're busy, but if you wouldn't mind handling one other little matter for us, we'd appreciate it." Miss Dickce nodded as her sister spoke.

"I'd be happy to do whatever I can, Miss An'gel." I smiled, though I could feel the start of a dull ache across my forehead.

"It's the money for the gala, you see." Miss Dickce leaned forward in her chair. "Usually everyone gives us their contributions before the end of the evening."

Miss An'gel took it from there. "With the events of that night, naturally, not everyone fulfilled their promises. Dickce and I will be calling upon most of them, except in one case. We would like you to handle that one."

"Besides," Miss Dickce broke in, "it will give you a chance to snoop around a little."

"Dickce." Miss An'gel glared at her sister. "You make it sound sordid."

"Don't be so persnickety, Sister," Miss Dickce said. "We asked Charlie to be a snoop, so call it what it is."

That ache in my forehead grew stronger. "Whom would you like me to call on, ladies?"

"Sissy and Hank Beauchamp," Miss An'gel replied.

"And good luck getting the money out of them," Miss Dickce said.

That remark started another squabble about manners, and I let them carp at each other while I considered what they wanted me to do.

Lovely, I thought. *Now I can add* bill collector *to my resume.*

TWENTY-FIVE

|||||||||||||||||||||||||||||||||||||||||||||||||||||||||||||||||||||||||||||||||

If the sisters sensed my hesitation, they didn't let on when they stopped dickering after a few minutes.

"Can you go this morning, Charlie?" Miss An'gel smiled at me while Miss Dickce sulked.

"I don't see why not." Might as well get it over with, then perhaps I could get back here and start looking in their family papers for information about Essie Mae Hobson. I felt a surge of guilt over that, but I quickly suppressed it. If I were going to investigate thoroughly, I couldn't afford to overlook anything, no matter how tenuous it might seem.

"Thank you. We promise to leave you alone the rest of the day." Miss An'gel glanced at her sister. "Though my sister phrased it poorly, we are aware that the Beauchamps are having certain financial difficulties. If they aren't able to come up with their contribution, we can overlook it."

"We are also aware"—Miss Dickce matched her sister's prim tone—"of the talk about Morty Cassity and Sissy, and we certainly remember the scene she and Vera caused at the gala. We hate to think of Sissy as a common gold digger, but we understand the depth of her loyalty to her brother and to her family name."

I could understand it, too, though I couldn't condone going to extreme lengths to preserve the family honor.

"What is so surprising," Miss Dickce continued, "is that Sissy has never behaved like this before. She has always been a sensible girl, the kind of Southern lady she was raised to be. Why would she turn her back on everything her parents taught her?"

"Where certain kinds of men are involved, anything is possible. Sissy is only human, after all, and Morty is an attractive, virile man." Miss An'gel rose. "Come along, Dickce. We have more calls to make, and Charlie is a busy man. Good-bye, Diesel. Make sure Charlie brings you to visit us soon."

Diesel followed them to the door, warbling and meowing the whole way, to the sisters' evident delight. I called my good-byes after them.

The cat padded back while I stared blankly at the top of my desk. Might as well get it over with, I figured. "Come on, boy, we're going home to get the car and then take a little ride." I decided to call Melba rather than stop by her office to let her know I had to go out for a while. That way I could forestall questions more easily.

Twenty minutes later Diesel and I were in the car headed for Beauchamp House.

Built over a decade before either River Hill or Ranelagh, at around the time Mississippi became a state in 1817, the Beauchamp family home occupied a large lot on Main Street a few blocks from the town square. I had always admired the simple, graceful Federal-style architecture, but I noticed the house looked decidedly shabby as I pulled the car to a stop in front of it. I wondered how long it had been since the house was painted. The grounds seemed to be suffering from neglect as well, though the autumn weather obviously had taken a toll. Hedges were uneven, and some of the elderly oak trees had dead branches. In fact there was one whole tree that needed to be cut down. Sissy's pink convertible provided the only color in the whole drab landscape.

Diesel trotted beside me up the walk, gazing curiously around. There was no verandah, but a small portico protected the front door. I knocked, and Sissy Beauchamp opened it moments later.

Her eyes widened in surprise as she recognized me, then saw Diesel. She smiled. "I think this is the first time Beauchamp House has ever had a cat come calling. Morning, Charlie, y'all come on in."

Sissy led us through a bare hallway into a parlor that also seemed short of the usual furniture. Had they been selling antiques? I'd not been inside the house before, but according to local legend the Beauchamps had a fine collection of early American and Federal-style furniture.

Dressed casually in Capri pants, flat shoes, and a snug-fitting T-shirt, Sissy appeared comfortable though I found the room chilly. She patted Diesel's head for a moment but didn't seem all that interested in him.

"Have a seat." My hostess plucked a man's rumpled suit jacket from the back of a chair and indicated I should sit there. She draped the jacket over the arm of a threadbare sofa and sat on a particularly bald spot. "What can I do for you, Charlie?"

"I'm sorry to barge in on you unannounced and uninvited," I said as Diesel settled on the floor beside my chair. "It's about the gala."

Sissy interrupted me. "Wasn't it wonderful? All those gorgeous costumes and the food was awesome! It was a great party." Her face clouded. "But the way it ended was real awful. Poor Morty. Losing his wife like that."

"Yes, that was a shock," I said.

"And how humiliating for Vera," Sissy said with a frown. "I mean, if she had any idea how she died, she'd be mortified. Falling down the back stairs at River Hill. The *servants'* stairs, that is. Imagine that."

I hadn't thought of Vera's death in that light, but I realized Sissy was right. Had the killer planned it that way? One final humiliation in death? That extra bit of viciousness was disturbing to contemplate.

"Sissy, have you seen my jacket?" Hank Beauchamp wandered into the room but pulled up short when he saw that his sister had company. "Oh, morning, Charlie. I see you brought your cat with you." He didn't sound pleased about it.

"Yes, he goes almost everywhere with me." I kept my tone light and cheerful. "He's well behaved, so you don't have to worry about him scratching the furniture or causing any damage."

Hank nodded, then his eyes lighted on his jacket. "There it is." He picked it up, shook it in a vain attempt to get rid of some of the wrinkles, then slipped it on.

"That looks pretty messy," Sissy said. "Are you sure you want to go to court dressed like that?"

"I don't have any choice. Everything else is at the cleaner's, *remember*?" There was an unpleasant edge to Hank's voice and an odd emphasis on that last word.

Sissy stared at him blankly for a moment. "Sorry, forgot about that." She turned to me with a bright smile. "What were we talking about? Oh, the gala."

I nodded. "Yes, and we were saying how awful it was for Vera to die like that." I watched Hank as I spoke, interested to see his reaction.

He winced. "The woman is dead. Why can't everyone let it go? She was probably drunk and fell down the stairs. She was knocking back the booze the last time I saw her."

I couldn't believe either of them was naive enough to believe it was an accident. They had to be putting on an act for my benefit. I decided to drop a little bomb and see what happened.

"What if it wasn't an accident?" I asked. They'd probably think I was a gossipy idiot, but that didn't matter. "Know what I heard? I heard her husband pushed her down the stairs because she wouldn't give him a divorce."

"Who told you that?" Hank's face reddened as he snapped out the words.

I shrugged. "Oh, it's just something that's going around."

"That's awful," Sissy said, her voice cool. "Vera was a giant pain in the rear, but surely nobody would murder her."

"Don't be an idiot." Hank glared at me. "The whole thing is ridiculous. I told you, Vera was drunk as a skunk. She fell. Morty would never kill her, no matter how much she provoked him."

Sissy shrugged and addressed me. "No point in arguing with him." She opened her mouth to continue, but Hank interrupted her.

"Has the garage called about my car?"

"No, not this morning," Sissy said.

Hank swore. "They've had it for almost two weeks now. It can't be that hard to fix." He sighed. "Then I'll have to borrow yours again. Before court this morning I have to run over to Oxford and get a deposition."

"You know where the keys are." Sissy turned to me.

"What was it you came about, Charlie? I don't think you ever said."

"No, I hadn't gotten around to it yet." I offered them both a self-deprecating smile. "I'm here on behalf of the Friends of the Library. Miss An'gel asked me to help collect the pledges people made at the gala. With everything that happened, quite naturally some people forgot to make good on them that night."

"I see." Sissy shared an uncertain glance with her brother. "I thought you already took care of that, Hank."

Hank responded in a testy voice, "I thought *you* took care of it. I have to get going or I won't get to Oxford and back in time for court. You deal with it." He whirled around and stomped out of the room.

Sissy glared at his retreating back. "You'll have to excuse him. He's in the middle of a really difficult case right now, and he's always tense when he has to go to court. He'd be a lot happier doing something else."

I didn't know how to respond to that, but Sissy didn't appear to need an answer. She excused herself, saying she'd be back with a check in a minute.

Diesel had moved under my chair during the tense moments between the Beauchamp siblings, and I almost wished I could join him. It hadn't been pleasant. As I surveyed the room, I decided the rumors about financial problems were actual fact. The threadbare, skimpy furnishings and the chilly indoor temperature spoke loudly. Apparently they couldn't even afford firewood.

Sissy came back, check in hand. I rose to accept it and thanked her. "We'll be on our way now. I'm sure you have lots to do." I tucked the check into my pocket without examining it.

She nodded and escorted us to the front door. "See you at the next board meeting."

"'Bye until then." I stepped off the portico and headed for the car, Diesel loping alongside.

As we drove back to the library, I replayed the whole thing in my mind. I had the odd feeling there was something I'd missed, but whatever it was, I couldn't get it to surface. The best thing would be for me to get back to the archives and get on with my research in the Ducote papers. If it were truly important, whatever I had missed would come to me later.

Right now I was anxious to get back to the archives. I honestly didn't expect to find anything that would shed light on Vera's death, but the sooner I could rule this possibility out, the better.

TWENTY-SIX

||||||||||||||||||||||||||||||||||||||||||||||||||||||||||||||||||||||||||

I stuck my head in Melba's office to let her know we were back. She was on the phone so I was able to escape temporarily. I figured she would be up later to grill me.

Diesel went straight to his water bowl when we reached the office. He meowed loudly to let me know it was empty. I took care of that, checked my e-mail and voice mail, and realized happily there was nothing that couldn't wait. I left the cat napping in the window while I went to the room next door where most of the archival collections were stored.

Before I looked for the boxes of Ducote papers, I checked the climate control system. To maintain the materials properly required a constant temperature of no higher than seventy degrees Fahrenheit and a humidity level between thirty and fifty percent. Otherwise irreparable damage could occur. Both temperature and humidity were fine. I left the door closed but not on the latch, in case Diesel should come looking for me. He was strong enough to push the door open and enter.

I had checked the records earlier to find out how many boxes of materials made up the Ducote archives. I was relieved to discover that there were only eighteen. All but two of the boxes had been gifted to the archives before my tenure started nearly four years ago. I had looked through the two newer boxes when I accessioned them and listed their contents, and they contained papers from the last twenty years. I decided to leave them till last.

My search might be tedious, but each box contained a list of contents and approximate dates of materials, and I was hoping that a scan of the lists could save me time. I reasoned that Essie Mae Hobson could have been a maid or some other kind of employee at River Hill, and account books should reveal that. I had also narrowed the time frame to between seventy-five and eighty-five years ago, based on Vera's age. I figured it reasonable that any association that Essie Mae Hobson had with the Ducotes probably occurred within the decade before Vera was born.

Boxes one through eight I ruled out quickly because of the age of the contents. They covered the early years of the Ducotes in Mississippi up through the end of the Civil War. I itched to read some of the letters and other materials, but they would have to wait.

The next four boxes contained a hodgepodge of dates and types of items. There were letters from the 1880s and the 1920s, as well as postcards, photos, and several account books. I would have to check each of them carefully, and I figured that would take me a couple of hours. Might as well bring them into my office next door where I would be more comfortable and could be with Diesel as well.

The cat eyed me sleepily as I settled into my chair.

When he saw me open the first box, he perked up. He always wanted to investigate any kind of container, and that reminded me I should weight down the tops of the other three boxes while I searched this one. That way I could keep my nosy feline in check.

Diesel hopped onto my desk, and I had to grab a stack of papers to keep them from sliding off. He poked his head in the open box and was about to climb in—despite the lack of space—when I told him not to do it. He looked at me with that "who, me?" expression that cats have perfected over the millennia since they first decided to domesticate themselves.

"Back to the window." I pointed. He meowed, but when I repeated my command, he jumped back onto the sill. "Good boy." I gave him a treat from the stash in my desk as a reward for his good behavior.

Now to delve into the box. I started with the letters and skimmed them quickly. There were a few from Richard Ducote to his wife, Cecilia, the parents of Miss An'gel and Miss Dickce, from the first year of their marriage. I felt like a voyeur, but I scanned them so quickly for any mention of Essie Mae that I didn't really absorb their meaning.

No luck with the letters, so I moved on to the account books. The Ducotes were meticulous record keepers, particularly when it came to household expenses. I resisted the urge to go through and compare 1920s prices to current ones. I had to focus on my goal. There were periodic entries for wages with employees listed by name, but I couldn't find names or initials to match either Essie Mae Whoever or Essie Mae Hobson, nor even an Essie or a Mae.

I finally put that box aside. A check of the time revealed that it was a few minutes past noon. Thanks to the skimpier-than-usual breakfast I'd eaten that morning, I felt hungry.

If I started on another box I could spend an hour or more with it, and I was ready for some food right then.

I remembered that I might have to provide my own lunch because Azalea was home sick. If no one else had beaten me to it, there might still be some of that delicious ham and potato salad I'd had the day before. That would do nicely.

When Diesel and I walked into the kitchen, appetizing odors, along with Laura and Stewart, greeted us. Stewart presided over the stove while Laura prepared a salad.

"Just in time for lunch." Laura pecked me on the cheek. "And there's my big beautiful boy." She blew a kiss to the cat, and Diesel rubbed against her legs, warbling happily.

"Howdy, Charlie." Stewart said. "Hope you're hungry."

"I sure am. I thought you were going to be a bum today, and here you are cooking." I walked over to the stove to see what was cooking. "Beef stroganoff. I do hope that's for lunch."

"It is." Stewart grinned. "When you told me Azalea wouldn't be here today, I couldn't resist the chance to get into the kitchen on a weekday."

"I'm glad your resistance was low," I said. "I was figuring on having leftover ham and potato salad."

"Too late for that anyway." Laura giggled. "I think Justin must have had it for a midnight snack last night."

"Then I'm doubly thankful Stewart had the urge to cook." I sat down at the table. I hoped the stroganoff would be ready soon. The aroma was driving me crazy with hunger.

"Sean is lunching with Alexandra," Laura said as she placed the large bowl of salad on the table. "Justin's gone to see his father, so it's just the three of us." She began to set the table.

"This will be ready in just a minute." Stewart added a heaping tablespoon of sour cream and stirred it in. "Any further leads on who killed Vera?"

"Nothing concrete," I said. "I think Morty is the best suspect, though. Get rid of Vera, no need for a divorce, and then he could marry Sissy."

"Speaking of our beautiful Miss Beauchamp, I ran into her yesterday afternoon." Stewart began ladling noodles and beef onto plates. "I was walking around the square, and out she popped from the Atheneum. The poor thing looked upset about something—which I never could winkle out of her though I certainly tried—so I invited her over to the ice cream shop for a milk shake to cheer her up."

While Stewart related his story, I'd been watching the cat pace back and forth near the counter where Laura had prepared the salad. She hadn't put away the bag of grated cheese when she finished, and the cat could smell it. All of a sudden he leaped onto the counter and tried to stick his head into the bag.

"Diesel, no! You get down from there. You know better than that." At my sharp tone the cat turned to glare at me. Laura retrieved the bag and returned it to the fridge. Diesel grumbled as he jumped to the floor and disappeared into the utility room.

"Poor kitty," Stewart said. "He's going to waste away to absolutely nothing if you won't let him eat." He set a plate of stroganoff in front of me, and Laura dished out the salad.

"Yes, he's always on the point of starvation. Or at least he thinks he is." I had to smile. After all, it did take a fair amount of grub to keep a thirty-six-pound cat in decent shape.

"How about some iced tea, Dad?" Laura held up a glass, and I nodded. She put it on the table and then took her seat.

"I'm sorry Azalea wasn't feeling well today. Do you think she's really sick? Or just worn out from all she's been through?"

"I think she was probably exhausted," I said. "If she was truly ill I'm sure Kanesha would have called to let us know."

"If she's not back tomorrow I'm going to check on her," Laura said.

"You might be able to get away with it," Stewart said. "But you're the only one. She really likes you. The rest of us she only tolerates." He grinned.

Laura smirked. "Can I help it if Azalea is such a good judge of character?"

"Where is Dante?" It finally dawned on me the little dog was nowhere in evidence. Usually he was within a foot of Stewart at all times.

"He's at the doggy beauty parlor, getting all fabulous," Stewart said. "He was overdue for a cut and a shampoo. I'll go pick him up after we finish lunch. Pardon the change of subject, but to get back to the murder for a moment. Laura told me about Azalea's ordeal in the back stairs Tuesday night. Poor woman. I think that would give me nightmares."

"Me, too," Laura said. "Stewart and I have been discussing the case, Dad. He's part of the family now, so he might as well be part of the investigative team, right?"

Stewart looked at her adoringly, and I grinned. He *had* become part of the family, though I certainly hadn't expected it when he moved in the previous year. I didn't think of him in a paternal way, however. He was more like a kid brother.

"Of course it's okay, but I'm not sure about this *investigative team*. That makes us sound like a family of private eyes." I wiped my mouth and put the napkin down beside my empty plate. "I know I can count on both of you not to go talking about this to anyone outside the family, though." I gazed sternly at each of them in turn.

Neither of them paid any attention to that attempt at humor.

"Do you think she actually saw anything other than Vera falling?" Stewart picked up my plate and took it to the stove for a second helping. I didn't protest.

"It's hard to say. It must have been pretty dim in there. The one lightbulb gives off very little light, and it's at the top of the stairs." I tucked into my second portion of stroganoff.

"Have you thought about a reenactment?" Stewart asked. "I don't know that Azalea would go for it, but you could try it to test whether a person at the top of the stairs would have been visible enough to identify."

"That's a terrific idea," Laura said. "I'll lend a hand, Dad. It will probably be creepy, but if it will help, I can handle it."

"It is an excellent idea," I said. *Why didn't I think of that myself?* Then I realized there could be a problem. "The stairs might still be sealed off, and if they are, we'll have to wait."

"Can't you call Miss An'gel and ask?" Laura said.

"Of course. Let me look up the number." I got up from the table and went to the drawer where we kept the local phone book. I handed it to Laura. "Find the number and call it out to me. You can read those small numbers more easily than I can."

Laura took the book eagerly and thumbed through the pages. "Here it is."

I punched in the number and after four rings, the housekeeper answered. I identified myself and asked Clementine whether one of the Ducote sisters was available.

"Miss Dickce here somewhere. Let me get her." Clementine set the phone down with a slight clunk, and I waited.

It took almost two minutes, but Miss Dickce eventually came on the line. We exchanged greetings, and then I asked whether the back stairs were still sealed off.

"No, they're not. A nice young officer from the sheriff's department removed everything this morning, as a matter of fact. Why do you ask?"

I explained Stewart's idea, and she squealed into the phone. "Of course you must do that. How exciting. When can you come?"

"How about half an hour from now?" Laura and Stewart nodded enthusiastically when I glanced their way. "Good. We'll see you soon."

"Don't you have to go pick up Dante?" Laura asked.

"It's barely noon now," Stewart said. "He won't be ready until two at the very least, and they won't mind keeping him an extra half hour or so. Besides, do you really think I'm going to miss out on this?"

We quickly finished lunch and put everything away. I drove, and on the way we discussed who would do what. I would play Azalea's role, Laura would be Vera, and Stewart would be the killer.

Miss Dickce was waiting on the verandah when we arrived. She was fairly hopping with excitement, but she took time to coo over Diesel for a moment. Then she hurried us into the house and up the stairs to the second floor. We followed her down the hall to the back of the house, and she pointed out the entrance to the back stairs.

"You turn the light on here. There's another switch downstairs to turn it off." She pointed to a switch on the wall next to the door, then flipped it. "The fixture is on the wall to your right. There is another light down at the bottom, but there's something wrong with the wiring. Since we don't use these stairs anymore, though, we haven't had it fixed."

"Thank you." I turned to my two assistants. "Give me at least two minutes before you open the door. I want my eyes to have time to adjust the way Azalea's would have."

Laura and Stewart nodded.

"Diesel, you stay here with Miss Dickce." He meowed as if he understood, and Miss Dickce stroked his back. I took a deep breath before I opened the door and stepped into the stairwell.

The door shut behind me, and I peered down through the murky light to the bottom of the stairs. The light on the wall beside me did little to illuminate any farther than about a third of the way down, from what I could see. The musty odor made my nose twitch, and I hoped my sinuses wouldn't pay me back later for this.

I started cautiously down the stairs, mindful of what I knew about the state of the wood beneath my feet. I reached out to grasp the handrail but then realized there wasn't one. I had maybe two inches' clearance on each side of me, and, as I discovered, not even that much space over my head. Claustrophobia began to kick in, worsening as I went further down, counting each step.

At number twenty-six I reached the bottom. These antebellum homes had higher ceilings than most houses did these days, and that accounted for the longer-than-usual staircase. I felt for the knob and grasped it. By now my eyes had adjusted to the lack of light, and I discovered that it was pretty dark at the bottom.

I turned to look up. Deep shadows covered the lower

two-thirds of the run of stairs, and the light appeared even weaker than before from this vantage point. I turned and faced the door again, because I remembered Azalea's telling me she was in that position when she heard someone enter at the head of the stairs.

The seconds stretched out, and I breathed in the damp air. I couldn't wait to get out of there. I sympathized with Azalea.

Finally I heard movement above me, and the floor creaked as Laura and Stewart entered the stairwell. I counted to five before I turned and looked up.

Laura was only a silhouette, and I couldn't see Stewart at all. They were approximately the same height, so that wasn't surprising. Laura started down the steps, and then I could see the edge of Stewart's silhouette behind her, outlined by a faint nimbus of light. As I watched, I saw the silhouette behind Laura change shape slightly.

"I'm pretending to shove her down now," Stewart said, and I could just see the movement of his arms behind Laura. They were dark projections of his body. Then I focused on Laura as she pretended to pitch forward, and without thinking I started up the stairs toward her to break her fall.

She called out to me. "I'm okay, Dad. I'm not really falling."

I stopped where I was, and as I did I realized I could no longer see anyone behind her on the stairs. Evidently Stewart had slipped back up the stairs and out the door while my attention was focused on Laura.

"Jeez, it's dark in here," Laura said. "That lightbulb must be an antique itself. Did they ever make ten-watt bulbs?"

"I don't know, but we can look it up when we get home.

Stay where you are for a moment." I went back down to the bottom door and twisted the knob. It opened, for which I was deeply thankful. I stepped out into the kitchen, blinked rapidly in the bright light, then turned back to peer up the stairs.

With the added light I could see more, but this made me realize how difficult it would have been for Azalea to see much that night.

But what exactly *had* she seen?

More than she was telling, I was pretty sure.

How could I get her to tell me everything?

TWENTY-SEVEN

||||||||||||||||||||||||||||||||||||||||||||||||||||||||||||||||||||||||||||||||||||||||||

Laura joined me in the kitchen. "How eerie was that?" She rubbed her arms.

I nodded. "I'd hate to get stuck in there. Poor Azalea."

Stewart called down to us from upstairs. "Are we done?"

I stepped back into the stairwell and shouted up to him. "Yes, come on down."

"Okay."

Laura and I moved out into the hallway and met Stewart, Diesel, and Miss Dickce at the foot of the main staircase.

"Was that helpful?" Miss Dickce asked.

"I think so," I said. "At least now I have a better understanding of what it was like for Azalea in there."

"Could you see anything?" Miss Dickce peered anxiously at me. "I'm glad you didn't ask me to go in there. I can't abide dark places. An'gel should either have the wiring fixed and the stairs replaced or shut the whole thing off permanently."

"It's hard to see anything," I said. "I doubt Azalea could see much, either. I think the sheriff is going to have to solve this thing without a full eyewitness account."

"That's too bad," Miss Dickce said. "I wish this were all over." Diesel rubbed against her legs, and I tried not to notice the trail of hair he left on her navy blue dress. Our hostess didn't seem to mind, however. She scratched the cat's head and smiled down at him.

Stewart patted her arm. "We all do, Miss Dickce. But Charlie will figure it out, don't you worry."

"I appreciate your faith in me," I said. "But it's not going to be easy. Thank you, Miss Dickce, for letting us come do this. We'd better get going, though. I need to get back to work, and Stewart has an errand to take care of, too."

"You're so welcome, Charlie," Miss Dickce said warmly. "I wish you had time to stay longer, but I understand."

I suddenly remembered the check I collected from Sissy Beauchamp that morning. I pulled it from my pocket and handed it to Miss Dickce. She accepted it, glanced at it, and frowned. I wondered whether the amount was for less than what the Beauchamps had pledged, and given what I suspected about their finances, it probably was.

"Thank you for taking care of that, Charlie." Miss Dickce showed us to the door and bent to give Diesel a kiss on the nose as a good-bye.

Laura and Stewart chatted on the drive home, but I paid scant attention. My thoughts focused on that dark stairwell, bouncing back and forth between our reenactment and the events of Tuesday night. I had to talk to Azalea again, and this time I had to persist until she finally told me everything.

Diesel and I made it back to my office at the library by a quarter to two. He showed brief interest in the box I opened, but another treat distracted him. He munched it and then snoozed on the windowsill while I delved into the box's contents.

According to the list there were only letters here, more correspondence, chiefly business matters, from the 1920s and 1930s. I scanned letter after letter, gradually emptying the box, but found nothing of interest to my current quest.

Near the bottom of the box I felt a hard lump underneath the last inch of paper. Curious, I pulled all the letters up to reveal a small leather-bound book lying beneath. Slightly larger in dimension than a paperback and half as thick, it had a monogram stamped in gold on the cover. The letters were *KCD*.

Why wasn't this listed as part of the contents? I picked up the little book and opened it. An inscription in cramped, tiny handwriting adorned the front flyleaf, and I had to pull out a magnifying glass in order to read it. *The Private Journal of Katherine Cecilia Ducote.*

Cecilia Ducote was the mother of Miss An'gel and Miss Dickce. I had a sudden feeling that this little book could hold the answers to Vera Cassity's quest to know more about her mother. I also wondered whether the sisters knew about the existence of their mother's journal.

I turned the page. There was no date, but the first sentence revealed that the keeper of the journal was on her honeymoon.

My darling Richard has brought me to Paris on our wedding trip. Paris! The city of my dreams. And then Vienna and Rome! Was any girl ever so fortunate? Richard is so attentive and so passionate. I blush to

*write of such things here, but dear Maman should have
told me that a woman's duty could entail such delightful feelings!*

Oh, my. I probably blushed a little, reading the most private thoughts of this young woman. I hoped she wouldn't
rhapsodize in any further detail.

I began to skim and worked my way through the splen-
dors of Paris, Vienna, and Rome. By the time the young
couple left Rome to return to the United States, they had
spent nearly five months in Europe. Near the end of the trip
Cecilia confided to the journal that she suspected she was
going to have a baby.

Home again in Athena Cecilia wrote about the events of
daily life at River Hill and her developing pregnancy. She
began to have problems around the fifth month, and her
doctor put her on bedrest for the duration of her pregnancy.

I read with sadness the account of the stillbirth of the
child, a boy, in the eighth month. Then came the shocking
news that the doctor feared Cecilia would never be able to
bear another child, at least not to full term.

Shaken, I put the journal down. Cecilia was heartbro-
ken over the loss of her baby, and as a father, I could only
imagine the depth of sorrow and despair she and Richard
felt. Sean and Laura were both such healthy babies, and
Jackie and I could have had more children, had we chosen
to do so. But we were happy with our two and decided they
were enough.

I brightened at that thought, because I realized that
long-ago doctor had been proven wrong. Cecilia and Richard went on to have two daughters.

Thus heartened, I picked up the book and took up where
I left off.

Cecilia was evidently ill for some months after the death of the baby, and her entries in the journal were sporadic at best. Then I hit an entry that gave me a tingling of excitement.

Richard insists I need a companion. He's so busy now and can't be with me during the day. He worries that I'll be bored and lonely with only the housekeeper and the staff in the house. I finally consented and began to consider who might be suitable. Someone who will not fatigue me unnecessarily and whose face I can bear to see day after day, naturally. I considered various family members, but they are mostly too old and depressing. Cousin Lavinia has the face and disposition of a prune, and I should go mad after one day in her company. Aunt Berenice isn't much better, nor is her whiny daughter, my cousin Mary Elizabeth. Then I thought about a distant connection, Esther McMullen. If I recall it correctly, she is the granddaughter of my mother's great-aunt Matilda, or something like that. I have met her a couple of times, and she is a quiet, modest young woman. Richard has arranged for her to travel here from Georgia for a trial period. She is apparently quite grateful for she is alone with very little money.

Esther McMullen. That wasn't the same as *Essie Mae*, but Essie could be a nickname for Esther.

After a few entries Cecilia mentioned her cousin again.

Cousin Esther is here and is so far proving satisfactory. She is as quiet and modest as I remembered and so pathetically grateful as to be embarrassing. I have managed to extract certain details from her about her

*reduced circumstances. Her mother married against
her family's wishes, and her choice was a charming but
faithless Irish rogue named Mick McMullen. He abandoned Esther and her mother when Esther was only
five years old! How terrible it must be not to have a
father one can rely upon. Esther's maternal grandpar-
ents turned their back on her and her mother as well.
That was not the Christian thing to do!*

The tale of Esther and her mother was a sad one, but not
uncommon. I read further.

*My cousin has settled in well, and I am quite pleased
with her. She is a comfortable and unobtrusive companion. I have discovered that she prefers to be called
Essie Mae, however. It was her father's pet name for
her. I should think she would find it abhorrent, given
that the man abandoned her, but she clings to her
memories of him. So she will be Essie Mae henceforth,
though I wince at the common sound of the name every
time I hear it.*

So Vera Cassity was a distant cousin of Miss An'gel
and Miss Dickce. I put the journal down and considered
that.

I wondered if Vera suspected anything like this. If she
had, that might have been why she was so determined to
snoop in the Ducote papers.

But what would she have done with the proof that she
was related to the Ducotes of River Hill?

She would have crowed about it to everyone she met, I
decided. Her blood had a tinge of blue after all.

I didn't think Miss An'gel and Miss Dickce would be all that thrilled to have to acknowledge the connection.

Suddenly my mind was abuzz with the possibilities.

Did they already know?

And could they have killed Vera to prevent anyone else from ever knowing?

TWENTY-EIGHT

The more I thought about it, the more I considered the blood relationship between Vera Cassity and the Ducote sisters a weak motive for murder. Miss An'gel and Miss Dickce would have to be the other side of crazy to want to kill Vera to stop her from claiming kinship to them.

Besides, I had no proof that the sisters were even aware of the relationship. They had the means and the opportunity, though. Even at their ages—early eighties, I suspected—they appeared vigorous and healthy enough to give Vera a hard shove down the stairs.

I also realized that I simply didn't want to think the sisters would do any such thing. I liked and admired them tremendously, and I would be both horrified and disappointed if either of them turned out to be the murderer.

How could I prove that they did or didn't know Vera was a distant cousin?

Then I realized how odd it was that Vera didn't already

know herself. She must have suspected something; otherwise, she wouldn't have sent me the photograph of her mother. She at least had no proof, or the whole state of Mississippi would have known.

Essie Mae McMullen, later Hobson, evidently kept the knowledge of the relationship from her daughter. Why? Was she forced to do so by the Ducotes? Or did she not want to claim kinship for her own reasons?

I stared at the journal. The answers to those questions might lie within its pages. With a certain amount of reluctance I picked it up and found the last entry I'd read.

Essie Mae figured often in Cecilia's journal. The young Mrs. Ducote relied more and more heavily on her cousin-companion, and within months Cecilia pronounced her indispensable. One typical entry summed up the situation.

Essie Mae is the dearest girl on earth. And so grateful to Dick and me for giving her a home, one where she feels appreciated and useful. She is more like a sister to me now, the sister I never had. She is only fifteen months older, but sometimes seems so much younger. For her birthday three days ago, Dick and I gave her a silk dressing gown, and she actually cried. She told us both over and over there wasn't anything she wouldn't do for us. So very sweet! She has spoken only rarely of her life before she came to us, but I suspect it was far more dreadful than I first realized.

Essie Mae had really wormed herself into Cecilia's heart.

That thought brought me up short. Why did I think of it in those terms? I realized I was projecting backward, based on my distaste for Vera. That was not fair to Essie Mae, and I resolved not to fall into that trap again.

I returned to reading. There were occasional references to the baby, but judging from the tone of the entries, Cecilia seemed determined to be more cheerful, particularly with her husband, who still felt the loss of the child keenly.

Dick so desperately wants a child. I know he would love a son to carry on the Ducote name. He is an only child, and now that his father is gone, he is the only male Ducote left. I want so much to give him a son and am quite willing to try, but he is terrified that another pregnancy will be dangerous. I suspect the doctor told him things that neither of them shared with me about my health. I have taxed him with that, but he always evades the questions. Once I suggested that we adopt a child, but he was adamant. I don't think I have ever seen him so furious. Only a child of his blood would be good enough to inherit River Hill. The Ducote bloodline must carry on.

I frowned. Had Cecilia been able to overcome Dick's objections to adoption? Or was the doctor wrong after all? I began to have suspicions that the answer to both questions was *no*.

I skimmed through ten pages of routine journal entries, mostly accounts of social engagements. I found an amusing reference to Hester Beauchamp, who I figured must be the grandmother of Hank and Sissy. According to Cecilia, Hester was a homely frump and a vicious gossip. Neither Hank nor Sissy inherited his or her looks from Granny Hester, that much was obvious.

I turned a page, and my eyes widened in shock, even though I had begun to suspect what I read.

There is to be a child with Ducote blood after all. Essie Mae is with child, and Dick confessed shamefacedly that the child is his. I am sick over this double betrayal. Not one, but two vipers I have nursed in my bosom!!!

Poor Cecilia. Perhaps my assessment of Essie Mae's character hadn't been off after all.

The next entry was dated four days later.

I am trying to reconcile myself to the fact that my husband and his concubine are having a child. I tried to insist that Essie Mae be sent away forever because I can't stand to have her near me, but Dick refused. He has grown callous in a way I never suspected he could be. He is determined to have a child. What am I to do?

I felt heartsick for Cecilia. I could only imagine the depth of her outrage and her hurt. I also realized that Essie Mae's child had to be Miss An'gel, and that was hard to grasp. Vera and Miss An'gel were half sisters.

What about Miss Dickce? I read on.

Essie Mae and I are going to North Carolina for the next six months. Dick is telling everyone that I am "in an interesting condition," and that I need time in the clear mountain air to be sure to deliver a healthy child. No one besides the three of us knows the truth, and we will leave before Essie Mae grows large enough with child to reveal the shameful secret. When we return, the child will be considered my own. Essie Mae has agreed to this. She is terrified, of course, that she will be sent away once the baby is born, but I will reserve judgment on that.

The next entry came six months later.

Essie Mae was delivered of a girl this morning. One glimpse of that angelic little face, and I was lost. The child is the innocent in all this, and I will not visit the sins of her father and mother upon her. She is so like a little angel that I have decided that shall be her name. It should have a French sound, however, so her name will be An'gel. An'gel Ducote. Dick will not dare argue with me over this. He of course will be disappointed that my An'gel is not a boy, but perhaps the Lord has decided to repay him in this way for his perfidy.

I was so absorbed in my reading that I completely forgot my napping cat. Diesel took care of that by butting the back of my head several times to get my attention. I took a minute to reassure him that he was still wonderful and that I adored him, and he purred in satisfaction. When he'd had enough he went back to napping, and I returned to the journal.

From that point on I skimmed even more rapidly, searching for mention of a second child. Cecilia grew reconciled to the presence of Essie Mae in the household, and everyone within the house and without apparently accepted An'gel without question as the child of Cecilia and Richard. At first Dick had little to do with his daughter, severely disappointed that she wasn't a son. Eventually the child won him over, however.

I was rather glad to read that. I would have hated to think that Miss An'gel wasn't cherished by her father.

When An'gel was a year old, Cecilia began to long for another child. Richard continued to refuse to risk her health and at last confided in her that the doctor had said another pregnancy might kill her. She battled with her emotions in the pages of her journal, but she finally resolved to ask Dick to father another child with Essie Mae.

That shocked me, but I could understand Cecilia's longing for another baby. At least, as she reasoned to herself, a second child would be a full sibling to little An'gel. Richard readily agreed to the scheme, but Essie Mae took more persuading. She soon consented, however, and within two months was with child again.

They followed the same procedure as before. Away Cecilia and Essie Mae went to the mountains of North Carolina, and six months later came home with another baby, again a daughter, this time named Richelle after her father. I knew that at some point Richelle became Dickce, a nickname formed from the names of her legal parents, Dick and Cecilia (often called Kitce by Dick, I discovered, *Kit* for Katherine and *Ce* for Cecilia).

I had a slight headache now from reading the cramped handwriting, and I set the book aside even though there were more pages left to read. I wanted to consider the implications of the true relationship between Vera Cassity and the Ducote sisters.

Being a distant cousin was one thing. Being a full sister or a half sister—especially if Vera had been able to prove the relationship—was quite another.

If she were their full sister, Vera might have some claim to her father's estate—worth millions, if rumors about the Ducote fortune were accurate.

That was not a crazy motive for murder.

TWENTY-NINE

||||||||||||||||||||||||||||||||||||||||||||||||||||||||||||||||||||||||

Slow down, Charlie, I told myself. Vera was the half sister of An'gel and Dickce, but only half, and it was because they shared the same mother. As far as I knew, Vera's father was Jedediah Hobson, not Richard Ducote, and I couldn't see Richard Ducote allowing a child of his to be passed off as the child of another man.

There was a simple way to settle this. I knew Richard Ducote died in an accident while Miss An'gel and Miss Dicke were very young. If his death occurred long enough before Vera was born, that would settle the issue. All I had to do was find out the exact dates of Richard Ducote's death and Vera Hobson's birth.

The former was simple enough. The archives kept a file of information about notable citizens of Athena, and the Ducote family figured prominently in it. Digitized a couple of years ago, it was accessible via computer.

In less than five minutes I had the information I needed.

Richard Ducote died in a hunting accident seventy-five years ago, when Miss An'gel would have been about nine and Miss Dickce seven. I also checked Cecilia's death date. She outlived Richard by nearly forty years. I recalled someone telling me that Vera's mother died when Vera was about thirty, and that meant that Cecilia had outlived Essie Mae, more than likely.

Now to find out exactly when Vera was born. I checked an online genealogical database but that yielded no results.

That meant I would have to go to the courthouse and check the public records. As long as I was going to do that, I reckoned I might as well look up Richard Ducote's will. It would be interesting to see whether there was any provision for Essie Mae. Come to think of it, I should also check for wills for Cecilia and Essie Mae. I remembered that Vera had inherited money from her mother, money that Essie Mae in her turn had allegedly inherited from a relative. Could the money have come from the Ducote estate?

My head ached from trying to sort out who died when and the possible implications of wills and inheritances. I'd better get down to the courthouse as soon as possible.

I checked the time. Too late to go today; it was already seventeen minutes after five. The courthouse would have to wait until tomorrow morning.

"Come on, Diesel, let's go home." I shut down the computer, put the journal away in my desk and locked it, thought about it a moment, unlocked the desk, and pulled the journal back out. *Maybe I should take it home with me to finish reading tonight.*

No, that wouldn't be right. Materials from the Ducote Collection were not supposed to leave the archives. Back into the drawer went the journal again, and this time it stayed there.

Diesel, impatient to be on the way, meowed loudly at me. He was already by the door, and I didn't linger.

On the walk home my head buzzed with questions. A new one that occurred to me was whether I should share the revelations from Cecilia Ducote's journal with Kanesha. If one of the Ducote sisters did turn out to be the killer, then the information about the relationship with Vera would have to come out.

But if they were both innocent, there was no point in anyone else knowing the story. It was a private family matter, and I felt guilty enough as it was for having pried into it myself.

I couldn't share this with Kanesha yet. If I found some proof that either Miss An'gel or Miss Dickce pushed Vera down those stairs, I would have to. But until then I would keep quiet about what I'd learned.

That one decision made, I felt better. Diesel and I turned into the driveway and headed for the back door. I let him open the door, and while he did, I pulled my ringing cell phone from my pocket.

Kanesha. That was eerie. I had just been thinking about her, and now she was calling. I stepped into the empty kitchen as I answered.

"I'm about five minutes away from there. Okay if I stop by?" she said after barely giving me time to say hello.

"Sure, come on by."

I had just enough time to shed my coat and read a hastily scrawled note from Laura, informing me that everyone would be out for dinner tonight and I was on my own, when the doorbell rang.

"Thought it would be good to check in with you, share information," Kanesha said without preamble the moment I opened the door.

I stood aside for her to enter and then followed her into the kitchen where Diesel was waiting. He meowed loudly three times, and I understood the message.

"Please have a seat, and I'll be back in a minute," I said with an apologetic smile. "His Majesty has informed me that the Royal Food Bowl is empty and in need of filling."

Kanesha scowled as she pulled out a chair and sat.

I hurried into the utility room to take care of Diesel's needs. He watched anxiously as I added fresh dry food to his bowl—not completely empty, by the way—then warbled to let me know I was dismissed now that I had fulfilled my duty.

Smiling, I went back to the kitchen to join Kanesha. "Can I offer you something to drink?" I asked. I went to the fridge to fetch a can of diet soda for myself.

"No, thank you. Have you turned up anything else?"

"I'll get to that in a minute. First, how is your mother? She didn't come to work today." I explained about the note I'd found this morning.

Kanesha frowned. "When I talked to her, she was fine, or so she said. She didn't say anything about not coming to work today. That's how she is, though. She won't ever tell me when she's not feeling good, because she doesn't want me to worry."

"Aunt Dottie was the same way," I said. "I hope Azalea got some rest." I decided to start with the reenactment as I sat down across the table from her. She leaned forward in her chair as I told her what we'd done.

"That was a good idea," she said when I finished. "Any conclusions?"

"Mostly that Azalea would have had a hard time seeing much. It was even darker in there than I realized."

"Do you still think there's something she's holding back?"

I nodded. "It's a feeling I can't shake. I know it doesn't sound rational, but there was simply something about her manner the first time I talked to her. And the second time as well. I want to talk to her again, and this time I'm determined to find out what she's not telling us."

"Good luck." Kanesha leaned back in her chair. "Anything else you can tell me?"

"I went to visit Sissy and Hank Beauchamp today, too. Miss An'gel and Miss Dickce came by again this morning and asked me to go see the Beauchamps to collect the money they promised for the fund-raiser."

"Did you actually get money from them?"

"A check from Sissy," I said. "Why do you ask?"

"I wish Miss An'gel luck in getting it cashed. I've been doing some checking into people's money, trying to see what the financial angle could be in this case. The Beauchamps are in bad shape. There's actually a mortgage on the house, and they're behind three months already. Hank's law practice isn't doing well, and Sissy has never worked a day in her life."

"Any idea why they're so short of money?" I asked. "I thought the Beauchamps were wealthy."

"They used to be," Kanesha replied. "Their father was rich, left them a lot of money from his own law practice. But Sissy has expensive tastes, and so does Hank. He also has a gambling problem."

I nodded, remembering again what Helen Louise had told me. That was a fast way to run through a fortune. I felt sorry for them, but I realized that, in terms of motive, they had to be considered prime suspects in Vera's death.

"I thought the house looked rather sad, needs new paint, and there's not a lot of furniture, at least in the hall and in the front parlor."

Kanesha nodded. "Aunt Lily told me they had started selling the furniture. She said it like to have broke her heart, seeing all those family heirlooms go. Then they had to let her go, too. They couldn't pay her, and she couldn't work for free."

"I didn't know your aunt worked for the Beauchamps."

"For nearly forty years." Kanesha made a sour face. "And now she has to go out looking for a new job, at her age. She can't afford to retire."

"I'm sorry she's lost her job." I was about to add, *If there's anything I can do, let me know*, but I realized in time that wouldn't go over too well. Kanesha would bite my head off.

"What about Morty Cassity?" I asked. "Is his financial position solid?"

"From everything I can find out, he's in excellent shape. Worth about twenty-five million or so."

"Money that the Beauchamps could certainly use, and with Vera out of the way, Morty is free to marry Sissy."

"That could wrap it up pretty neatly," Kanesha said. "But there's a matter of proof. Motive is there, but we still have to make sure one of the three of them had the opportunity."

"Morty was upstairs with Vera," I said. "We know that from Azalea's evidence."

"He was upstairs with her part of the time, but we don't know for sure that he was still upstairs when she got pushed. Unless Mama can swear in court that she saw him do it, of course."

Her cell phone rang as I was about to pose a question.

Kanesha held up a hand to forestall me as she answered her phone. "Right," she said. "On my way right now." She ended the call and put the phone back in her pocket. "Three-car accident about three miles out of town. We'll talk more later."

That was fine with me. Maybe by the time we talked again, I would know enough to make a decision about sharing what I'd learned about Vera's connection to the Ducote family. I showed Kanesha to the door, then wandered back to the kitchen to figure out what to have for dinner.

Diesel waited by the fridge and peered inside the moment I opened it. I never could figure out what it was he looked for, but he inevitably wanted to see inside whenever someone opened the door.

I found a casserole dish with a note on it. "Found this in the freezer, so I took it out to let it thaw for you. Love, Laura." I pulled the casserole out and peeled off the foil and plastic wrap. It looked like one of Azalea's chicken, broccoli, rice, and cheese casseroles. Good rib-sticking food. Not exactly healthy, but definitely tasty.

I put it in the oven to warm. While I waited for dinner to be ready, I went upstairs to wash up and fetch the book I was reading, the latest Ellery Adams Books by the Bay mystery. This was a relatively new series, but I loved the characters and the North Carolina setting.

Downstairs again, I checked the casserole, but it needed about another fifteen minutes. I tried to read, but I couldn't block my worries about Vera Cassity's murder from my mind. I put the book aside for now and focused instead on the thoughts that wouldn't leave me alone.

I kept coming back to Miss An'gel and Miss Dickce. What if one of them had killed Vera? For the sake of the family honor. Would an eighty-year-old scandal be that much of a scandal now? All the principals involved were long dead.

Miss An'gel and Miss Dickce might be embarrassed by the revelation that Cecilia Ducote was not their birth mother. They might be even more embarrassed to have to acknowledge Vera Cassity as a half sister.

But I couldn't see embarrassment as a compelling motive for murder.

Then again, my family had never been as prominent as the Ducotes, though they had been in Athena about as long. I was proud of my ancestors, and I knew of some skeletons in the family cupboards that were rather embarrassing, but still.

A lot would hinge on what I found out about the wills of the three principals, Richard, Cecilia, and Essie Mae. And whether Vera could possibly be a third daughter of Richard Ducote. I think if I could have broken into the courthouse right then and there to get to the information I wanted, I would have. Patience had never been one of my virtues, particularly when the stakes were this high.

The casserole was as delicious as I expected, and I ate rather more than I should have. That was what happened when I was anxious. I fetched Diesel some of the treats he liked rather than letting him have any of the casserole. There were also onions in it, I realized, and he didn't need onions or cheese. He for once seemed satisfied with the treats, perhaps because I pretended they came from the casserole dish.

The Ducote sisters. I couldn't stop thinking about them. Every which way I turned, there they were. They'd orchestrated Vera's "retirement" from public life, and I had to wonder how much else they might have orchestrated. Now that I thought about it, they had certainly been directing my footsteps. First they asked me to involve myself in the case, then they sent me off to talk to Morty Cassity. This morning they had me going to talk to Hank and Sissy Beauchamp.

Were they purposely directing me so that I wouldn't have time to think about them as possible prime suspects in Vera's murder?

THIRTY

The Ducote sisters were definitely devious enough to be pulling the puppet strings, and I had been all too willing to let them.

I found it difficult, though, to think of them in that way. They would have to be fine actresses to dissemble that well—the Olivia de Havilland and Joan Fontaine of Athena.

No, I just couldn't see them that way.

All this speculation was fruitless. With a sigh I got up and started to clear the table. Once that was done, I went to the den to watch television, but that failed to hold my interest. Diesel was not pleased when I roused him from the couch and told him I was going to bed.

He followed me nevertheless, and by the time I was ready to slip under the covers, he was sound asleep, sprawled over his half of the bed. More like two-thirds, really. I made myself comfortable, picked up the Ellery Adams book, and this time I focused on the story and was soon absorbed by it.

When I woke in the morning, after a surprisingly restful night's sleep, I was alone in bed. Diesel could be quite the nocturnal gadabout, but I was used to it by now.

As I came down the stairs, I sniffed and happily detected the smell of bacon. Azalea was back today, and I could look forward to a nice, full breakfast. No making do with cereal and toast today.

Once I had fortified myself with a stout breakfast I would try to convince Azalea to talk to me and tell me everything she'd seen in that dark stairwell on Tuesday night.

When I walked into the kitchen I thought for a moment I was seeing double. There were two Azaleas standing at the stove, their backs to me. After the first moment of shock passed I realized that one of the Azaleas was slightly taller than the other and wore a different-colored dress.

"Good morning, Azalea."

The two figures turned, and Azalea turned out to be the shorter one. The resemblance between the two of them was eerie. Then I noticed the other woman looked older than Azalea and tired. Deep lines scored her forehead, and I realized this must be Azalea's sister Lily.

"Morning, Mr. Charlie," Azalea said, wiping her hands on her apron. "This is my sister Lily Golliday. I brought her with me to help with some of the heavy cleaning today. She used to help me out some when Miss Dottie was alive. I sure hope you don't mind."

"I don't mind at all," I said warmly. "Good morning, Mrs. Golliday. I'm glad to meet you." I advanced and extended a hand.

Lily's hand trembled as she placed it in mine. She ducked her head shyly. "Thank you, Mr. Charlie. Nice to meet you, sir."

"Lily, why don't you go on and be sorting out that laundry," Azalea said. "Soon's I finish up with breakfast we gonna start on the upstairs."

Lily nodded and glanced at me before she disappeared into the utility room.

Azalea poured me a cup of coffee, then returned to the stove to plate my food. As she set it down, she said, "Thank you, Mr. Charlie. I appreciate you letting Lily help me today. She done lost her job and she can't stand not being busy."

"Lily can help you as much as you need her," I said. "I heard about her losing her job." Belatedly I realized that was probably a mistake.

Sure enough, Azalea glowered at me. "How you be hearing about Lily losing her job? Ain't nobody knowing about that but me and her and the Beauchamps."

"Actually I heard it from Kanesha," I said meekly. "I talked to her yesterday when I mentioned I'd been to see the Beauchamps about something. When I told her I was surprised the house was in bad shape and there wasn't much furniture, she told me about your sister being let go. That was all it was." I probably said too much. Azalea had that effect on me sometimes.

She appeared to be mollified, however. Maybe she wouldn't rake Kanesha over the coals later for blabbing to me. "I forgot Kanesha knew. She and Lily be real close."

That was a bullet dodged. Azalea turned away, and I tucked into my breakfast of scrambled eggs, bacon, biscuits, and gravy. While I ate, Azalea followed her sister into the utility room, and they emerged several minutes later and headed upstairs.

There was still no sign of Diesel. I wished I could lie in bed till all hours sometimes, but this morning I had too much to do. Before I reported for my volunteer shift at the public library at eleven I needed to get to the courthouse. And before I left for the courthouse I wanted to talk to Azalea.

I checked the clock. I had two hours and forty-three minutes to do all that. I chewed my final mouthful of bacon and biscuit, had a last sip of coffee, then hurried upstairs to get dressed.

I heard movement on the third floor when I came out of my bedroom ten minutes later, and I headed up the stairs. There were four bedrooms up there, an empty one on either end. Stewart and Justin occupied the other two, also at opposite ends of the floor. Azalea and Lily must be working in the vacant ones.

As I neared the open door of one bedroom I could hear voices.

". . . such nice things Miss Dottie had," Lily said with a catch in her voice. "Miss Sissy and Mr. Hank used to have, but they's all about gone now. My heart be just about breaking for them, 'Zalea. That house look so pitiful now."

I paused about three feet away from the door. Perhaps now wasn't the best time to interrupt the sisters for my conversation with Azalea.

When I heard Lily start sobbing I beat a hasty retreat. I would talk to Azalea later.

Diesel greeted me on the second-floor landing. Laura's door stood open, and she poked her head out. "Morning, Dad."

"Morning, sweetheart. How are you this morning?"

"Fine." She yawned. "Still sleepy, but okay. How are you?"

"Fine also, but I have a busy morning, and I need to leave Diesel here. I have some business at the courthouse, and I can't take him with me."

"I'm going to be here until lunchtime," Laura said. "Is that long enough?"

"Should be. Thank you." I looked down at the cat. "Diesel, I want you to stay with Laura this morning. I would take you if I could, but the person I need to see is allergic to cats."

The one time before I had tried to take Diesel with me to the vital records section had been a disaster. The poor woman there sneezed so much that I took Diesel away after about three minutes. I explained this hurriedly to Laura.

"No problem, Dad. Come on, Diesel, come back in here with me."

Diesel looked from me to her before, tail in the air, he turned and strode in majestic leisure down the hall to my daughter's room. Laura and I exchanged grins before I hurried downstairs.

I couldn't remember the name of the woman in the vital records office, but a nameplate told me that she was Laurel Sanders. I greeted her, and she looked up from her desk. Her eyes narrowed as she recognized me.

She frowned at me. "Did you bring your cat with you?"

When I assured her I hadn't, she relaxed. "I actually do like cats," she said. "I'm just horribly allergic."

"No need to apologize," I said. "I need your help this morning."

She approached the counter, peering over the glasses that had slid down her nose. "What are you looking for?"

"Birth and death certificates, and also several wills." I jotted the names and approximate dates down for her.

She scanned the list. "Some prominent names here." She nodded. "This will take a few minutes, but I'll find what you need." She pointed to a desk in the corner. "Just wait there."

"Thank you." I sat down at the desk and divested myself of my coat and briefcase. I pulled out a pen and a notepad, ready to jot down details.

Twenty minutes passed before Ms. Sanders returned. She was remarkably efficient, but I knew she had worked in this office for over twenty years. She had to keep everything properly organized in order to be so effective, and I respected that. In many ways she was like a reference librarian, and a first-rate one at that.

I had to sign a receipt for each document she handed me, and that took a few minutes. Finally I was able to sit down at the desk again and start my research.

I checked the birth and death records first and noted them on my pad. Once that was done I checked the dates and determined that Richard Ducote could not have been the father of Vera Cassity. She was only seventy-three when she died, three months past her birthday, according to her birth certificate, and he died about two years before she was born.

One question resolved. With no blood relationship to the Ducotes, Vera could not have laid claim to Richard Ducote's estate, although she and the Ducote sisters shared the same mother.

Now for the wills. Richard Ducote first.

I skimmed through the legalese and found the pertinent information. Other than small legacies to some of his household servants—not including Essie Mae McMullen— he left the bulk of his estate in trust for his two daughters, An'gel and Richelle (a.k.a. Dickce). When they each turned twenty-one they would inherit half the estate. He settled a substantial amount on his wife, Cecilia, in a trust for her lifetime. His two executors were named administrators of the trust. Should Cecilia remarry, the money would revert to the estate to be divided between her daughters.

That was it. Not a single mention of Essie Mae anywhere.

Frankly I found it odd. Not to leave anything to the mother of his two children? It was cold, not to mention callous.

Did he trust Cecilia to provide for Essie Mae? And had that trust been fulfilled?

I turned to Cecilia's will. No surprises here, and no mention of Essie Mae. Cecilia left everything to An'gel and Dickce.

The lack of provision for Essie Mae disturbed me even more. Had Cecilia booted her out of the house after Richard's death? I could understand Cecilia's feelings in the matter, naturally, but still.

Perhaps there was an explanation in the journal. I had read about two-thirds of it, I estimated, and if the journal extended to the time of Richard's death and after, the answers to my questions could be within its pages.

The last document was the last will and testament of Esther Mae McMullen Hobson. She left all her worldly goods to her daughter, Vera Micaela Hobson, and her son, Amory McMullen Hobson. I wondered where the *Micaela* came from, and then I remembered reading that Essie Mae's father was called Mick, probably short for Michael.

No answers in Essie Mae's will, either.

It all came down to the journal, then.

I returned the documents to Ms. Sanders. She checked them carefully, one by one, to make sure they were not damaged in any way. After she was satisfied, I thanked her again and left the courthouse.

I checked my watch. It was a quarter to ten. I had accomplished a lot in a surprisingly short amount of time.

On my way out of the courthouse I spotted Hank Beauchamp down the hall. He wore that same rumpled suit, and I recognized it as the one he had worn to the gala. Evidently it was the only one he had. He was busy chatting with someone and didn't see me, and I had no reason to interrupt his conversation.

Instead, blessing the efficiency and speediness of Ms. Sanders, I hopped into my car and headed for the archives office.

Seven minutes later I sat at my desk, Cecilia's journal in my hands. I found the place I'd left off and began to read again.

Cecilia professed to be ecstatic over her two darling girls, and Richard adored them as well. There was no mention of Essie Mae for several pages. There were accounts of social events, a short trip to New Orleans with Richard, and then the entries grew more sporadic. Months passed without one, and in a few pages two years sped by. Evidently Cecilia was too busy with the children or with the social activities entailed by her position as Mrs. Richard Ducote to have much time to spare for her journal.

I persisted, however, in hopes that I would find another mention of Essie Mae. The first one I found shocked me.

I am in complete despair. I thought Richard was happy with our two dear little angels, but he confessed to me this morning that he still longs for a son. He needs a son, he says, to keep the Ducote name alive. He owes it to his ancestors to make sure the name goes on. I was furious with him, because I knew what he wanted. Essie Mae is still here, though I do my best to forget her completely, and apparently willing to bear him another child, but I WILL NOT HAVE IT!!!

The next entry occurred on a date I recognized. Cecilia wrote simply that Richard was killed in an accident that day.

Two months passed before she wrote in her journal again.

I still can't believe that Dick is gone. The house seems surprisingly empty now. There is so much quiet. I hadn't realized how alive and vital a man he was, the flurry of activity that always seemed to surround him. He was the love of my life, despite his transgressions. What shall the girls and I do without him?

We will do without Essie Mae, however. I will have her out of this house as quickly as possible. There is a local farmer who has been trying to court her, Jedediah Hobson. He is rough and uneducated, but he seems very much in love with her. I have told her that if she will marry him and leave this house and never come back, I will see that she will be rewarded. She does not know that Dick wanted to change his will to settle a large sum on her, in addition to his provisions for me and my darling angels. I managed to stall him, and then he was killed before he had the lawyer draw it up.

Conscience nags at me. I would love to kick her out of this house without a cent, but every time I look at my sweet girls, I would be reminded, and I cannot have her on my conscience. Dick would reproach me from the grave. Therefore I have made her write and sign a statement that once she leaves this house she will never

return, nor will she ever have any contact with my
daughters. If she does she will forfeit the money she
will be paid every month. Now I wait only to hear
whether she has decided to marry Hobson, and the
sooner she does so, the better.

I turned the page and found a small, folded sheet of
paper. I opened it and read the contents—Essie Mae's
agreement to leave River Hill and never return. She stated
that she would never see or speak to An'gel or Dickce
again, on pain of forfeiting her annuity, as she called it.

I folded the paper and tucked it back inside. I set the
journal down. There was something so sad and so touching
about that spidery handwriting. A mother renouncing all
claim to her children forever.

My heart ached for her.

THIRTY-ONE

I forced myself to pick up the journal and glance through the remaining pages but found nothing of further interest. I put it back in my desk and locked the drawer.

A check of the time alerted me that I had about twenty minutes to get home, pick up Diesel, and make it to the public library if I didn't want to be late. I didn't dare go to work without Diesel, because if the staff and the patrons had to choose between the two of us, I knew which one they would prefer.

There was no sign of Azalea or Lily when I entered the kitchen, and I assumed they were upstairs somewhere. I still needed to talk to Azalea, but that would now have to wait until I was done at the library.

I found Diesel and Laura in the den watching television. I explained to Laura that I was in a hurry, and she gave us each a quick kiss good-bye.

My four hours at the library passed quickly enough.

Fridays were generally busy, and today was no exception, despite the approaching Christmas holiday. Diesel was in his element, spending time with his friends Bronwyn Forster and Lizzie Hayes, going between the reference and circulation desks. I spent a couple of hours cataloging before finishing up with a stint at the reference desk.

I tried to keep focused on the tasks at hand, but I did find my mind wandering occasionally to the tragic—at least, that's how it seemed to me—story of Essie Mae McMullen. It wasn't that I didn't have sympathy for Cecilia Ducote, because her husband's determination to carry on his family bloodline at all costs had put her in a nearly untenable position. But she had wealth, social position, and two daughters everyone believed were hers.

Essie Mae had none of those things. She did have another daughter, Vera, and a son, but I couldn't believe she could completely get over the loss of those two children. I wondered if she ever violated that agreement and spoke to the girls. I could imagine the temptation. She must have been a strong woman to survive such loss.

From the angle of the Ducote sisters and their motives for doing away with Vera, I came to the conclusion that they didn't have one strong enough. Vera had no claim on their parents' estate, and with no compelling monetary motive, I didn't think they would resort to murder. There was no proof that Miss An'gel and Miss Dickce knew the truth about their birth mother, nor that Vera did. She might have suspected something, but I doubted she would have been foolish enough to make claims she couldn't back up.

It was rather odd, though, that I had found the journal at all. How did it wind up in that box? I should check to see if it was listed as part of the contents of any of the unopened boxes. Perhaps it was simply misplaced.

I would have thought, however, that Cecilia would be careful not to let it be read by anyone else. Why didn't she destroy it? Had she meant to but simply forgot?

What about Miss An'gel and Miss Dickce? Should I tell them of the journal's existence? If I showed it to them, I might be able to discover whether they already knew about it.

Then again, if they didn't know about it, I didn't think it was my place to give them the means to discover their true parentage. This bore further thought, but like Scarlett O'Hara, I decided to think about it tomorrow.

By the time Diesel and I reached home, shortly after three that afternoon, I had a pounding headache—from tension. The last thing I felt like doing at the moment was talking to Azalea and trying to convince her to confide in me, but I really shouldn't put it off any longer.

My decision was moot, as it turned out. Diesel and I found Lily in the kitchen, and she explained that Azalea had gone home early. She was still feeling "a mite poorly," as Lily expressed it.

"I'm sorry she's not feeling well," I told Lily. "I hope she's feeling more herself soon."

In a way I was relieved, but I was also frustrated. Yet another delay. Unless I went to Azalea's home—which I didn't think she would appreciate at all—I would have to wait until she came back on Monday. I decided that was too long and resolved to call her in the morning and insist on talking to her.

Lily thanked me and then assured me that I wouldn't have to worry about dinner. She knew what Azalea was planning to cook and she would prepare it for the family.

"I appreciate that, Lily. I'd rather not have to eat my own cooking." I smiled and felt a little of the tension melt away.

"I'm mighty glad to help out," Lily said. "Better to keep busy. Idle hands can get you in trouble." She gazed down at Diesel, who in turn regarded her with interest. "Azalea told me about your cat. He sure is the biggest cat I ever did see."

"He's a Maine Coon," I explained. "They can get to be pretty big, but Diesel is bigger than usual."

"He sure is pretty, too." She stretched out a tentative hand and stroked his head. Diesel pushed against her hand and purred, and Lily smiled. "He's sweet. Can't think why 'Zalea fusses about him."

"I don't think she likes cats all that much," I said.

"Reckon not," Lily said. "This one here is something special, though."

"Yes, he is."

"Miss Sissy and Mr. Hank had them a little dog, but he got sick and died about two years ago. He was a mess, but I sure did miss him." Lily sighed. "Can't believe I got attached to him the way I did. Like to broke Miss Sissy's heart. Mr. Hank, too." Suddenly she turned away, and I heard a barely suppressed sob.

I felt awkward. Lily obviously needed comfort, but I barely knew her. "I'm so sorry, Lily. I know what it's like to lose a pet."

"Not that, really," Lily said, her voice muffled by the handkerchief at her mouth. "I done about raised Miss Sissy and Mr. Hank. I been with them since they was real little, and now I ain't got no job no more." Diesel meowed and rubbed against her leg, worried because she was upset. He obviously liked Lily or he wouldn't have stayed near her.

All I could do was repeat how sorry I was. I wished I could offer her some other comfort, but I didn't know what else to say.

"Don't pay no mind to me, Mr. Charlie. You go on now,

and I'll be fixing your dinner." She put away her handkerchief and straightened her back. "You a sweet cat," she told Diesel as she patted his head.

"Okay, Lily, but if you need anything, let me know. I'll be upstairs." As I walked out of the room I glanced over my shoulder to see whether Diesel would follow.

He didn't. He stayed near Lily, and I saw her smile down at him. I knew he would help her feel better, more so than I could, so I left them together.

I decided a hot shower and some aspirin might take care of the tension headache, and they did. I felt much better a half hour later, and I headed back downstairs to see what was cooking and to get some iced tea. As far as I knew, Diesel was still in the kitchen with Lily. He hadn't put in an appearance in the bedroom.

As I approached the kitchen I heard Stewart's voice.

"So good to see you, Lily. It's been way too long."

"Mr. Stewart, I sure do miss you coming over to see Mr. Hank. Just ain't been the same, you not visiting like you did." Lily sounded truly regretful.

I paused in the hall, not wanting to interrupt, yet curious to hear more. I should have been ashamed of eavesdropping, but I couldn't help myself.

"Well, Lily, things just didn't work out. Hank and I saw things differently, I guess." He sounded regretful, too. "Tell me, is he doing okay? Is he still gambling?"

"He swears he ain't going to no more, but he said that before. I'm afraid they go'n' lose everything, Mr. Stewart. They had to let me go, and they been selling the furniture. They ain't hardly nothing left."

"I didn't know it had gotten that bad. If I could help, I would, but I'm the last person Hank would accept any help from."

"And you the best friend he ever had. I can't think what's wrong with that boy. Now he done took up with, well, he done took up with somebody else, and I don't think it's right."

"I didn't know that. Who is this new 'friend' of his?" Stewart sounded both annoyed and curious.

"I don't rightly know. You have to ask Mr. Hank that yourself," Lily said, and she sounded evasive to me.

"Are you sure you can't tell me, Lily?" Stewart would have his most winsome, wheedling expression on full force now, I was sure.

"No, I can't, Mr. Stewart. Like I said, I don't rightly know. You have to ask Mr. Hank." Lily was stubborn in her refusal. I was sure she did know the identity of Hank's new boyfriend, but for whatever reason she wasn't going to tell Stewart.

Not that it was any of my business, or Stewart's, for that matter. I had eavesdropped long enough. I backed up a few steps, called out, "Diesel, where are you?" then strolled into the kitchen.

"Hi, Stewart," I said brightly. "Lily, is Diesel still here with you?" Diesel answered that question himself by warbling loudly as he walked around the table to greet me.

"Evening, Charlie," Stewart said with an odd expression. Was he wondering whether I had overheard his conversation with Lily? "How are you?"

"Fine," I said. "Are you going to be in for dinner?"

"Now that I know Lily cooked the dinner, I am," Stewart said. "Lily is a fabulous cook, even better than Azalea. But don't either of you dare tell Azalea that or she'll never let me touch her food again." He wagged a finger at Lily and me in turn.

Lily laughed. "No way I'm go'n' tell 'Zalea that, Mr. Stewart. She like to think she the best at everything, and I ain't about to argue with her."

"Good," Stewart said. "Now, if y'all will excuse me, I'm going to run upstairs and get Dante and take him for his walk."

As he left the kitchen I turned to Lily and said, "I hope Diesel hasn't pestered you. He always acts like he's on the point of starvation and likes to beg food."

"No, he been real good," Lily said, her attention once again focused on the stove. "Friendly, but he ain't been begging."

"That's good," I said, "because there are some things that are bad for cats."

"I know they ain't supposed to have chocolate, but what else can't they have?"

I gave her the quick list: raisins, grapes, onions, cheese, milk, green tomatoes, and raw potatoes.

"I be sure and remember all that," Lily said. "Don't want to go making no cat sick."

"Thank you," I said, "and Diesel thanks you, too." Diesel meowed right on cue, and Lily laughed.

My cell phone rang, and I excused myself and walked into the hall to answer it. Kanesha was calling, strain evident in her voice when she spoke.

"I'm at the hospital with Mama, and she's asking for you. Can you come?"

THIRTY-TWO

|||||||||||||||||||||||||||||||||||||||||||||||||||||||||||||||||||||||||||

"What happened?" I asked, so startled I almost dropped the phone.

"They think she had a mild heart attack," Kanesha said. "She's going to be okay, but she wants to talk to you."

"Of course. I'm on my way." I ended the call, then speed-dialed Stewart. He answered right away. I asked him to come downstairs immediately.

I turned to Lily to tell her about her sister. "Would you like to come to the hospital with me?"

She nodded, her lips already working on a silent prayer, and went to fetch her coat.

When Stewart ran into the kitchen I told him quickly what had happened. He said he would keep an eye on the stove and on Diesel.

Lily and I made it to the hospital in about ten minutes. I'm sure Lily prayed the entire way, and I silently added my prayers to hers. Kanesha said it was a mild heart attack, but that didn't make it less worrisome.

Dr. Sharp stood waiting at the emergency room reception desk when we arrived, and he escorted us to the small room where Azalea lay in bed. She had various monitors hooked up to her, and Kanesha sat in a chair near the bed, her whole body taut with tension. Azalea appeared to be asleep, but her eyes popped open as we approached her.

I hung back to let Lily talk to her sister first. Kanesha joined me and Dr. Sharp in a corner of the small room.

"How is she?" I asked. Azalea looked exhausted, and her skin had a gray tinge to it that alarmed me.

"Doing better than she looks," Dr. Sharp said. "It was a minor cardiac incident, and fortunately Kanesha was with her when it occurred. She's going to be fine, but she's going to have to cut back on the salt and fried foods."

Kanesha muttered something that sounded like "Ain't gonna happen." Sharp slipped an arm around her, and she leaned against him for a moment.

"I'm glad she's in such good hands," I said, greatly relieved by the cardiologist's confidence.

Lily called to me. "Mr. Charlie, 'Zalea wants to see you."

I moved toward the bed, and Lily stepped out of the way. I squeezed one of Azalea's hands gently. "How are you feeling?"

A ghost of a smile flitted across her face and then disappeared. "Tolerable, Mr. Charlie. Tolerable." Her stock answer when I inquired about her health. I had a sudden lump in my throat and couldn't speak for a moment.

"Looks like they're taking good care of you," I finally said. "If there's anything I can do for you, you let me know."

Azalea nodded. "Thank you, Mr. Charlie. They say I

got to take it easy for a while. Can't do no lifting much and things like that. Be okay with you if Lily come help me awhile?"

"For as long as you need her," I said firmly. "The important thing is for you to get to feeling better. Nothing else matters." I would make sure she didn't have to worry about the hospital bill, either. Unbeknownst to Azalea, Aunt Dottie had left money for just such a contingency, with firm instructions to me to take care of Azalea and not to let her talk me out of doing it. This was one battle with Azalea I would win, I promised Aunt Dottie silently.

"Can you pull up a chair and sit close?" Azalea said. "Need to tell you something."

I glanced at Dr. Sharp, and he nodded as he approached the bed. "It's okay as long as you don't talk too long. You need to rest." He smiled down at her. "I don't want Kanesha carrying me off to jail if something happens to you. All right?"

Azalea nodded, and Sharp withdrew, taking Lily and Kanesha with him.

"What did you want to tell me?" I asked as I scooted the chair close to the bed.

Azalea's eyes were closed, and one hand plucked at the blanket covering her. She sighed heavily. "I sure am sorry, Mr. Charlie. Should've told you this earlier, but I was feeling like a foolish old woman." Her eyes opened, and she blinked at me.

"Don't worry about that," I said and risked patting her restless hand. Her fingers curled around my hand for a moment and squeezed briefly. "Is this about what happened in that stairwell the other night?"

She nodded. "I did see something I didn't tell you about. It like to scare me to death, though. Ain't never seen nothing like it. I thought it must be the old devil himself coming after that woman."

I felt a chill along my spine. I could hear the terror in her voice, and I squeezed her hand again.

"What did it look like?" I asked.

She shuddered. "Horrible. I looked up those stairs when I heard that woman up there, and this shadow come up behind her. I saw it move and strike her, and I turned away and tried to hide myself so it wouldn't come after me."

How bizarre. "What did the shadow look like? I know it's scary for you to think about, but if you can describe it for me, maybe I can figure out what it was."

"All right." She paused. "Reckon it was like a great big ole hand, 'cepting it had horns on it."

What on earth could it be? I wondered. "How big was the hand?"

"Really big." Azalea sketched out a shape in the air with one hand.

Even allowing for the distortion caused by light and shadow, it sounded like whatever Azalea had seen was larger than I would have expected a normal hand and arm to look like as they cast a shadow.

"That does sound really strange," I said, "but I'm sure there's a logical explanation for it. Don't worry about it anymore. I promise you I'll figure it out, but you will need to tell the sheriff about it later, when you're feeling up to it."

That seemed to reassure her. "Okay, Mr. Charlie. Thank you. I be all right now."

"Good. You get some rest, and we'll come see you tomorrow."

I didn't wait for any acknowledgment. I pushed the

chair back as quietly as I could and slipped from the room. Kanesha and Lily waited right outside the door.

"Can I go in now?" Lily asked her niece.

"Go ahead. I'll be with you in a minute." Kanesha glanced at me.

Kanesha and I moved away from the door to talk. I shared with her what Azalea had told me, and Kanesha frowned. "That doesn't make any sense," she said. "Maybe she was so frightened of the dark she imagined it. It's so bizarre."

"Yes, it is," I said. "But she seemed convinced of what she saw. It wasn't the devil, obviously, but it was something with a distorted shadow. We just have to figure out what it was."

Lily came out of the room and interrupted further conversation. "'Zalea says I should go back with you and finish up dinner." She smiled, though her eyes were wet with tears. "She go'n' be okay, she ordering me around like that."

"You really don't have to, Lily," I said. "I'd rather you stay here with Azalea."

Kanesha nodded. "I'll take you home later."

Lily shook her head. "No, 'Zalea be like to have a fit, she find out I didn't do what she done told me to do. Besides, I be feeling better if I got something to do. You don't worry 'bout me, 'Nesha."

Kanesha hugged her aunt, and Lily clung to her for a moment.

"Thank you, Charlie," Kanesha said, her voice husky.

I nodded and waited for Lily to compose herself. "Call if you need anything," I said. "Anything at all."

Lily was quiet on the ride home. I had plenty to think

about, too. Azalea's revelation puzzled me. What on earth
could she have seen?

Whatever it was, it had to be part of someone's costume,
I figured. I needed to sit down and think carefully about
what everyone wore that night and decide what could have
made such an odd shadow.

Stewart, Dante, and Diesel were busy in the kitchen
when we arrived. Lily took over at the stove and announced
that everything was ready. I filled Stewart in on Azalea's
condition while Lily dished up the food. Dante and Diesel
watched her with great interest, and Dante pranced around
on his back legs for a moment. Lily grinned at the little
poodle, and I was pleased to see it.

Diesel chattered to me while I talked to Stewart, and I
patted his head and stroked his back until he finally calmed
down. He obviously wasn't happy that I had left him behind
for the second time that day, and he had to tell me all
about it.

I asked Lily to eat with us, even though I halfway
expected Azalea to rise up out of her hospital bed and
come after both of us if Lily accepted. She declined politely
and said she wasn't hungry but might eat later.

That was that, so I thanked her for the delicious-looking
meal of pork chops, green beans, mashed potatoes, and
homemade rolls.

"You're welcome," she said, ducking her head shyly.

"Why don't you go on home," I said. "It's been a long
day, and Stewart and I will clean up afterward."

Lily looked like she wanted to argue, but I think tiredness won out. "All right, Mr. Charlie," she said. "Now, if
you need me this weekend, you just let me know."

I promised I would, and after making sure she had a

ride home—she had Azalea's car—I bade her good-bye. Then Stewart and I tucked into the meal. It was every bit as tasty as it looked.

After a few mouthfuls I put my fork down for a moment. "You weren't kidding earlier," I said. "About Lily being such a good cook. Everything tastes wonderful."

"Yes, I had more than a few opportunities to sample Lily's cooking," Stewart said.

"When she was working for the Beauchamps?" I said.

Stewart nodded. "You might as well know, Hank and I were together for a couple of years. It didn't work out."

"I sort of gathered that from that little episode the night of the gala," I said, trying to make light of it.

"Not one of my better moments, I'll admit," Stewart said. "It's too bad, because Hank can be a really great guy. He just has this little problem. Oh, well, he's moved on, according to Lily, though I don't know to whom." He shrugged. "Good for him. And good for Sissy, too. We all thought she would never have a life of her own."

"What do you mean?" I asked. "I really don't know her, but as gorgeous as she is, surely she's never lacked for attention from men."

"No, I guess not," Stewart said. "But she was stuck in that house for years, looking after that nasty grandmother of hers, then it was her mother, and finally her father. Old man Beauchamp was too cheap to hire extra help besides Lily, so poor Sissy got stuck being the dutiful, unpaid drudge of a daughter. Made Hank angry, but Daddy was the one with the money, and whenever he said 'Leap, frog,' they just asked, 'How high?'"

"That's too bad. Beauchamp Senior died about three years ago, didn't he?"

"Yes, and it was about ten years too late, if you ask me."
Stewart grimaced. "Nasty, unfeeling old bastard. He gave
Hank hell for being a *pansy*, as he called it. Hank did his
best to stand up to him, but it was hard. Of course, Sissy
helped. She's always done anything and everything for her
little brother." He fed Dante a bite of pork chop, and the
dog barked excitedly. Stewart told him to hush.

"I'm sorry things were so rough for them," I said. "Their
father sounds like a nightmare. At least they can live their
own lives now, and according to the gossip I've heard about
Sissy and Morty Cassity, she's making up for lost time."

Stewart shrugged. "I guess so. But that's the strange
thing to me. I always figured Sissy was just as queer as her
brother. Surprised the heck out of me when I heard she was
slipping around with a married man."

"She doesn't have to slip around any longer," I said,
"with Vera permanently out of the way."

"No, she doesn't. Well, it's no business of mine." Stewart attacked his food, and conversation languished. Dante
barked occasionally, and Stewart admonished him, but as
long as he kept rewarding the behavior with bits of food,
the dog would never learn not to do it. I didn't share this
with Stewart, however.

We worked together once we finished eating to clean up
the kitchen and put everything away. Diesel had several
bites of pork chop, just like his little buddy Dante, and he
was a happy kitty as we trudged up the stairs later on.

I got ready for bed, Diesel already comfortable on his
side, and found a notepad and pen. I wanted to make notes
about the costumes my chief suspects wore the night of the
gala. I was hoping that inspiration would strike as I worked
on remembering everything I could.

I started with the Ducote sisters, a.k.a. Amelia Peabody

and Jacqueline Kirby, then moved on to Morty Cassity, Hank Beauchamp, and finally Sissy.

As I scanned the details, one item leaped out at me. I focused on creating a mental image of that dark stairwell, and then I was convinced I was right. I was pretty sure I knew what Azalea had seen and who had worn it.

THIRTY-THREE

|||||||||||||||||||||||||||||||||||||||||||||||||||||||||||||||||||||||||||||||||||||||||

That absurd stuffed Yorkie Sissy had attached to her like a wrist corsage had to be what Azalea saw. It was the only thing on the list that I could imagine would cast a shadow like the one Azalea described.

That settled it in my mind. Sissy had pushed Vera to her death on those stairs.

With Vera out of the way Sissy was free to marry Morty—and gain access to Morty's millions. No more genteel poverty for her or her beloved little brother, Hank.

A fairly simple solution after all. Money lay at the root of it.

The motive was easy, but where was the proof? Azalea would tell the sheriff what she saw, and I could explain it, but a good defense lawyer would probably make nonsense of it in court.

The explanation did sound faintly ridiculous, even though

I was convinced of the truth of it. It all came down to the accessories of a costume.

Costume.

Something else was niggling at me, something to do with another costume.

I looked at the list again, poring over the descriptions I'd compiled. What was nagging at me?

I lingered over the details of Hank Beauchamp's costume as the rumpled but clever Victorian policeman, Thomas Pitt.

Rumpled. That was it.

Poor Hank was reduced to wearing that same suit, because all his other suits were at the cleaner's. Probably a euphemism for having to sell them, or else he owed the cleaner's so much money they wouldn't release his clothes until he paid them.

Either way, Hank had only the one suit. No wonder it looked like it did.

There was another elusive memory. Where else had I seen that suit, or part of it?

It took me a minute, but then I had it.

Morty Cassity was wearing the jacket when he came to the door the day I went to take Vera's plaque to him.

But how?

Then I remembered a chance remark Stewart had made. I sat up in bed and looked at the clock. It was only a few minutes till ten, and I knew Stewart stayed up late.

I slipped out of bed, trying not to disturb Diesel. I hurried up the stairs to the third floor and knocked lightly on Stewart's door.

"Come in," he called.

He was sitting cross-legged on the bed, still dressed as he had been at dinner, with Dante napping beside him.

He put aside the book he'd been reading. "Hi, Charlie. What's up?"

"Remember the other day, when you were talking about how you ran into Sissy Beauchamp on the square?"

Stewart nodded. "Sure."

"Can you tell me approximately what time it was when you ran into her, and how long the two of you were together?"

"Okay, let me see. I'm sure you'll tell me why you want to know this?" At my nod he continued, "Well, it was around one o'clock, as I recall. We must have spent about an hour together over our milk shakes, so it was probably after two when I left her."

"I see." If Sissy had been with Stewart while I was with Morty Cassity, then it wasn't Sissy driving that pink car that day. It had to be Hank instead.

Hank.

Sissy wasn't Morty's lover, Hank was.

I sat down abruptly on Stewart's bed.

"Charlie, what's the matter? Are you all right?"

I nodded, my thoughts running amok in my head. "Give me a minute." I started recalling the various things I'd heard about Sissy.

The Ducote sisters telling me how surprised they were to hear that Sissy was running around with Morty, when she'd never been known to do that kind of thing before.

Helen Louise saying much the same thing.

Stewart telling me, earlier this evening, that he was surprised to hear that Sissy was running around with Morty because he'd always thought she was gay like her brother.

It all made sense, though. Sissy was known to be willing to do whatever she could to help out her beloved little brother.

Even pretending that she was having an affair with a
married man so that no one would suspect that Hank and
Morty were lovers.

And, finally, pushing Vera down the stairs to clear the
way for her brother and Hank—and on top of that, access
to those millions for her brother and herself.

"Charlie, you're beginning to worry me. What's going
on in that head of yours?"

I surfaced from my whirlpool of thoughts to see Stewart
regarding me with concern. "I'm okay," I said. "Just a bit
stunned, that's all."

"You've figured it out, haven't you?" Stewart started
bobbing up and down on the bed. "Tell me, tell me, or I'm
going to bust a gasket right here and now." Dante sat up,
disturbed by the bobbing, and started barking. Stewart put
a hand on him to calm him, and he shut up.

"Okay. Here goes." I launched into my explanation.

Stewart's eyes looked like they were going to pop out of
his head at first, but then he started nodding. When I finished, he said, "I think you have to be right, Charlie. I
never could see why Sissy would take up with Morty, but I
sure can see why Hank would. He always did seem to have
a thing for older men, and powerful men, too. Morty is
certainly that, with all that money. I can't believe I didn't
see it myself."

"They were extraordinarily careful," I said. "Sissy was
the key, the smokescreen."

"Pretty effective," Stewart said.

"Yes, she was." I felt drained all of a sudden.

"Charlie, do you think Hank and Morty were in on the
murder, though? Was it Sissy acting completely on her
own, or do you think they egged her on?" Stewart sounded
troubled, and I was sure he didn't want to think a former

boyfriend of his was capable of inciting his own sister to murder.

"I honestly don't know," I said. "I bet they've figured out by now that she did it, but the other day Hank seemed awfully convinced that Vera was drunk and fell down the stairs on her own."

"He's a terrible actor," Stewart said, his face clearing a little, "and a terrible liar. Trust me, I've had plenty experience with it. He must have really believed it was an accident."

"Maybe so." I was going to reserve judgment on that one.

"What are you going to do now? Call Kanesha?"

I shook my head. "Not tonight. For one thing, Azalea is in no condition right now to talk to the sheriff, and Kanesha can't do anything about it without involving Tidwell. It can wait until morning."

I was probably cavalier in making that decision, but I felt that it was the right one. Convincing Kanesha, and then Tidwell, could be a monumental task, and I didn't have the mental or physical energy to tackle it at ten thirty at night.

"Not a word to anyone else about this," I said as I got up from the bed. "Okay?"

"No one will hear it from me," Stewart said. "It's going to be one hell of a mess, though, when it all comes out. Morty Cassity turning out to be gay will be a huge scandal."

"No doubt," I said wryly. Athena would be buzzing for months to come, if not years.

Diesel sat up sleepily when I got back in bed. He meowed at me, and I reassured him that everything was fine. He settled back down, and I tried to emulate him. My stomach churned, and my head buzzed, and it took quite a while that night for me to calm myself enough to fall asleep.

After a restless night I woke up at six the next morning. Too nervous to think about food, I also decided that caffeine wouldn't help, so I settled on a cold glass of milk. Diesel was disappointed that there was no bacon to cadge, and he wandered off, probably in search of another bed to snooze on.

I kept glancing at the clock, waiting until a decent hour to call Kanesha.

Finally, at eight o'clock, I couldn't stand it any longer. I called Kanesha's cell phone and was relieved when she answered straightaway.

"How is Azalea doing?" I asked.

"She had a good night," Kanesha replied. "I think she's really going to be okay, thank the Lord. They moved her into a room not long after you left, and they'll probably keep her until tomorrow. But if she keeps on doing well, she can go home then."

"That's wonderful news," I said. "If she can have visitors, I'll come visit later this morning."

"I think she'd like that," Kanesha said. "Aunt Lily's with her now, but she won't stay long."

"Are you at the hospital now?"

"No, I'm at home. Why? What's up?"

"I've got it figured out," I said. "I need to talk to you right away."

"I'll be there in ten minutes," Kanesha said.

I felt a little better now and decided that I could eat something. I didn't have the energy to cook, so I settled for cereal and toast. Probably better for my waistline, anyway, so long as I didn't load down the toast with any of Azalea's homemade apricot preserves or strawberry jam.

Kanesha was as good as her word. Ten minutes from when we hung up, she was at the front door. I set down the last bit of toast and went to let her in.

"Come on into the kitchen," I said. "Can I offer you anything to drink?"

"I could use some coffee," she said. She looked like she hadn't slept much, and I could sympathize.

"Sure, won't take but a few minutes. I was about to make some for myself," I added to forestall any objections.

"Thank you," she said. "So tell me. What was it that Mama saw that night? I thought a lot about it, but I couldn't get it."

As I prepared the coffeemaker, I reminded her about Sissy's Yorkie wrist corsage, and she nodded. "Got you. It *would* make a weird shadow. And maybe it shed some of its hair on Vera when she pushed her. That could help prove she did it."

I hoped she was right. Then I went on to explain the realization I had come to about the true nature of the relationship among Sissy, Hank, and Morty.

Kanesha apparently didn't have any trouble believing it. "Makes sense to me," she said. "The main question will be whether they were accessories."

"I'm glad I won't have to be the one to decide that," I said. The coffee was ready, and I poured cups for both of us. She took hers without cream or sugar. I had to have both in mine.

"What will you do now?" I asked after she'd had a few sips of her coffee.

"I'll have to go to Tidwell," Kanesha said. "Not looking forward to that, but he's in charge. I just don't want him to harass Mama about this."

"I don't imagine either you or Dr. Sharp will let that happen."

Kanesha smiled faintly. "You're right about that." She

drained her coffee and put the cup aside. "Thank you, Charlie. For the coffee and everything." She stood. "I can't put this off. I'll give you a call later, but the sheriff may be in touch with you first."

"That's fine," I said. "I'll be here."

I showed her to the door and walked tiredly back to the kitchen. I debated whether to go back to bed but decided I might as well stay up.

I poured myself more coffee and thought about Vera's murder. A terrible tragedy all the way around.

Most of all I felt sorry for Vera, and also for her mother, Essie Mae. I thought about the Ducote sisters and wondered whether they knew the truth about Essie Mae, or if they even remembered her at all.

Should that skeleton stay in the closet? Was it my place to tell the sisters about it? Whatever I decided, I knew I would be haunted by Essie Mae for a long time.

THIRTY-FOUR

IIIIIIIIIIIIIIIIIIIIIIIIIIIIIIIIIIIIIIIIIIIIIIIIIIIIIIIIIIIIIIIIIIIIIIIIIIIII

I spent a restless morning as I continued to debate with myself whether I should give the diary to the Ducote sisters, and once I had decided that I must, how I should explain my having read it in the first place. Poor Diesel watched me pace around my bedroom for an hour before he had enough and abandoned me for someone who would give him more than the occasional pat on the head.

When I came downstairs around ten I found Laura in the kitchen, Diesel in her lap as she thumbed through a magazine.

"Morning, Dad." Laura frowned. "You look rough. Bad night?"

"And morning." I smiled tiredly. "Too much to think about."

"You've figured it out all, haven't you?" Laura closed the magazine and shifted Diesel out of her lap. He grumbled as he stalked off in the direction of the utility room. "Sit down and let me get you a drink. How about hot tea?"

"Sounds lovely, thanks." I subsided into a chair, feeling about a century older today than yesterday. "I talked to Kanesha this morning, and it's all in her hands—and the sheriff's—now." I gave her a rundown of the case against Sissy Beauchamp while she prepared my tea.

Laura waited to comment until I finished and had a few sips of the hot drink. "Talk about sacrifice. She spent her whole adult life taking care of one member after another of her family. You almost can't blame her for snapping and pushing that awful woman down the stairs."

"I certainly have a lot of sympathy for her plight." I drained my cup, and Laura poured more tea. "That doesn't excuse murder, however."

"Of course it doesn't," Laura said. "But surely her lawyer will use her situation somehow in her defense. I'd hate to see her executed, despite what she did."

"I agree with you. A competent defense attorney will do everything possible for her."

"Finding the answer can be painful." Laura came over and bent to wrap her arms around me, her head against mine. "The truth has to come out, though, doesn't it?"

"It does." I sighed as Laura gave one more squeeze before letting go. "Now I have to face causing more pain."

"How so?" Laura resumed her seat at the table and regarded me with a frown.

Diesel returned from the utility room and padded over to me. He butted his head against my leg, and I stroked his head and back. I didn't feel I could share the whole story of Vera and Essie Mae with Laura, and I thought for a moment about how to explain what I meant.

"As part of my nosing around," I began, "I had to consider everyone, including the Ducote sisters. I had to figure out why Vera sent me that picture of her mother, and what connection, if any, her mother could have to the Ducotes. I found out by searching through the Ducote archives at the library, and I don't think the sisters are aware of what I discovered. It's something private, and I can't share it with you. I have to tell Miss An'gel and Miss Dickce, and they may be livid over what I did."

Diesel's rumbling purr filled the silence as I waited for my daughter's response. Her curiosity rivaled mine, and not knowing would irk her, but she was mature enough to handle the situation.

"Did what you discovered help you reach the solution to the murder?"

"No," I said.

"But you had no way of knowing that when you were going through their archives."

"I didn't."

Laura sighed. "They are intelligent women, and they ought to understand why you did it. They wanted you to find out the truth, although they might not have thought you would consider them suspects."

"Exactly. Plus as it turned out, I meddled in their family's affairs for no reason." I rubbed Diesel's back, and the purring continued.

"Do Miss An'gel and Miss Dickce have to know whatever it was you discovered?"

"I believe so," I said. "It's an important piece of their family history. They should know, but it's up to them what they do with the knowledge. I will never reveal what I found out to anyone else."

"They have respect for you," Laura said with a gentle smile. "You simply have to tell them and trust them to do the right thing."

I had reached the same conclusion earlier, but hearing those words from my bright and sensitive daughter reassured me. "Then I guess I have a phone call to make."

Three hours later Diesel and I drove out to River Hill, Cecilia Ducote's precious journal wrapped in acid-free paper. Large butterflies cavorted in my stomach as the time for the dreaded interview loomed closer. I hated the thought of causing pain to two women I admired so deeply, but I didn't see any other way. This was the right thing to do. Clementine opened the door to admit us, and we followed her into the front parlor where Miss An'gel and Miss Dickce waited, side by side on the sofa. Diesel scampered to them immediately and jumped onto the sofa. There was no point in my remonstrating with him because the sisters were already smothering him with attention. I took the seat proffered by Clementine and waited for one of the sisters to greet me. I held the journal in my lap.

Miss An'gel spoke first. "Afternoon, Charlie. Dickce and I are devastated by the news. Poor Sissy."

"And Hank and Morty Cassity." Miss Dickce's cheeks reddened. "Why, I don't think anyone ever suspected such a thing."

"Still waters and so on." Miss An'gel frowned. "One can't blame Morty for turning elsewhere, I suppose, but dear Hank is not the most stable person he could have chosen."

"Now, Sister," Miss Dickce said, "Hank and Sissy both had a lot to put up with. If anyone's to blame it's that jackass of a father and his witch of a mother."

"That's true," Miss An'gel responded. "Two more selfish, mean people never roamed the good Lord's earth, and I hope they are both roasting in hell as they so properly deserve for the terrible things they did to those children and their mother."

Diesel warbled loudly to regain their attention, and Miss An'gel patted him fondly on the head. "Quite right, Diesel, enough of that." She glanced my way. "You have something you need to tell us, Charlie. I suppose it involves that package you have."

"Yes, ma'am," I said, one hand on the wrapped journal. "Before I show this to you, I need to explain how I came to find it and what it is."

" 'Curiouser and curiouser.' " Miss Dickce grinned as she quoted *Alice's Adventures in Wonderland.*

I doubted either one of them would be smiling by the time I finished what I had come to say. After one deep breath to steady my nerves, I launched into my explanation, starting with the photograph of Essie Mae Hobson that Vera had sent me.

Miss Dickce's expression remained alight with curiosity while I talked, but Miss An'gel's countenance grew stonier by the sentence. As the elder sister she might have vague memories of Essie Mae, whereas Miss Dickce would have been only an infant when their biological mother was forced to leave them.

"I never truly thought either of you killed Vera," I said as I neared the end of my story. "But to be thorough I had to consider any possible angle to get at the truth, and that's why I examined your family archives. What I found turned out not to have anything directly to do with Vera's murder, though it had a lot to do with her life." Now the only sound in the room, besides our breathing, came from my cat. His purr rumbled as I watched the sisters carefully for a hint of their reaction. Miss An'gel's head could have been carved from granite.

When at last she spoke, Miss An'gel sounded neutral, to my great surprise. "Thank you for your honesty, Charlie. Had you not told us we would never have known what you did, and I appreciate your position. I certainly don't relish the idea that you considered us as suspects, but I can see that you had to be thorough."

Miss Dickce nodded. "Certainly, Charlie, you did the right thing." She flashed a quick grin. "Unlike my iron-drawered sister here, I am frankly tickled that you might have thought for a moment that I would push Vera down those stairs."

Miss An'gel shot her sibling what should have been a quelling look, but Miss Dickce returned it with a defiant glare instead.

I breathed a little more easily, now that I had successfully negotiated one hurdle. The most difficult one remained, however.

"Thank you both," I said. "Now I need to share with you something I found while I was looking through your family papers." My hands trembled a bit as I unwrapped the journal. I let the paper fall to the floor, and Diesel immediately scrambled off the sofa to investigate the paper. While he played with it, I handed the journal to Miss An'gel.

The Ducote sisters stared at the book but neither moved to open it. "What is it?" Miss An'gel asked.

"Your mother's journal," I said, feeling my chest tighten. I took a deep breath before I continued. "There is information in those pages that I think you both should know, and I will leave you to read it. Before I go, however, I want you to know that I will never reveal what I read."

"Must be pretty serious, whatever it is." Miss Dickce frowned. "Can't you just tell us?"

"I could," I said, "but I think you need to read the whole thing so that you can see it all through Cecilia's eyes. It's her story to tell, not mine."

"Thank you, Charlie." Miss An'gel handed the journal to her sister as she rose from the sofa. "We will read it, and naturally both Dickce and I have every confidence in you. No matter what is in Mother's journal, we trust you to do the right thing."

"Bless you both." I stood and took Miss An'gel's hand. To my consternation she leaned forward and kissed my cheek. Miss Dickce didn't move from the sofa. Her hands caressed the book in a constant motion. "Come along, Diesel." I bent to take the paper away from him, and he glared at me. "Come on, I said, it's time for us to go." I placed the paper on a table, and he reluctantly followed me as Miss An'gel walked with us through the parlor and to the front door.

Neither Miss An'gel nor I spoke again, and even Diesel was subdued. He sensed the gravity of the situation, ever sensitive to mood.

On the drive home I thought about the contents of Cecilia's journal and the stunning revelations it held for Miss An'gel and Miss Dickce. Both had an impressive mental toughness, but the truth of their parentage would rock them to the core. I hoped and prayed they would be okay.

THIRTY-FIVE

A week later, on Christmas Day, I woke early with Diesel curled against my side. I savored the warmth and lay there for a while, recalling other Christmases.

When Sean and Laura were small, they would burst into our bedroom, faces aglow with excitement, eager to tell us what Santa Claus had brought them. Jackie and I would exchange secret smiles over their heads as they climbed into the bed with us, each clutching a precious new toy.

The first Christmas after Jackie's death had been tough for all of us, but we made it through the holidays. I felt her presence near me every day during that time. I often felt it here, too, along with that of Aunt Dottie. I liked to think that those we loved best never completely left us. I knew they would always be in my heart, but somehow I believed it was more than that.

There were no excited childish voices to savor—until there were grandchildren, and I looked forward to that. I would be a doting grandfather, I knew, and I would have to try hard not to spoil my grandchildren terribly.

Diesel sat up and stretched, so I threw aside the covers and went over to the window. Dawn had arrived, and with it, the snow. I smiled. We hadn't had a white Christmas in several years, and seeing the dusting of snow on everything added a lovely touch of magic to the day.

This would be a happy day, with my children and friends here to celebrate with me. Helen Louise would be here, as would Stewart. Justin had gone to spend the holidays with his family, and though I would miss him, I was pleased to know that he would be with his father. Alexandra Pendergrast and Frank Salisbury were coming as well. Alexandra's father was off somewhere on a hunting trip with his cronies, and Frank couldn't bear to be apart from Laura.

A happy day for me and my family, certainly. I thought about Sissy and Hank Beauchamp, though, and the sad holiday they would have with Sissy in jail, awaiting indictment on a murder charge.

Kanesha had an easier time than she expected, convincing the sheriff to consider the solution that I had put together. He talked to Azalea and then to me, and finally confronted Sissy Beauchamp and arrested her for the murder of Vera Cassity. Kanesha said Sissy confessed, that she seemed almost relieved, while Hank appeared devastated by the knowledge of what his sister had done.

I felt sorry for Sissy Beauchamp, despite what she had done. For decades she'd served as a caretaker for others, without any opportunity to get free and live her own life. She sacrificed herself for her family, including her beloved younger brother. She might have to make the ultimate sacrifice, depending on the outcome of the trial.

Azalea had come home from the hospital, and that was

a blessing. Lily was looking after her, and I wished Lily well, because I was sure Azalea was a difficult patient. Lily helped out here as much as she could, but it was more important for her to take care of her sister. We would manage until Azalea was healthy enough to return to work. In the meantime Helen Louise and I vowed we would not rest until we found Lily a new full-time job. Perhaps Morty and Hank would need her.

I had thought about Miss An'gel and Miss Dickce a lot the past few days. I hoped to hear from them because I was concerned how they would handle such a stunning bit of news. I realized, however, that they would need time, perhaps a long time, to come to grips with Essie Mae's story. If they wanted to talk to me about anything, they would. And if they decided never to refer to any of it, then I would respect their decision.

Each day, though, I couldn't help but wonder.

My answer came on Christmas Eve, through the mail, in a smallish, cream-colored envelope. I recognized the handwriting at once and knew it was a card from Miss An'gel. My fingers refused to work at first as I tried to open the envelope, but finally I managed it. I withdrew the card inside and discovered that I had been invited to a party at River Hill on New Year's Eve. "To meet our brother Amory Hobson," I read, and suddenly I felt tears sting my eyes.

Then I had to smile, for Miss Dickce had scribbled a brief note at the bottom: "Don't dare leave Diesel at home!"

Diesel and I went down to the kitchen, and I began preparing breakfast. I was no match for either Azalea or Lily as a cook, but I could manage pretty good scrambled eggs, toast, and sausage. That should be hearty enough. The real eating would come later. Helen Louise was coming over at nine, and Stewart would assist her in preparing the turkey and other goodies, with some help from Laura and me.

After lunch we settled in the living room to open presents, and Frank acted as Santa Claus. "I am the only one with a beard, after all," he said. "Though I apologize it isn't white."

We had a great time delving into packages and sharing the contents. Helen Louise gave me two more sweaters, and I had found a beautiful necklace and earrings for her. We shared a kiss or two under the mistletoe Sean had hung earlier, and I noticed that my children spent a fair amount of time beneath it with their partners.

By late afternoon we were all full, tired, happy, and sleepy. Diesel and Dante had worn themselves out playing with boxes, wrapping paper, and ribbons, though we all had to be vigilant to make sure none of the paper or ribbons were eaten.

Around five I went into the kitchen to put on a pot of coffee. I needed a little caffeine to perk me up. As I stood at the sink filling the pot with water, I felt two arms slip around me, and my daughter whispered in my ear, "Merry Christmas, Dad."

"Merry Christmas, sweetheart. I'm so glad you're here." I didn't add that I dreaded her leaving after the holidays and heading back to California.

"I have a little surprise for you," she said with an impish grin. "I wanted to tell you first, and then I'll tell Sean and the others."

"What is it?" I set the coffeepot down. My hands trembled a little. I knew what I hoped she was going to tell me.

"I'm not going back to California, Dad. I'm going to stay here. The college offered me a full-time job. The woman who was out on maternity leave decided not to come back, and they want me to take her place."

"That's wonderful," I said and swept her into a hug. "I'm so happy you're staying here."

"Me, too," she said as I released her.

"You're sure you're not going to miss being a glamorous Hollywood star?" I couldn't help teasing her a little.

"Nope, not a bit. I actually have another role in mind," she said with that same impish grin.

"And what would that be?" I asked.

"Let me put it this way," she said. "How would you like to help me plan a wedding?"

FROM *NEW YORK TIMES* BESTSELLING AUTHOR

Miranda James

OUT OF CIRCULATION

- A Cat in the Stacks Mystery -

Small-town librarian Charlie Harris and his Maine
coon cat, Diesel, are famous all over Athena, Mississippi, for their charming Southern manners and
sleuthing skills. When a tiff between Athena's richest
ladies ends with one of them dead, it's up to Charlie
and his feline friend to set the record straight before
his own life is stamped out.

**"James should soon be on everyone's
favorite list of authors."**
—Leann Sweeney, author of the Cats in Trouble Mysteries

catinthestacks.com
facebook.com/MirandaJamesAuthor
facebook.com/TheCrimeSceneBooks
penguin.com

M1374T1113

"(A) kindhearted librarian hero . . . and a gentle giant
of a cat that will steal your heart."
—Lorna Barrett, *New York Times* bestselling author

FROM *NEW YORK TIMES* BESTSELLING AUTHOR
Miranda James

FILE M FOR MURDER ·

- A Cat in the Stacks Mystery -

Athena College's new writer-in-residence is native son
and playwright Connor Lawton, known for his sharp
writing—and sharper tongue. After an unpleasant
encounter, librarian Charlie Harris heads home to a
nice surprise: his daughter, Laura, is subbing for another Athena professor. Unfortunately, her old flame
Connor Lawton got her the job. But before Connor
finishes his newest play, he's murdered—and Laura is
the prime suspect. Charlie and his faithful cat, Diesel,
follow Connor's cluttered trail to find the true killer
before his daughter is forever cataloged under "M"—
for murderer.

facebook.com/TheCrimeSceneBooks
penguin.com

FROM *NEW YORK TIMES* BESTSELLING AUTHOR
Miranda James

- The Cat in the Stacks Mysteries -

MURDER PAST DUE
CLASSIFIED AS MURDER
FILE M FOR MURDER
OUT OF CIRCULATION

Praise for the Cat in the Stacks Mysteries

"Courtly librarian Charlie Harris
and his Maine coon cat, Diesel,
are an endearing detective duo.
Warm, charming, and Southern as the tastiest grits."

—Carolyn Hart, author of the Bailey Ruth Mysteries

"An intelligent amateur sleuth with a lovable sidekick."

—*Lesa's Book Critiques*

facebook.com/TheCrimeSceneBooks
penguin.com